Strange Love in America

JC Howell

Strange Love in America, Published April, 2018

Editorial and proofreading services: Kathleen A. Tracy and Karen Grennan

Interior layout and cover design: Howard Johnson

Cover artwork: oil on canvas, created by Randi Jane Davis,

www.randijanedavis.com

 **SDP Publishing**

Published by SDP Publishing, an imprint of SDP Publishing Solutions, LLC.

To obtain permission(s) to use material from this work, please submit a written request to:

SDP Publishing

Permissions Department

PO Box 26, East Bridgewater, MA 02333

or email your request to info@SDPPublishing.com.

ISBN-13 (hardcover): 978-1-7321115-0-9

ISBN-13 (paperback): 978-0-9992839-6-7

ISBN-13 (e-book): 978-0-9992839-7-4

Library of Congress Control Number: 2017963380

Copyright 2018, JC Howell

Printed in the United States of America.

To my readers who direct their attention to share strange love.

This book would not have been possible without the encouragement and support of Jacki Flynn, Alice Rachel Bottoms, Lisa Akoury-Ross, Karen Grennan, and Kathleen Tracy. Kathleen elevated this manuscript with her trenchant observations, suggestions, and edits. And last, special thank you to Randi Jane Davis and Howard Johnson for giving this story majesty through the storyline cover artwork and elegant paging.

Philosophy is not about the love of wisdom.
It's about the wisdom of love.

Prologue

Alex ran ahead, up the stairs and across the porch. When Polly and I stepped onto the landing area, Alex approached. "This is it," he said with tearful eyes.

"No, we promised. We're not going to cry," Polly said. "Alex, you're going to play Fred, and I'm Holly Golightly tonight. Antonio, you're Doc."

Polly and her crazy imagination. She wanted to play *Breakfast at Tiffany's* on our last night together at our home. Alex grinned and reached to embrace Polly, lifting her and giving a twirl.

I shook my head at them. "Come here you two thespians." We wrapped our arms around one another and embraced for a long moment.

"Only tears for joy," Polly said, wiping her eyes as we released. Alex and I agreed.

We found our favorite rocking chairs on the homey balcony porch of the school building at Essence, the international orphanage in Andorra where we'd grown up together.

"This is going to be our best sunset ever," Polly said.

I shot her and Alex a smile.

Enjoying a summer breeze, we moved to-and-fro gazing at rock-faced mountains that shaped the southeastern horizon in nearby France. The view from up here on this porch, on top of Mount Essence, was breathtaking. We'd enjoyed so many evenings here under the awning, watching sunsets and then rocking through twilight till the stars emerged. It seemed impossible that tonight would be our last night.

Glancing over my left shoulder, I noticed Polly and Alex

slowing as they rocked side-by-side. Polly spoke softly about places where they could dine on their trip tomorrow.

I looked in awe at Alex, my orphan brother, a handsome young man, one hundred eighty-three centimeters, six feet, almost as tall as me, with brown hair and brown eyes, wearing khaki slacks and a baby-blue dress shirt, just like me. Polly continued in a small voice about tomorrow's affairs. She was my orphan sister, now a beautiful young lady with red hair, blue eyes, and tiny freckles, wearing her favorite Paris-green dress. I turned my chair toward them, taking them both in, wanting to commit their majestic faces and this moment to memory.

A heavy, shaky sensation traveled from my chest to the top of my head then, a quivering wave of sadness almost producing tears. I felt another wave and swiveled to my right, to avoid being noticed. I leaned back and directed my attention at the clouds.

Finally the waves passed. I let out a deep breath in relief and rocked slowly. Dark clouds had gathered above the green mountaintops of Andorra, the stage for our sunset. I could see the wind—

"Antonio, where will you go when you arrive at Harvard?" Polly asked.

"Just a second," I said while watching the tops of pine trees swaying, and then traced the wind to the northwestern blue yonder—not a cloud in sight.

Feeling better and satisfied the horizon would soon be clear, I swiveled back around to answer Polly, who'd turned her attention toward Alex. She called him *Fred* and playfully caressed his cheek. Alex murmured *Lulamae Barnes, Holly Golightly's* former name, and then giggled as Polly tickled him. Alex retaliated by tickling her. They seemed so in love with each other. I thought in amusement about the sunset a few years earlier when Alex had tried so hard to get Polly to pay attention to him, the memory recalling so many other glorious sunsets since we were children. Now at eighteen all three of us were leaving our home to begin our journeys so we could lead the world to freedom through Sentio.

I knew my mother, Marie, and Sister Josephine wouldn't attend tonight's sunset because they would feel too sad about Alex and Polly leaving tomorrow and that I would be departing the following day.

Polly turned toward me—her long, red hair cascading past her shoulders. "*Doc*, I mean Antonio, what will you do when you arrive at Harvard?"

"I'm supposed to meet with the dean of admissions. He's made arrangements for my temporary residence on campus. What will you and Alex do when you arrive in London?"

"First, we'll meet our new housemates, and tomorrow evening we'll tour the Barbican multi-arts center. Can you believe we'll live in a beautiful home in the city? Uncle Poulou has been so generous to us."

I nodded. "He's the greatest."

Poulou was a loving, caring, fun person and uncle to all orphans. He'd arranged for them to board with a family in London, and he'd also given me money to find a place to live in Boston.

Polly sat back, and asked Alex, "Do you remember that odd woman's name who's supposed to meet us at London Heathrow Airport? Lancelotta? Lolitotta?"

I rotated forward and glanced at the sun near the horizon. It looked dim, hazy. Several moments later, the waves of sadness returned, and a tear released down my cheek. I stopped rocking and turned into Polly's gaze. I was thinking about how much I would miss them, and she could see that I was crying. She got up and pulled me from my chair into an embrace. We hugged for the longest, and the quiver in my chest calmed. When we let go, she said, "*O King Arthur, my King Arthur, don't let your beautiful blue eyes be sad.*"

Alex approached us. *"Never let it be forgot that there once was a spot, and for a brief shining moment it was known as Esselot."*

I smiled at Polly and reached to hug Alex. They'd recited lines from our play *Esselot*, a takeoff on *Camelot*, which we performed a couple of years earlier. After embracing Alex, I noticed Polly's smile had disappeared, her blue eyes sad. I knew why; she believed Essence was Camelot and our brief, shining moment was coming to an end. I pulled her and Alex into a group hug.

"We are going to lead humankind to freedom through Sentio," I said, giving a squeeze to their shoulders. "We will find a way to free their attention from language-thinking consciousness. We know what we must do, and we'll discover what we must know to lead them to freedom. I'll lead the Americans who according to Aunt Helen are the most difficult because they think they are free. And you two will lead actors to freedom. They'll be difficult too."

Polly added, "Josephine says that many actors believe they have found Sentio, but most really haven't." Polly squeezed me harder, her arms wrapped around my waist. "Antonio, I'm worried about you. How will you find strange love in America?"

"I will," I said, and hugged her tighter. She was worried because I would need the strange love given for freedom, greater freedom for all, to maintain my Sentio sensitivity— strange love, the love we'd grown up giving and receiving at Essence. Alex and Polly could love each other. That thought comforted me.

Releasing from our group embrace, Alex stepped back and met my eyes. "You promise you will visit us this Christmas in London?"

"I'll be there," I said. "I love you both more than you'll ever know."

"We love you," Alex and Polly said in unison.

"Here it comes, our last sunset together at Essence," I said softly.

A lump gathered in my throat as we stepped toward the balcony rail. We stood with our arms around one another, savoring the majesty of nature and each other, staring at the orange-yellow glow shrinking on the horizon. No words were said. The turquoise sky faded into darkness. We embraced once more with sadness in our eyes, not wanting to let go of each other, knowing we'd never be together here like this ever again.

"Remember our plan. We'll live together again in Paris in a few years. I promise," I said through my tears and recited Polly's favorite quote from *Breakfast at Tiffany's*. "'Cross my heart and kiss my elbow.'" She tightened her hug and pressed her head against my chest.

Alex looked at me with tears in his eyes, produced a beautiful and contagious smile, and said, "We will live together again."

Polly released and smiled, wiping tears. "Let's go find Marie and Josephine."

We held hands and strode across the moonlit porch toward Villa #4.

"Please hurry and free the Americans," Polly said. "Then Alex and I will help you free the rest of the world."

I assured them there was nothing I wanted more than that.

CHAPTER

1

The airplane dropped, bounced, and wobbled, waking me from a beautiful dream. After rousing for a moment, my eyes closed, and I drifted back to the images of a gorgeous sunset where the violets and pinks gleamed from the Mediterranean-blue sky. Mother, Polly, and Alex rocked alongside me on the porch, and as we watched in collective silence, the yellow-orange sun disappeared behind the purple mountains of Andorra. The dream was the memory of the sunset I witnessed four years ago at age fourteen when I experienced the Compass of Freedom and saw my path to greater freedom for all. In my vision I was doing medical research at Harvard.

We dropped and bounced again. I turned my head toward the nice man in the aisle seat, a gray-haired professor from MIT. Before boarding the flight to Boston at Charles de Gaulle, I'd experienced a tearful farewell with my mother, and the professor comforted me.

I rubbed my eyes. "Where are we?" I asked in a low voice.

He looked at me over the top of his reading glasses. "By my calculation we are somewhere over the North Atlantic, flying through turbulence—"

The airplane wobbled. A chime rang out as the fasten-seat-belt sign lit up.

The professor fastened his belt. "You've been asleep for several hours."

"Yes, I needed to dream," I said softly.

"Did you have a nice dream?"

"Yes, of a beautiful sunset over Andorra."

I gazed out my window, where the billowing clouds obscured the view. A warmness in the air stirred below my window seat. I could barely sense it, which meant most people would never know it was there. It rose around me in a uniform fashion. I turned toward the professor and told him the sun-heated ground of America was below.

The professor peered out my window for a moment. "The clouds are blocking the view. I can't see land, but we should be getting close."

A few minutes later the captain's voice crackled through the intercom. "We've received permission to land at Logan International and are making our final descent. Please return your seat back to its upright position."

"You were right," the professor said, sounding surprised. Then he grinned. "Ah-ha! You deduced we were over America because of the turbulence, caused by thermals rising from the coast."

I gave a little smile, shook my head to disagree, and gazed out my window. The professor suggested I'd used deduction. But in truth, I experienced the heat directly from the solid ground through my Sentio consciousness.

I leaned back against the headrest and from the corner of my eye could see the professor staring at me with an arched brow and questioning expression. When I didn't make eye contact, he resumed reading. I sighed, relieved he didn't ask me to explain how I'd known the solid ground was below.

From the time I was a premature baby, my mother, Aunt Helen, Uncle Poulou, and the Sisters of Freedom had nurtured me into a Sentio being, and that was why I experienced the world differently. I attend to the immediate projection of sense data in my Sentio, my pure sensory consciousness. The same sensory data experienced in Sentio continues through my brain, passing through an inhibitory filter where it's altered by various phenomena. Then a few milliseconds later, the altered data wave projects into my Cogito—language-thinking consciousness—where I can direct my attention when necessary. But most of the time my attention dwells in Sentio, the first consciousness and the source of all truth.

The institutions of America had enslaved the professor's attention to experience the world through his language-thinking consciousness, and he didn't know his sense data was dulled and altered. I wanted to tell him the truth, but I couldn't—not now. And the truth might upset him. I peeked again, and his eyes remained glued to his book, perhaps searching for the truth of the ages, which I knew he couldn't find. Most likely, he'd never experienced his attention in pure sensory consciousness, his sense of being in Sentio. Or if he had, he probably wrote it off as a mystical experience. He didn't know his attention was trapped in Cogito like an addiction.

When the professor wrinkled his brow and turned the page of his book, the thought that I would soon free his attention and give him the freedom to experience the truth of the ages played in my mind.

I would deliver pure sensory consciousness to him and all the Americans. How I experienced the rich texture of colors, especially during sunsets. How I saw ripples in the air streaming around Alex's body when he ran like a deer. How I saw Brownian motion in the clouds. And how I could sense temperature, pressure, and the velocity dynamics of fluids, like when I looked out my window and watched the air rushing over the top of the curved wing, reducing the air pressure above the wing and allowing our plane to lift—sensate causality.

My brilliant aunt Helen, who discovered Sentio, warned me that the only way to free the Americans from Cogito was by delivering Sentio experientially, like helping someone learn to ride a bicycle. I needed to provide a freeing sensory experience and then help them keep their attention dwelling in pure sensory consciousess while they learned to use Cogito as a plowshare for freedom instead of as a weapon for power. Then I'd need to find a way to restore their Sentio sensitivity, which in turn would restore their vision for freedom.

I knew my aunt's language-thinking ideas alone could not free the Americans, could not free their attention from Cogito, and using language ideas might work against my efforts to free them, as she had warned.

I looked over at the professor's wrinkled face, the face of Cogito, and remembered my aunt's words. *There's no language solution for internal freedom. Proposing language-thinking solutions will make it more difficult to free attention from Cogito.*

The professor closed his book and folded his glasses into his pocket. I turned my eyes up toward the ceiling, stretched my arms, and yawned.

"There's the famous harbor," the captain's voice announced over the intercom, "where America began her march toward freedom, home of the Boston Tea Party. And on our left is Cambridge, home of Harvard and the Massachusetts Institute of Technology, MIT. Once again, it has been our pleasure. Thank you for flying with Air France, and enjoy your stay in America."

I smiled to myself and glanced at the harbor through a window across the aisle. The Boston Tea Party had been a seminal moment in the history of humankind's march toward freedom. And soon I would lead the Americans on a new journey toward greater freedom.

"There it is, young man," the professor said with excitement and pointed at a large, gray-white building through my window. "That's where you'll be treating patients someday."

I gazed at the majestic building on the horizon, and a warm, tingling sensation filled my chest and spread to the top of my head. Staring for several moments, I thought, I'll discover the pathway to freedom there. My head tingled again, and I turned my eyes toward the streets below.

Everything on the ground looked clean and flawless—a curvilinear masterpiece. The tree-lined streets formed perfect circles, rectangles, and squares. And as we got lower, the colonial style buildings came into view, surrounded by green lawns and white sidewalks.

The professor talked about the architecture of the buildings on Harvard's campus, and a tear streamed down my cheek. I'd dreamed of this moment many times over the last four years, and now it was here. I was arriving in the United States two weeks before medical school was to begin, the Harvard Medical School Class of 1986. I wiped another tear from my cheek, shot the professor a smile, and checked my watch. My meeting with the dean of admissions was in two hours.

The professor handed me a card with his name and phone number. Norman Romsky. "Antonio, if you need anything or just need to talk, give me a call."

"Thank you. I will," I replied, and felt a warm glow from the professor's face. I would not forget him.

I glanced at his card again and put it in my back pocket. He was an expert on the genetics of language. Hmm. I furrowed my brow. I'd always thought language was learned. After a long moment, it dawned on me. If language was innate, the current institutional forces enslaving attention to language-thinking consciousness could propagate through natural selection, the driver of evolution. Humans with language-gene mutations—allowing their attention to be more easily enslaved to Cogito—would emerge preferentially. Then human attention would become permanently trapped in the mendacity of language-thinking consciousness. That inescapable conclusion replayed in my mind: humans, permanently trapped in the mendacity of Cogito.

A chill ran down my spine. I gasped and turned toward my window, shocked by the idea that humans might evolve further from the truth projected in Sentio, from the truth rooted in nature. The gravity of my mission was far greater than I'd ever imagined. If I wasn't successful in restoring pure sensory consciousness, Americans and humankind might be enslaved to Cogito forever.

The wheels of the plane touched ground in America then bounced again and again as the jet's engines revved, reversing their thrust. We slowed then came to a stop.

2

After taxiing to our gate, the passengers rose and gathered their things from the overhead storage bins. The professor wished me well. I said goodbye, and then he hurried on ahead. I stood and brushed the seat of my new jeans, a going away present from Polly. I fastened the button below my collar and tucked in my white shirt, a gift from Alex, and waited for an opening to exit my row.

A polite, French lady in the aisle paused. I thanked her with a smile, slipped out of the row, and stepped off the plane quickly. I walked into a large waiting area where a burly man in a red blazer called for foreign citizens to queue. I fell in line toward the middle, and we inched forward like a giant caterpillar.

Staring at the back of a man's gray-haired head in front of me, I reflected some more about the genetics of language. Sentio could be lost forever, and America would not fulfill her potential. I felt a pang of sadness, and then I thought about the American Revolution. My resolve grew.

I thought, I will ignite an American revolution for Sentio consciousness, in some ways similar to Paine, Hume, and Locke, the great empiricists who catalyzed the American Revolution by providing the vision to break free from British legal authority and monarchy rule, which violated the rule of equality and the truth rooted in nature. I will provide a way to break free from institutional Cogito existence—

The burly man called me forward. It was suddenly my turn. I stepped up to the counter, looked into the immigration official's glassy eyes, and handed him my student visa and passport. He stamped my passport and waved me onward as if it were no big deal, as if he knew the state of freedom in America. Once past immigration I was directed to follow the corridor to the claim area.

I marched behind several passengers from my flight and stopped to gaze at the large open area on my left, filled with gift shops and small restaurants strung like Christmas lights on both sides of the concourse. The smell of grease on tap streamed through the air, and voices overhead filled with urgency, calling for passengers to return to their gates. And more noise, more than idle chatter of a crowd—incomprehensible sounds and loud conversations—echoed through the concourse.

I realized then my Sentio was overloaded with unfamiliar sensory data, and Intentios, attention waves, were oscillating neurons all over my brain, searching my memory files for comparison data, reference information to help me understand the new and strange phenomena of my surroundings.

Intentios arose with every incoming sensory packet for recognition and safety, traveling much faster than consciousness, and then moments later they'd settle within my consciousness where I could control them by using the agency of selective attention.

Full of uncertainty, I turned and directed my attention to a couple of familiar faces walking past me: two garrulous Frenchmen who'd been on my flight. I followed them to the claim area.

My luggage appeared on the carousel, and I grabbed my red duffle bag, brown suitcase, and green backpack. Then an elderly female attendant directed me to the customs line.

"Passport?" asked the young gentleman in blue.

I put my bags down, pulled it from my back pocket, and handed it to him.

"Antonio Dasein?" he asked.

"Yes."

He looked me over, matching my features with my picture: long, brown hair; blue eyes; long-jawed face; and square chin with a small dimple. "One hundred eighty-eight centimeters, eighty kilograms?"

"Yes, six feet two and 180 pounds."

He glanced at his co-worker, and they both stared at my face. My hands began to sweat. What was wrong? Was it the stubble on my chin?

"Where is Andorra?" the young man asked his older partner, who shrugged.

Neither gentleman knew where Andorra was. Was that the problem?

They escorted me to a windowless room where they searched me and my belongings. I had nothing to declare and wondered what they thought I was hiding. The older man received a phone call, listened, then nodded to his partner who stopped searching through my things. I gave the young man an inquisitive look.

"Your long hair is why we searched," he explained. "You can go."

Strange. I wanted to tell him the reason for my long hair—two years earlier I vowed not to cut my hair until I freed the Americans—but realized he wouldn't understand. I exhaled a sigh of relief and thanked him for letting me go. I gathered my belongings from the table, dashed through the doors to the outer terminal area, and found an escalator to the ground level. I followed the moving sidewalk to the exit, passed through the automatic door, and took a deep breath of summer air.

I continued down a sidewalk into the sunshine to where yellow cabs choked a double-wide asphalt lane. A strong rush of salty wind blew my hair into my face, turning me sideways. I took out a red bandana from my duffle bag and wrapped it around my head. After tightening the straps of my back-pack, I gazed at the long row of cabs and stepped toward the crosswalk.

A man in a blue suit moved ahead of me. "Taxi!" he yelled.

When the yellow car pulled up, the man appeared to change his mind and turned away, so I approached the vehicle and looked through the open window. The driver's green eyes peered at me from under the visor of an old ball cap. He had a deep, jagged scar running from the corner of his mouth into his scruffy sideburn on the left side of his face, producing a sardonic twist to his mouth.

I cringed at his asymmetry and focused on his eyes. After a few moments, an Intentio, which his face had gener-ated, found my memory files of Ogie, the one-eyed man in Pierre—the town by the Essence orphanage—a nice man disfigured during the war. I smiled.

"Where ya goin?" the driver garbled, moving only the right side of his mouth.

"What?"

"Where ya going?" he repeated more slowly.

"Harvard."

"Back up," he said. When I moved back, he raised his leg and kicked open the handle-less front door. "Get in!"

I jumped in with my backpack behind me, placed my suitcase on the floor and duffle bag on my lap, closed the door, and held on for dear life as he sped away. He drove fast and close to the cars ahead. I wondered what he was thinking and what his reason was for changing lanes. The changes had produced no advantage. I kept quiet with my eyes on the road. About twenty minutes later, he stopped the cab near a tarnished bronze statue of a man sitting in a chair with a book in his lap.

"This is it," he said. "Harvard."

"Wow! Thank you," I said, gazing at the three-story brick building, the green-leaf trees, and the white-brick sidewalk leading straight to the tarnished statue.

"Who is the guy in the chair?" I asked.

"John Harvard. Eighteen dollars," the driver said. He took my twenty-dollar bill and searched his pockets for change.

"Keep the change," I said, and got out. Before I could turn around and ask for directions to the administration building, the cab had sped away.

CHAPTER

3

With my backpack pulled tight and bags in hand, I passed the statue of John Harvard and strolled down the sidewalk surveying my new home, looking for the medical school's administration building. My stomach growled as I pivoted east, south, west, and then north. The ivy-covered brick buildings—Georgian style, according to my professor friend from MIT—surrounded the campus and created a historical atmosphere. I walked until I saw the *Science Campus* sign, pointing north. I searched for my destination, which I knew from the pamphlet was a tall, glass building.

The Science Campus smelled like baked beans, making me crave beans with brown sugar on top and warm bread. I sniffed, trying to identify the source of the smell. As I walked past the biochemistry building, I detected a familiar, putrid odor of rotten eggs, like the compost pile at Essence. I lost my appetite and quickened my pace till I smelled the beans again. I took a big whiff. They smelled delicious.

I slowed to gaze at two attractive adults with bright green eyes and knitted brows moving toward me. I said hello to the couple, but they averted their eyes from mine, and I received no reply. They skirted around me as if I were not there. They seemed preoccupied—language thinking no doubt—American slaves of Cogito existence. They were all around me, and I wanted to tell them that I'd come to set them free. But for now I kept walking.

A red-haired young lady gained my attention when she dropped her books on the sidewalk. I approached her thinking of Polly, and she smiled at me. When I knelt to help, her boyfriend stepped forward.

"What do you want?"

I looked up at him and then turned toward her. "I want to help and say hello."

Her kind, blue eyes asked me to forgive her boyfriend as I handed her a book. The boyfriend pulled her arm and led her away. She looked over her shoulder at me with sadness, her expression reminding me of a new orphan girl arriving at Essence. She and her boyfriend disappeared behind a brick building. I hoped we would meet again when I could set them free.

I got to my feet and in the distance saw the sun reflecting off the administration building, which rose on the horizon like the horn of a unicorn. Made of glass, steel, and concrete, it was different from the other buildings. I picked up my things and ran to it, hauling my bags up the front steps and through two large glass doors. Once inside I put my bags down, caught my breath, and scanned the lobby. There was no one to ask for directions, no one to show me to the dean's office.

I followed the gray, slate floor and stepped into the lift just as the doors were closing. I'd been instructed to go to Room M10, but I saw no M button. Just G, B, and one through twelve. Suddenly the lift jumped then plunged. My stomach did a somersault. Stopping abruptly, the lift rattled, and the doors opened. A middle-aged black man in crimson scrubs rolled a stretcher into the lift, pushed the number six button, and asked, "What floor?"

I showed him my letter.

He smiled at me. "Room M10 is on the mezzanine, which is the second floor." He pushed the button marked two. "When you get off the elevator, M10 is all the way down the hall. You can't miss it. The office has a glass door entrance."

I thanked the nice man then looked down at the stretcher. What was under the plastic sheet? The smell was making my eyes water.

"What's on the gurney?" I asked.

The man explained that it was a cadaver. He'd fixed a woman's body with formaldehyde so it could be used in the human anatomy lab. I held my breath and tried not to think about the woman's body. When the lift stopped at the second floor, I said goodbye and scampered down the corridor, exhaling a sigh.

I entered M10 through its glass door, glanced around the room for signs of the dean, and saw another glass door at the end of a short hallway. The pale-yellow office was bright from sunlight coming through a large wall window. An older, plump lady with a hoarse voice sat behind the counter at a green desk talking on the phone and greeted me with a glare. I looked away. A fake palm tree stood next to the water fountain in the short hallway to my left, and I recognized two reproductions of Monet's garden paintings hanging on the wall to my right.

A blue-haired lady appeared from a glass office behind the counter, but she seemed reluctant to greet me, so I turned toward her and cleared my throat to gain her attention. Americans were more guarded than I had imagined. I set my bags down, leaned on the counter, and cleared my throat again.

"Are you Antonio Dasein?" the blue-haired lady asked.

"Yes," I said, surprised she knew my name.

She grinned and explained that I had arrived early, and the dean of admissions was out of the office. Then she said some things about me that were inaccurate—she believed that I was from Max Planck University in Munich—but I was afraid to correct her. Her authoritative demeanor made me jittery, so I listened in silence and then took a seat near the glass entrance door, where she'd directed me.

As I waited, I thought about the American predicament, their addiction to Cogito. How would I free their attention? I shook my head and looked down at the black and white tile floor—checkerboard—as if it held the answer. The blue-haired secretary approached. She walked past me, opened the door, and ambled down the hall. The door let in the delicious smell. The beans must be close, perhaps inside the building. My mouth watered.

I stood, garnering the husky lady's attention. "Can you smell that? Is someone eating beans?"

She frowned, her face turning bright red. "What?"

It occurred to me why she was offended by my question about the beans. "Oh, nothing," I said, embarrassed for asking. I wanted to apologize, but she got up and walked away from her desk. I sat, turned toward the door, and anxiously watched for the dean.

4

I could see the stainless-steel doors of the lift—an *elevator* as they say in America—at the far end of the long hallway. About ten minutes later, an orange-haired man exited the lift in a nice gray suit and blue tie and made his way toward the office. He looked like a dean. When he entered, the husky lady pointed toward me.

He turned and produced a smile with his square face and probing gray eyes. "Are you Dasein?"

I stood with a cordial smile. "Yes, I'm Antonio Dasein." I was a head taller than him.

"I've been expecting you. Your uncle called last week and said you were coming today. I'm the dean of admissions, but everyone calls me Director, the one and only Director here at Harvard, my nickname," he said in a friendly tone, and shook my hand for several moments. He looked over at my bags. "We need to store your things. Come on."

He grabbed my suitcase and led me down the hall into another office. We placed my things in a closet and locked the door, and the Director made a beeline toward the elevators.

I caught up with his quick pace. "We'll find you a place to stay later," he said. "I have to lead a group of premed students on a tour."

"I'm from Essence, Andorra," I said, wanting to clear up any confusion.

He nodded in understanding and kept walking. When we reached the lift, he looked down at his watch.

"Follow me," he said.

We bounded down the stairs to the ground floor. Stepping out of the stairwell into the lobby, we joined a group of twelve students, all attractive and intelligent looking with darting eyes. A pretty young lady with black hair, blue eyes, and an arched brow smiled at me and then wrote something in her notebook. Out of curiosity, I leaned over to see what she wrote, but she gave another inquisitive look at me and closed her book.

"Follow me," the Director said, garnering our attention, then waved his hand, and off we went on a tour of the campus.

We visited the science library, the law library, and a brick building with a copper dome, a teaching facility. We left the empty classrooms, and the Director led us over a long concrete bridge above a waterway to an enormous building, the largest structure I'd ever seen. It was the building my professor friend from MIT had pointed at through the window of the plane. The Director stopped, and we gathered around him as he spoke.

"This is the city's finest hospital and teaching facility. It spans four city blocks and operates 1,450 inpatient beds. Two entire floors, seven and eight, constitute our transplant surgery center. Our transplant teams replace broken hearts, lungs, livers, kidneys, and even small parts of the brain."

Small parts of the human brain? Hmm, I thought. We turned our attention toward the street as three ambulances, one after the other, traveled down the busy street in front of the hospital, sirens fading. Where were the ambulances going? I wondered as they slowed and turned down an alley. The Director led us across the street and pointed to the front of the hospital, guarded by glass doors and a sign above that read: *No Admittance.*

Odd. Why would they have doors and then deny entrance? I wondered. How do you get in?

The Director gave me a look as if he'd heard my thoughts and wanted me to ask the question. I shook my head; I didn't want to ask a question.

The Director pointed to his left. "The donated organs arrive over there."

The entrance for organs looked nice and clean, and behind the glass doors I could see the faces of people dressed in crimson; their faces were pale with the corners of their mouths turned down and with blank incurious eyes. What was wrong? They looked unhappy. I believed I saw despair in their eyes. I wondered about the human organs and their donors. Then it occurred to me; you'd have to die to donate your brain or heart.

Suddenly I became aware of my heartbeat, and waves of nausea passed through me with each beat. For several seconds I held a deep breath then released. I lowered my eyes and stared at the concrete sidewalk. The Director finished his speech about donated organs, and away we went. Walking briskly, I felt better.

The Director pointed at two glass doors riddled with holes. "The ambulances carrying the sick and dying unload over there." Over the doors a sign in big red letters read: *Emergenc*, with *No Admittance* painted underneath in black. Our group cut through a parking lot and approached the doors. Two men towing an empty stretcher entered through the doors without hesitation. About a minute later, two more men entered with another stretcher.

How strange, I thought, that they entered through the no-admittance doors.

Americans had a strange way. I thought about that book *1984*. I tried to recall the word used by the author, George Orwell, to describe the peculiar use of language—I couldn't remember.

Our troop came to a stop.

"Bullets caused the holes in the doors," said a nice looking black male student. "I saw the same size holes at Chicago General Hospital. Only a .45 round can make those holes."

I gathered the courage to speak. "What about the missing letter Y from the *Emergency* sign above the doors?"

"Someone must have taken the Y from the sign as a prank," said the Director.

"But why?" I asked.

The students laughed as the Director twirled and waved his hand for us to follow him.

"What about the bullet holes?" I asked softly, walking beside the Director.

He shook his head, blushed, and whispered, "Not now." He came to a quick stop and waved for the students to gather in front of an alley.

"The ambulances carrying the trauma patients enter on the other side," the Director said. "Follow me."

He led us down the short side street where we saw six ambulances waiting in line, delivering their patients through a glass door entrance beneath a sign that read *Trauma*, written in large black letters, three meters high.

I still wondered about the missing Y, and why there were so many bullet holes and injuries in America. Trauma?

I looked around the corner of the building and saw a man on crutches smoking a cigarette and a couple of other men in wheelchairs who appeared to be waiting for something. I pointed at them and asked the Director, "What are they waiting for?"

"They are waiting to be seen in the emergency room, and they look *pitoyable*," said the pretty, blue-eyed girl in a French accent.

"*Oui*," I said, and stared at her for several moments.

"*Ca va?*" she asked.

"*Bien.* I'm good. I love listening to your voice. It reminds me of home."

"Where is that?"

"Essence, Andorra."

"En Dor," she said, and smiled at me. She was attractive and reminded me of Sister Amelia, my language teacher at Essence.

The Director led us down a sidewalk away from the trauma sign. "Our trauma care ranks among the best in the world. In an emergency the medical staff can treat sixty casualties as easily as one," he said with pride.

He swiveled toward the sign and talked about motor vehicle injuries. I moved closer to hear him better over the noise from a fire truck and an aerial ambulance set against the inner-city medley of buses and automobiles. For a moment the sound waves ricocheted off the tall buildings and merged into one cacophony, raising the decibels to a point that was deafening and painful.

"We now conclude our tour of the hospital campus," the Director said. "Are there any questions?"

Silence fell over our group. I wanted to ask about the beans but didn't. The other students rushed away in different directions. I was glad the tour was over.

The pretty French student lingered and smiled at me.

"What did you write in your book?" I asked.

She hesitated. "Red bandana. *Au revoir.*"

"Bye." I waved. She turned and strutted away.

"Dasein, are you coming?" yelled the Director.

I tore my eyes away from *la mademoiselle* and followed him, reflecting on what I had just witnessed on the tour: the peculiar use of language, the faces of despair, bullet holes, trauma, the missing Y, and the pitiful fellows waiting for care. America was in deep trouble.

CHAPTER 5

I ran to catch up and followed the Director across the bridge. We climbed stairs on the other side of the building—a shortcut—and entered his office through the other glass door. When we walked in, a group of seven white coats was queued behind the counter where two men and a woman, all nicely dressed with fixed smiles, were passing out plates of meat, lettuce, and bread. A large, cream-covered chocolate chip cookie, bigger than a pie, decorated the counter. My mouth watered, and I looked at the Director, hoping there would be enough food for us to eat.

He whispered that a pharmaceutical company had donated the food and drink. How kind, I thought.

"Let's grab a plate."

The Director had said the magic words. We filled our plates with beans and chips and sat together at the table in the glass conference room behind the counter. I took a bite of my sandwich and noticed the blue-haired secretary cutting the cookie and sharing it with the husky lady and two other women. I hoped there'd be some leftover cookie.

While we ate the delicious food and sipped on tea, the company representatives asked for our attention and talked to us about an important new drug, Niagara. Then the nicely dressed woman in a gray skirt and blue jacket stood at the head of the table and described the new, blockbuster drug—named after the waterfall—as an improved break-through product used to invigorate male sexual performance.

"Odd name," I whispered to the Director, who smiled.

"Niagara used to be a big honeymoon venue," he whispered, staring at the woman, now explaining how the drug worked.

I listened for a few minutes and wondered about this Cogito pharmacy lesson given during lunch and decided they were trying to condition us by associating the neuro tracks of pleasure activated by the delicious food with their new drug's Cogito information tracks. How sneaky, American conditioning.

I leaned back with a pleasant smile of satiety while the woman continued with her bubbly sales pitch. She gave a happy projection of more than fifty million new prescriptions by next year. I frowned at the news. The others smiled, nodding their heads and applauding. America was in deep trouble, worse than I'd thought.

After the presentation I decided to explore the Director's Sentio awareness. I suggested to him that something was rotten in Denmark and that Americans had lost their sensory awareness and sensitivity. The Director looked at me and shook his head no.

"The new pill really works," he whispered. "I've used it, and for two hours I performed like a stud." He grinned and glanced at the husky lady with cookie cream on her cheek.

I shook my head to disagree. The Director did not understand Sentio. He said that I didn't understand Americans, and he believed I would enjoy being around German students. I wanted to tell him I understood Americans—slaves of Cogito existence who experienced altered sensory data—better than him. I looked into the Director's dim gray eyes and felt a wave of sadness; he didn't know he was enslaved to Cogito and that his sensory experiences were dulled.

After the meal we left his office and walked to the undergraduate library. The Director wanted to introduce me to some happy students. We approached a table in the whisper section, but the three German students frowned at us and buried their faces in their books. They didn't look happy. The Director apologized for disturbing them, and we left.

He led me to a science building where he wanted me to meet cheerful faces of well-adjusted students, and we found three, completely bald German students at the school for engineers—quantum physics majors working on an integrated circuit board in a dark laboratory. The German fellows followed us into the lit hallway and said hello and then agreed to come with us on a tour. They marched behind as the Director led us to the soccer fields where he pointed toward three freshman frauleins. The pretty young ladies passing their soccer ball stopped, looked at us, giggled, and ran to the other side of the field, joining their team. The Director waved at them. We paused for a moment watching other young ladies taking shots at the goal. As we continued on, the Director asked me if there were pretty German girls where I lived.

I'm not sure why the Director thought I was German. I'd explained to him that I was from Andorra. I explained again, and he nodded again. Then it dawned on me; the Director knew me by my application documents, and my degree was from Max Planck. No matter what I said, I couldn't override my Cogito existence already established in his mind. Frustrated, I fell behind our group, thinking that documents had become very powerful in America, more powerful than personal experience.

As we continued along toward the student centers, the campus vibrated with laughter, high-pitched screams, and sounds of play. Everyone seemed to be enjoying life at the Harvard undergraduate campus.

There were so many pretty, young girls—especially

the ones jumping in short skirts. The Director called them cheerleaders. I found myself staring at one brown-eyed girl with long, honey-colored hair dressed in a skimpy green and white outfit. She was beautiful. She ran on the track and did three flips, landing on her feet. Immediately, she pulled her hair back from her face with the gentility of a princess, displaying her high cheek bones, and then turned to watch another cheerleader flip. I smiled and thought how my uncle Poulou would enjoy watching the beautiful young cheerleaders at Harvard.

"Dasein, are you coming?" yelled the Director who had walked on ahead with the bald German students.

I watched the cheerleaders for a few more seconds and then skipped to catch up with the Director.

We visited the German Student Center where I met more Germans cooking food inside their three-story house. The Director whispered that it would be fun for me to spend time with them and talk about the fatherland. He said he would see me at 5:30 p.m. in his office and then left out the front door.

I turned and faked a smile at four freshman German students, sitting on the steps of a large staircase next to the kitchen to my left. After a long moment of silence, I introduced myself to a pretty, blue-eyed, blonde-haired female named Eva, and she told me she was a premed student. She grinned and I grinned. Before I could tell her that I was a medical student, a big commotion had erupted in a room down the hall on my right. We looked down the hallway toward the noise, and the bald engineering students came running out of a room toward us laughing uncontrollably.

"No! No!" yelled the woman cooking in the kitchen.

"That's disgusting!" yelled Eva.

It was disgusting. I watched as the German students scattered, fleeing the stench, and shook my head in outrage at the bald fellows.

"Did you find the beans on the science campus?" I asked with indignation.

The stinkers did not answer as two older German fellows came running down the stairs and chased them out the back door.

The smell of knackwurst, boiled cabbage, and flatus was sickening. I pinched my nose, glanced into the kitchen, and waved to the older, hefty German woman boiling cabbage. She caught my eye and gave me a smile as I departed. There was something special and sacred about the woman who cooked for the students. She reminded me of the women who cooked at Essence, the women who'd cooked for my freedom.

Once outside I exhaled and sniffed for the scent of beans. I gazed at the clear blue sky and then the campus horizon. Andorra was my motherland; I had no fatherland. I walked toward the soccer field searching for the cheerleader with honey-colored hair, but she was not there.

I found the dorms and watched the groups of girls in short skirts perform acrobatics on the lawn while their partners yelled rhyming cheers. Dorm windows framed more smiling faces, shouting cheers from dorm to dorm—the campus was near climax. Their shouting battle shook the ground beneath my feet.

"Go team, go!"

"One, two, three, four . . ."

"Beat them!"

"Lick them!"

"Win!"

I looked up in horror as a blonde-haired, female cheerleader jumped out of a third-floor window; her short, red skirt lifted into a parachute.

"For goodness sake!" I shouted, then gasped in relief as she landed on a giant trampoline, bouncing high into the air, again and again.

When she rolled off the trampoline, I smiled at her,

and she beamed at me. I told her she'd frightened me. But now I felt the urge to jump. She explained that she had to run to their competition near the football stadium and invited me to join them. I looked at my watch; my meeting with the Director was in ten minutes. I thanked her but declined her invitation. Another cheerleader approached, lifting the corners of her mouth at me too, and then they both departed.

Warmed by their ways, I yelled, "I hope to see you again."

The cheerleaders seemed very kind. They reminded me of the Sisters of Freedom at Essence.

6

Hurrying through the soccer field, I headed back to the administration building. I checked in with the blue-haired secretary and sat down on the bench against the wall outside the office waiting for the Director to come out of the lift. A few minutes later, he surprised me by coming from the door labeled *Exit*.

"Did you meet some nice German friends?" he asked, making eye contact briefly, and kept walking.

"Yes, they were nice," I said, got up, and followed close behind.

I asked him about the cheerleaders and suggested that maybe I should try cheerleading.

He stopped and smiled. "It is a cheer camp. The cheerleaders come from all over the world."

Ah, that explained why there were so many different squads and why the campus seemed overrun by them. A cheer camp, I thought; what a great idea. And the cheerleaders seemed happy and free.

"How about in the school of medicine? Do we have cheerleaders?" I asked.

The Director wrinkled his nose and scratched his head. His perplexed face looked a lot like Uncle Poulou's when he was thinking. "Medicine has too many cheerleaders. We need bright, strong men like you who can focus on learning medicine and delivering healthcare," he said in a jovial tone. Then his voice grew serious. "I forgot about the cheerleading camp—there are no dorm rooms available." The Director looked at his watch. "We need to hurry and get you a name badge. They close at 6:00 p.m. Follow me."

Down the stairs and out the front door we went. I had wondered where I'd be sleeping, but I was confused about the name badge.

"Our Campus Security requires a badge for appropriate identification for the sake of security," he explained, remaining one step ahead of me.

"I can tell people who I am," I said, "and I have my passport."

He quickened his pace. "Passports are no good on campus. Without a name badge, our picture ID, you do not exist at Harvard. You could be anyone from anywhere. We cannot allow that."

I didn't understand how I could be anyone from anywhere. "No matter where I go, I'm me," I said, running to catch up.

He stopped, pivoted, and laughed for a moment. "Yes, but your understanding of who you are, Dasein, will not fly in America. We need your picture and name so that we can decide who you are."

He resumed walking at a slower pace, perhaps pondering his own words. I wanted to say that I'm my Intentio, Sentio, and Cogito—here and now—and my Intentio is free.

"I do not have an identity. I'm just me." I knew he was referring to intersubjectivity and how my identity is supposedly determined by how others see me in the Harvard domain.

"Don't be difficult, Dasein. Everyone has a past and present self. We have to know some point in your past to create your present existence. We have to know what caused you."

"But I do not know what caused me."

"I don't mean your original cause. I mean some point in your life when you dropped anchor. We realize you will change, progress up the student ladder, and require a new ID badge every year, and you'll create a past here at Harvard. Isn't that nice?"

I shook my head and remained silent. I wanted to answer his rhetorical question by saying, I've come to free the slaves of existence and to free humans from institutions. Instead, I let my silence speak. The Director knew I didn't agree with this idea that I should be reduced to a picture badge in Harvard's kingdom.

As the Director picked up the pace, I walked faster, thinking I'm a Sentio being with a vision for freedom projecting into the future, the future's ecstasy and infinity—complete freedom. I am now, moving toward now-not-yet. Now-no-longer seemed to carry too much weight in America. And I cannot be fairly represented by a number or static photograph. I'm me, here and now. My I-self, Intentio self, reconstitutes in each now, now . . . now. I'm a living, thinking, and feeling being on a journey to find greater freedom for all. I wanted to ask if the American president wears an ID badge. If America is the land of the free, then an ID badge should not be necessary. But I knew it was useless to argue with the Director, who was enslaved by Cogito existence and now-no-longer. I remained silent.

7

We approached the hospital complex, and the Director slowed. A lightbulb seemed to go off in his head.

"I know where you can stay for a few days: in the hospital on-call rooms."

"Where are these rooms? In the city's finest hospital?"

He nodded, seeming stressed. "Yes, the interns and residents sleep there when on call at night. You'll stay there while I work on getting you an apartment."

We walked up the steps and through the side door into the hospital to have my photo taken for my badge. A nice, short lady in the personnel office took my picture and typed my name. She said that my picture looked handsome, and I thanked her. I smiled to myself because her Sentio image had stimulated an Intentio that visited old memories of Sister Josephine. A couple of minutes later, the machine spat out a little plastic card with my name and picture. The lady fastened a clip on the back of the badge and handed it to me. I slipped the badge in my shirt pocket.

"Two more stops." The Director led me to the end of a hall where we took the lift to the basement and walked toward an office with a sign above the door: *Parking.* Once inside, an old, scrawny fellow with steely eyes and a wrinkled face greeted us from behind the counter. He asked if I was a medical student, and I responded yes with pride. He looked at me with anger in his eyes and delivered a list of warnings in a resentful tone, instructing me where not to park my car.

"What car?" I asked, and looked at the Director.

"I forgot. You don't have a car," the Director said. "Sorry, I'm used to bringing students to get their parking permits. Excuse me."

We left Steely Eyes in a hurry. The Director led me to the security office down the hall where I noticed a large selection of donuts in a box near a half-full coffee pot warming on a burner.

"Have a seat," he said. "The chief must be upstairs in the business office."

I sat on a cold metal chair and placed my hands underneath me as we waited for the chief of security. The Director paced nervously and looked at his watch several times. He picked up the phone and punched a number. He spoke for several minutes about my needing scrubs, personal items, and directions to the interns' rooms. He said something about a dinner meeting and exchanged pleasantries. Smiling, he hung up.

"The chief of security had to tend to something," he said. "That was him on the phone. He'll return soon and take you to your temporary home. I'll see you later in the week. Have a great one."

The Director had left before I could express my gratitude. He was already down the hall entering the lift when I yelled thank you and then goodbye from the security office entrance.

I walked back into the office, caught a whiff of cinnamon, and looked at the donuts again. The chocolate, cream-filled ones looked delicious. I wished I'd eaten some of the cream-covered, chocolate chip cookies earlier—

"Antonio Dasein?"

I turned to answer. Standing in the office doorway was a short, fat man in blue, wearing a Mountie hat.

"Let me see your ID badge," he said.

I handed it to him. He gave a look and hooked it onto my shirt pocket.

"Dasein, keep your badge visible at all times."

"Are you the chief?" I asked.

"Yes."

I was about two heads taller than him. His body was wider and rounder than anyone I'd ever seen. His shape intrigued me.

"Follow me," he said.

He led me through the hospital basement where we stopped off at the supply room and picked up a toothbrush, razor, soap, and toothpaste. I needed to brush and shave. He pointed to a shelf that held small, medium, large, and extra-large tops and bottoms.

"Here, pick out some scrubs. Let me know when you need some more."

I selected a four-pack of medium crimson scrubs and followed the chief. We took the lift to the second level and walked down the hall to the on-call rooms. The chief opened the door by waving my badge in front of the black box mounted on the wall adjacent to the door. He hooked my badge back onto my shirt pocket and turned to leave. I thanked him for helping me. He wheeled around, looked into my eyes, and produced a broad smile warming my heart. He pointed to my badge, reminding me to keep it visible. I grinned as he told me to be careful and watched as he marched away. In a strange way he reminded me of Sister Josephine at Essence. A genuine, caring person lived beneath the chief's stern veneer.

Once inside the entry door, I walked into a spacious gathering area for the interns. The brown leather sofas and recliners in the lounging area looked comfortable, and behind the counter I saw a sink, cabinets, a microwave, and a yellow fridge. I opened the fridge, and it was empty except for a single half-full bottle of water. I meandered down the hall to the sleeping area and saw bunk beds in small rooms. How fun. I used to sleep on the top bunk at the dorm with Alex at Essence. I found an empty room and set my scrubs and toiletries down on a desk.

I walked out to explore Ground Level 2 and ventured down the long hallway. I wanted to travel down to Ground Level 1, but the lift wouldn't allow exit on Level 1—odd. I was afraid to take the stairs because of the signs on the doors that read: *Emergency Exit Only*, yet I saw several people enter and exit through the doors, and none of them appeared to have an emergency. I wondered what kind of Cogito existence Americans had settled upon, such misuse of their language. I remembered then the word Orwell had used: doublethink, the idea that a word can have opposite meanings simultaneously, and we accept them both.

Turning from the emergency exit, looking out the long hallway window, I saw a helicopter platform with a windsock and colored lights—green, red, and yellow—that made me think about Christmas Eve at Essence. I stared for a long moment and wished I was home.

"Code blue ICU number six! Code blue ICU number six!"

The woman's urgent words had blared from overhead speakers, bringing me out of my daydream. I wondered what a code blue was and saw a young man and woman wearing short white jackets scrambling toward the elevators. They looked like interns.

I strolled back to the on-call rooms, tired from my long flight and the day's activities. I stretched out on the top bunk, out of deference for my soon-to-be new bunk mate, and waited to see who that might be, but no one came. Twilight turned into darkness through a double window opposite my bunk. I wondered what had happened to America—their peculiar use of language, the faces of despair, bullet holes, trauma, the missing Y, the pitiful fellows waiting for care, Niagara, the oddball German students, Steely Eyes, and intersubjectivity at Harvard.

I allowed myself to feel sad for a moment—but only a moment. I looked at the ceiling tiles, thinking America was in worse trouble than I'd imagined. Then I thought about the Director, the German woman cook, the chief of security, and the scent of beans. I visited the images of the cheerleaders in my Sentio and smiled internally. I felt hopeful again that I'd find what I needed to know here at Harvard to restore freedom to the Americans and then the rest of the world.

I rolled over and tried to sleep, but my belly growled from hunger. I thought about my mother, Essence, Polly, and Alex. Oh, how I missed them. I turned on my side, cuddled with my pillow and found a Sentio memory about a hearty meal of stew and warm bread. I fell asleep.

8

Early the next morning I awoke and peeked from my doorway into the gathering area that was full of interns—handsome young men and women in short white lab coats—some standing and others sitting in a large huddle. I tied the drawstring of my scrub pants, tied my hair back, fastened my name badge on my pocket, slipped into my shoes, and walked out to join them.

Two fresh interns were addressing a tired intern with voices of concern. I drank some water and washed my face in the sink while listening. I didn't like the tone of their voices. After drying my face with a paper towel, I walked over and introduced myself to the tired intern, who was jotting on an index card. He sounded exhausted and didn't have time to talk because he was preparing to present his patients who'd been admitted during the night to attending physicians and residents, during a ceremony he called morning rounds.

Trying to reduce the tension in the room, I addressed the fresh interns and explained that in Andorra, rounds was a playground ball game for children.

"My friend Alex and I called the game centrifugal bumble ball. A ball on a rope connected to a pole thrown high and around the pole for fun."

"In America, people call the same game tetherball," one of the fresh interns responded.

Then the other fresh intern asked me to be quiet and turned away.

It was clear that rounds in America were not for fun, and my attempt to lift their spirits had failed. The interns exchanged sullen responses as they asked about each other's patients. It seemed that they knew each other's patients and had treated them before. They continued sharing information, referring to their patients as medical problems rather than human beings. It occurred to me that they were objectifying their patients. My aunt Helen had warned me about dehumanizing patients.

"How's the guy we admitted with the big anterior MI? How about the lady in DKA? The old fart from prison with sepsis?" the energetic interns inquired, and the weary interns muttered and stared.

I figured out what was going on. The nighttime intern took care of the daytime interns' patients. The interns were catching up on what had happened during the night, and they appeared more concerned about how the attending physicians would receive their presentations than anything else. Then all at once they stood, exhaled a group sigh, and left for rounds.

I sat in the lounge by myself, waiting for someone— anyone. I thought about the interns and premed students I'd met. I'd noticed their eyes moved about quickly. It was hard to make eye contact with them for more than a split second. I wondered why. My stomach growled louder, and I got up and searched through the trays near the sink. I found half a banana and some crackers and chewed slowly to make them last. Then I brushed my teeth and shaved in the large bathroom on the other side of the gathering area. I returned to the recliner and turned on the TV.

Several hours later I awoke hungry, got up, searched for food, and found some new empty trays by the sink. A large man wearing a tall chef's hat entered the gathering area, approached, and gave me an odd look as I foraged for food.

"Have you missed lunch? Do you need something from the grill?" he asked.

"No, thank you," I sighed. I had missed dinner, breakfast, and lunch, but I didn't want to bother him.

The man picked up all the trays, and I hurried over and held the door as he pushed the large cart of empty trays into the hall.

"Thanks," he said, nodding at me.

"You're welcome," I replied.

I took a seat in a recliner and rocked, thinking about our Saturday night fish dinners back home during the spring and summer. I missed Essence, and I missed my mother. My stomach gave another fierce growl, and I remembered stuffing a meal ticket in my duffle bag, which was in the closet in the administration building. After rocking for a couple of more minutes, I got up to get my ticket and to pick up some socks and underwear.

The man with the funny hat opened the door and approached with a smile and a tray. I could sense the warm food. When I tried to explain that I couldn't pay, he waved his hand and pushed the tray toward me. He didn't expect payment. I sat down at the table with him, removed the plate cover, and dove into the meal. The man watched with a slight smile and made eye contact as I ate the fish, chips, bread, cookie, and fruit cocktail. I thanked him and told him that his food was just as good as the cook's in Andorra, and he thanked me for the compliment.

"I'm Antonio Dasein."

"You can call me Joe." He gave me a firm pat on the shoulder and told me that starting tomorrow, he'd bring an extra breakfast, lunch, and dinner tray for me every day, marked with my name, *Antonio D.* I grinned.

The kindness of Joe elevated my mood, as had the meal.

He'd lifted my spirits after my disappointing attempt to lift the spirits of the interns who were worried about presenting their patients. I sensed Joe had a powerful Sentio waiting to be restored to its position of authority. I felt new hope for Americans. Smiling at him, I sat back in my chair, comforted by a full belly and enjoying the freedom from the misery of hunger. I thanked him again as he took my tray and departed.

Later that night after picking up my extra clothes and visiting with the Director, I felt more at home and less alone. I heard people nearby and wondered if they were happy. I got up and strolled out into the hallway toward their voices. A male nurse and a female X-ray tech identified themselves. I asked what they were doing and got no response.

"Are you happy?" I asked.

The X-ray tech asked me to move out of the way. The nurse shrugged and cocked his head sideways. "What ward are you from?"

"I'm a medical student living in the interns' quarters," I explained.

He chuckled then warned, "We do not have time to chat."

"Watch out," said the X-ray tech as she pushed the gurney around me.

Returning to the on-call room, I jumped up on my bunk and thought about the predicament of the X-ray tech and male nurse. Both appeared unhappy. I wanted to help them. But how? I tried to think of a way and realized the only way was to help them find freedom through Sentio.

I rolled over trying to sleep but could still hear them in the adjacent hallway. The chorus of their feet and rolling stretcher wheels played in my mind. The stretcher wheels created a unique sound against the tile floor, and I memorized the musical pathway, which repeatedly replayed on Ground Level 2. Stretchers were pushed to specialty X-ray and then back to the lift in a crescendo drum roll. The last big bump as the stretcher was loaded onto the lift created the finale of the Level 2 symphony.

I closed my eyes and fell asleep. I dreamed about my mother and Essence, and then I was dreaming about the nurse and the X-ray tech and awoke with an urge to pee. That is when I noticed the bathroom had no door. A long curtain, like a shower curtain, hung ceiling-to-floor where the bathroom door had been removed from its hinges. How odd! America was full of surprises.

9

The next evening, I asked one resident about the lack of bathroom doors as I climbed up on my bunk bed. The resident had introduced himself to me earlier as Andrew Wink, but he said everyone called him Anal. He had blue eyes, short blond hair, long sideburns, and a cropped goatee, which framed his lips and made his mouth look obscene, just like his nickname.

Anal was about my size and only made eye contact with me for a split second after our introduction. His eyes darted around the room as he talked. I'd never met anyone like him—odd but friendly at the same time. He began to explain why the interns' quarters had no doors for the bathrooms.

"A year ago there was an intern from Kipsie. He jumped down from the top bunk, probably tripped, and broke his head on a half-open door. The hospital's lawyers got involved, and they had the maintenance workers remove all the doors. And we were stuck with these wobbling bunk beds," said Anal.

"What happened to the intern?" I asked.

"He was declared brain-dead," Anal said. "Yep, poor dude. His brain died from cerebral hemorrhage."

"How awful." I hesitated for a moment then asked, "What happened to the rest of his body?"

40

"His family donated his heart, liver, kidneys, and lungs. Of course, all doctors eventually give everything, if not all at once then measured out by the spoonful every day. That is unless one of the million starving humanistic attorneys gets his hands on you first, then you can lose everything in one day in court."

"What? Why is that?" I asked.

Anal shook his head sideways as if I should know about attorneys. "Attorneys have no way to make a living other than suing and divorcing people, or sometimes they defend criminals like politicians. They are a bunch of scoundrels."

Anal went on as he sat on the edge of his bed. "Our society gives attorneys predatory rights over doctors. If not by malpractice, then they get you in divorce. They swoop down and rob you of everything. It is all legal; you'll learn."

I sat up, mystified by Anal's passionate description of attorneys and concerned about the legal predators of doctors and the term *legal*. Calling something legal seemed to make it morally right; calling something legal, even though it might be bad, made it good.

According to Anal, Americans had put all their faith into attorneys and politicians, who were enslaved by a legal Cogito existence and who created broken families as the products of their labor, their sense of being—a lot of nothingness—a dismal existence.

I thought for a long moment. If I could free Americans to become Sentio beings driven by the will for freedom rather than Cogito beings driven by the will for pleasure and power, then perhaps they would do the right things without the need for so many laws and attorneys. I'd learned at Essence that all humans have a yearning for goodness and the potential for empathy, arising from Sentio.

Then I thought about doctors. I asked Anal, "What are doctors but fancy titles for human beings who feel an obligation to care about the needs of other human beings?"

"You cannot live up to the altruistic doctors of the past. Don't even go there," Anal said. "Those guys gave everything and more. If you ask me, their goodwill allowed the attorneys to get their feet in the door. They tried too hard to be good." He paused for a moment. "The obligation and altruism died several years ago, and I hope you understand why that's a good thing. Now doctors can focus on what matters most: getting reimbursed for what we do, for our years of enslavement in these death camps."

"Death camps?"

"Yes, death camps. To survive, you must decide to be a human in between seeing patients, or you'll end up donating everything all at once like the brain-dead intern." He got up and turned out the lights.

I was astonished at how much Anal seemed to know about attorneys and the sacrifice of doctors. He was so quick-minded. I wondered what had happened to him. He was trying to squeeze out a life in between patients, and I could sense his panic. I had nothing to offer him. His Sentio had shut down, and his medical training had filled his brain with scientific and legal Cogito, imprisoning his Intentio.

"Was there ever talk about putting the doors back?" I asked.

Anal sighed. "I need to get to sleep."

"I'm sorry. I'm just curious. I've never known doors to be so dangerous, and I can't stop thinking about the heartbroken intern's family in Kipsie."

"The intern served humanity, and now he is free from the drudgery of a life of servitude," Anal grumbled. "It depends on your beliefs as to where the intern is now, heaven or hell. I believe he is just dead. The hospital sued the builders for the incorrectly hung doors and the cost for replacement doors, never replaced. The intern from Kipsie donated his organs, which the attorneys used for leverage in unrelated cases. Later the hospital attorneys argued against the intern's family and convinced a jury the intern had died from a tragic accident."

I frowned as Anal continued.

"The attorneys won on both ends. The doors had been hung wrong, so the builders settled. Then the attorneys settled with two other families in unrelated suits. The other families withdrew their separate suits against the hospital when replacement organs became available for their loved ones." Anal finished the story matter-of-factly and with no show of emotion.

Waves of nausea passed through me. Feeling I might retch, I was afraid to speak. The intern from Kipsie had provided the replacement organs—what an awful story—and his family got nothing. The attorneys had won on both ends. Americans had settled upon a legal Cogito existence.

Releasing a deep breath, the waves of nausea subsided. I said goodnight and tried to sleep, but I couldn't. The next day I got up and could not get the poor intern from Kipsie out of my mind. I didn't even know his name. Anal couldn't tell me his name because of some law created to protect organ donors and their recipients. As I walked down the hallway, I felt the urge to cry every time I saw a door. I spent the day mourning the loss of the intern and hoped his family had found peace.

CHAPTER 10

Around midnight on my fourth night, I was snacking on red grapes by the sink in the gathering area. A brown-haired, brown-eyed, beautiful young lady in her long, white lab coat approached.

"Hello," she said, and reached to shake my hand.

I wiped my hand on my scrubs, took her hand in mine, and grinned. She seemed friendly and fearless. Her name was Linda Hedrick, a medical resident from Stanford Medical School in California. Her sparkling eyes touched my Sentio in a way I'd not experienced in America. I felt an immediate connection to her at a deep level through her eyes. She released her grip and our hands fell apart. She asked if I was a new intern. I smiled, shaking my head no. Her eyes seemed so curious, like my mother's, and she had an English accent like Sister Josephine. I shared some grapes with her and explained I was a new medical student.

"That's wonderful," she said. Then she encouraged me to observe her and learn as much as I could.

I smiled to myself at her concern about my education and her invitation to observe her. I agreed with her that I had a lot to learn and then she offered again. After a moment staring at her in silence, I accepted her invitation. She explained how I could follow her when she was on call watching over the interns. A little nervous and excited about

44

my new friend, I reaffirmed my acceptance of her invitation to follow her around and observe on Monday night. I thanked her and said goodnight. I put the grapes back in the fridge.

She seemed deep in thought when I left, and after a few minutes she walked into my room, surprising me, and asked if the bed below me was vacant. I almost blurted yes but instead nodded, trying to control my excitement. I wanted her to sleep beneath me and hid my enthusiasm behind my grin. She asked if it was okay if she turned out the light. I lifted my head and nodded several times, still too excited to talk. She winked at me and turned out the light.

She removed her lab coat, and I stared at her silhouette as the moonlight came through the window, tracing her beautiful, feminine curves. She shook her head causing her long, brown hair to release from atop her head twirling down her back. She unloaded her pockets, as Alex and I used to do after catching frogs, and created a little nest on the dresser with her stethoscope surrounding several personal items: keychain, whistle, bracelet, and a tiny flashlight, which lit up her nest for a few seconds.

She sat on the bunk, slipped out of her shoes, and then fell back into the bed. I squinted through a peephole between my mattress and bed frame. I could see her as I lay still and quiet, watching her every move as she pulled and loosened the covers around her feet. She fluffed her pillow then repositioned her head. She drifted off to sleep, breathing through her nose with no snoring. Warmed by her presence beneath me, I rolled over, inhaled her sweet fragrance—like Polly's lilac scent—and drifted toward sleep, visiting Linda's moonlit silhouette in my reflective Sentio.

I woke when her pager went off. She grabbed the phone under the bed and barely wiggled when she placed a call.

"Yes, you can give him two milligrams of morphine." She hung up and fell back to sleep.

She slept on her side like my mother.

A feeling of joy washed over me. Smiling, I drifted back to sleep.

When I awoke in the morning, I looked below. She was gone; all her things were gone. I could still experience her sensate reality, warmth, and sweet fragrance. I visited her image in my reflective Sentio for a long moment and then got up and showered.

After eating toast and scrambled eggs from my breakfast tray, I sat in the main room of the intern quarters, thinking about the night with Linda. I rocked in a recliner and visited her image again, which had remained luminous in my reflective Sentio. An hour later I felt tired but wasn't sleepy, so I got up and moved from seat to seat until I decided the three sofas and two large reclining rocking chairs were equally comfortable.

Around noon three interns approached, waking me as they argued about something and sat on the sofa. I'd fallen asleep in my recliner and had been dreaming about Essence. The interns stared at the big TV screen and grew silent as they ate from their lunch trays and then disappeared shortly thereafter. Two more interns appeared and watched a cable news channel that paraded disasters with lost humanity and mundane existence with criminality, and the news presenter offered jaded commentary. Many more interns came and went during lunch.

A couple of second-year residents joined me in the late afternoon and watched TV while eating meatball sandwiches. They made sarcastic comments about the breaking news, enjoying their own remarks more than the presenters' views. An obese, pompous attorney delivered insight about the breaking news story and how he planned to restore America's greatness with some new laws that would replace three thousand pages of failed recent laws. I enjoyed the residents' humor directed at the attorney, which embraced the idea that American legal Cogito existence was the problem; I felt hope for the residents and sensed they desired freedom.

The residents stopped laughing. The black-haired resident claimed that you had to think about laws just walking down the street in America, and when treating patients laws guided every conceivable interaction with your patient. I almost laughed until I realized he was serious.

During the commercial I changed the subject and asked the residents about the smell of beans on the science campus. They looked at me and laughed. The yellow-haired resident explained, "The smell is from the nasty shit cooked at the Quiche and Bean shop behind the administration building."

That explained the smell of beans in the Director's office. I said goodbye and went to my room to exercise. After doing one hundred pushups, I got up and walked around, preparing to do more pushups and some sit-ups. The yellow-haired, chunky resident walked by the door and saw me without my scrub top. He called my abdominal muscles a six-pack. He said he used to have abs like mine before his residency. But now his belly had grown full as if he'd swallowed a watermelon seed. I flashed a smile at the thought of a watermelon growing inside of him.

I did some more pushups, and he counted for me. After finishing, I asked him out of curiosity if he knew the chief of security. He nodded and left abruptly as if I'd offended him. Confused, I continued with my exercise. I'd only mentioned the chief because I thought that if the resident could figure out what had happened to the chief's body, perhaps he could help himself and the chief.

After exercising, I thought about Linda. She would be on call again Monday, and I was going to follow her around. I wanted to sound and look sharp because I wanted my image projecting into her consciousness for her pleasure. Wanting her to desire me motivated me to do more pushups.

Cooling down from the extra sets, I thought about

intersubjectivity, the term my aunt Helen had warned me about. I wondered if I was losing my individuality because I wanted Linda to have a pleasurable conscious experience and memory of me? I pondered my individuality and decided I was in no danger of losing my beingness and becoming what others projected onto me.

Later that night I lay on my bed thinking about Linda. There was something special about her, something that could perhaps help me deliver greater freedom for all. But what? I didn't know, but I could still experience her luminous image in my reflective Sentio. I pulled an old picture of my mother from my wallet and stared. My chest warmed and tingled. Linda looked like the picture of my mother when she was still Anna Simmons before she had changed her name to Sister Anna Marie Simmons Antoinette, which made Linda even more special. I turned out the lights and hit the sack.

CHAPTER

11

I'd spent a fascinating and busy night following Linda around as she interviewed and examined patients all over the hospital. I fell asleep on my bunk at about eight Tuesday morning.

Waking in the afternoon, I still felt exhausted, needing more sleep, but I couldn't sleep. I lay on my bunk, and my Intentio kept visiting my observations, my memories, while I'd watched Linda caring for her patients in her kind and gentle way late last night and early this morning. I remembered being in the emergency room around 2:00 a.m. I'd asked Linda a question about a patient in heart failure who couldn't seem to relax his heart rate, and she'd glanced at me and smiled, saying that's an intriguing proposition. Remembering her smiling brown eyes, I smiled to myself.

The memory of being with her this morning seemed so vivid now. I sat up in my bed and took a moment to visit the image of her face in my Sentio again. A warm glow emerged in my chest and spread throughout my body then. I got up and went for a walk on the undergraduate campus, thinking about Linda, Dr. Linda Hedrick. I wondered why she was different than all the other Americans I'd met.

In the early evening I returned to the hospital and watched from the hallway window in amazement. The helicopter whirred and dropped down to the ground, and then two helmeted medics in crimson dress jumped out of the side door and crouched as they lifted their patient onto a gurney. Two nurses joined them, and they rushed the patient on the stretcher through two large, automatic glass doors. The pilot waited with the blades turning, and when the crew in crimson returned, the helicopter rose and moved suddenly into the twilight sky.

I turned and found an intern named Jason standing beside me. "Amazing!" I said, and we resumed gazing out the hallway window from Ground Level 2.

Jason—tall, skinny, and wearing black horn-rimmed glasses—said the helicopters were used for local emergencies and did not concern him. He was on alert for air ambulances, taxicopters, which came from hundreds of miles away and delivered very sick patients who couldn't pay. I walked into the on-call area with him, talking about the taxes needed to pay for the sick patients flown in from miles away. Healthcare was very expensive in America.

We sat on the sofa, watched TV, and about twenty minutes later heard a distinct stirring sound—much louder and more forceful than a helicopter. Whatever it was, it must have landed because I could feel the vibration in my feet. Jason nodded that it was an air ambulance, the first one I'd ever heard. The sound resembled the noise made by a speeding train, and I sensed fear in Jason. He jumped like a scared cat when his pager went off and left in a hurry to check on a patient with fever in the ICU.

Anal, who'd been watching TV, turned and smiled at me. He got up from the recliner, walked to the kitchen area, and threw me a tired-looking banana. He explained that the air ambulances delivered patients who were complicated and that it could take hours to sort out how someone at another facility had screwed up their care.

"You have to assume the transfer patient has been

misdiagnosed and mistreated. The interns get spooked, but they'll learn," Anal said with a sly grin. "It's axiomatic."

"But what if the patients have not been misdiagnosed, and they get worse because their treatment is changed?" I asked.

"You blame the bad outcome on the other facility for not sending them sooner," Anal said with no sign of emotion or concern about the possible harm in his strategy.

Frustrated, I asked myself: How can I help Anal? He'd given me insight but also caused me to feel despair because he didn't care. I watched a banana disappear into his mouth and lost my appetite. I laid my banana on the counter, went to my room, jumped up on the top bunk, and lay there staring at the ceiling, wondering if I would be able to free the Americans.

Anal caused me to doubt my mission; his legal Cogito sense of being perplexed me. How can I free his attention from this cynical language-thinking existence? It seemed impossible to affect him. Then I remembered what my mother had told me about how to give love to orphans who did not like to be hugged: through eye touching—making eye contact with soft, gentle eyes. Anal needed love, and he reminded me of my orphan brothers who didn't want to be hugged when they first arrived at Essence. I needed to try to touch Anal's eyes and send him love. I drifted to sleep with that thought playing in my mind.

12

The next morning I lay in bed thinking about Anal and the doors. He'd slept below and had already left. I got up to exercise and went for a jog at the undergraduate campus track. While jogging, I ran into the Director who was leading students on a tour. He said he had good news about my apartment, and he'd see me in a couple of days. He waved goodbye, leading his group of students toward the bridge.

I jogged for another hour, and the young, smiling faces of the cheerleaders returned to the track, rejuvenating me. I took a seat in the upper deck of the empty stadium and watched them cheer. They left late in the afternoon, and then I watched a beautiful sunset. The sky was painted with my mother's favorite colors: violets, blues, and pinks.

A warm glow emerged in my chest and a tear released. I was thinking about my mother and the Sisters of Freedom. I missed them and Essence. Twilight faded into darkness, and suddenly large bright stadium lights came on. The cheerleaders ran onto the field. Excited by their return, I moved to a lower seat and watched them cheer under the lights, thinking how similar they were to the Sisters of Freedom—not in appearance but in their kind and happy dispositions, the way they treated each other. Amazing.

It was late at night when I returned to the interns'

quarters. I was famished. I ate my dinner—spaghetti and garlic bread—and finished off a quart of milk. I ate an ice cream sandwich and met my new bunkmate, Dr. Bock, who was a six-foot-six, 250-pound former Yale football player. We talked in the gathering area. He finished his second ice cream sandwich and joined me in our room.

"You want me on top?" he asked.

"Oh, no. I'll sleep on top."

Dr. Bock fell asleep immediately and began to snore like Sister Phillips at Essence—very loudly.

I brushed my teeth then climbed the ladder and eased over onto my mattress. His snores grew louder. I tried to sleep by thinking of his snores like ocean waves, a trick Sister Josephine used to teach the orphans at Essence. But his snoring was too irregular, and every time Dr. Bock produced a really loud snore, he'd soon toss and turn, causing the bunk to wobble. After one particularly loud snore, he breathed in silence, no tossing or turning. A couple of minutes passed, and I relaxed.

Then an urgent *Code blue, room 601. Code blue, room 601* blared from the ceiling speaker in the hallway. I knew it meant an emergency was in the works for a patient near death in Room 601, and Dr. Bock knew too. When he tried to stand, he almost fell, pulling me and the bunk beds with him. I grabbed the railing next to my mattress and leaned opposite to him as a counterbalance, sweat beading at my temples. The bunk rocked back and forth several times and almost toppled. I didn't want to end up like the intern from Kipsie. After the bed stopped shaking, I waited about thirty seconds, then leaned over the edge, and noticed that Dr. Bock had rolled onto his abdomen and fallen back asleep. I'm not sure that he ever fully awoke. Several minutes passed, and his snoring had stopped. He was breathing without effort and slept serenely.

I lay on my bed trying to sleep, hoping there'd be no

more code blues, and thought about the word blue: a color of calm and serenity but used to condition anxiety and despair. I wondered what other conditioning Americans had adopted and who was looking out for the citizens. Who was in charge in America? I thought about the attorneys, those dirty scoundrels; they must be in charge.

I drifted off to sleep.

13

Waking after only a couple of hours of sleep and feeling exhausted from my restless night with Dr. Bock, who'd already showered and left, I got up, ate breakfast, returned to my bunk, and fell asleep.

Later that afternoon I awoke and realized it was Thursday. I needed to talk to the Director. I showered, changed into fresh scrubs, and ambled out to the gathering area. I grabbed a soggy, toasted tuna sandwich from my lunch tray, took a bite, and tore open a bag of Fritos. After chewing on the last bite of my sandwich, I crunched the last of the chips and washed them down with a carton of milk. I went back to my room and called the Director to inquire about my apartment. He said he'd found someone to help me find an apartment and wanted to see me in the morning. He reminded me that medical school was starting next week, so if I couldn't find an apartment tomorrow, I would need to move into the dorms this weekend. I hung up knowing it was probably my final night in the interns' quarters.

A wave of sadness passed through me, and I looked over at the bunk beds. I thought about the sad lives of my new friends. I had to help them and the others find freedom through Sentio.

How? Leaning back in my desk chair, thinking, I had

no idea and then remembered Linda was on call tonight and was comforted by the thought. Her image had become my most frequently visited Sentio memory. She was such a kind person, and I was secretly falling in love with her.

I walked down the hallway and found her in the gathering area where she was standing in her crimson clogs. She turned and looked at me with her fathomless, brown eyes. Her beautiful, long, brown hair was pulled atop her head, and she was wearing a white lab coat and crimson scrubs underneath. Her black stethoscope hung around the collar of her coat.

"Are you ready for another busy night?" she asked with a smile.

I returned the smile and nodded. "I'm ready."

I thought how grateful I was for Linda and how I would miss her. When I told her that it was our last night, she arched her brow, looked sad for a moment, and then teased me with a serious look. "Let's make it one to remember. We're on the cardiac arrest team tonight. We'll respond to all the code blues."

I grinned. Linda knew I wanted to see a code blue.

After Linda received a report from the daytime residents, she waved for me to follow. She led me up the stairs and across the ninth floor to a small office to check on an intern. I'd learned how to shadow Linda and stay out of her way when the excitement—or the arguing—began. After telling the exhausted intern she needed to answer her pages, Linda gave her an encouraging pat on her back and offered to help any way she could. The intern thanked her.

We left the small office, took the lift down to the first floor, and walked toward the emergency room. When we heard the words *code blue, room 604*, we ran into the stairwell and sprinted up five flights. Linda pushed open the stairwell door and ran down the hallway, and I followed toward Room 604 where several nurses came out into the hall waving their arms. The plump nurse said, "It was a mistake. It was a mistake; there's no one in that room."

I'd caught up with Linda, and we slowed to a stop, both winded. She leaned against the wall, caught her breath, and said, "Sometimes code blue is called by mistake."

I took some deep breaths with my hands on my head.

On our way back to the lift, we heard the call again, hurried into the lift, and exited on the tenth floor, looking for room 1013. We entered the room where a crowd of interns and nurses had gathered to resuscitate an elderly lady with blue lips, lying supine in her bed.

"She stopped breathing," the nurse said to Linda.

The lady looked like the picture of Sister Lenina in the Big Bell Chapel in Andorra. Over the erratic beeps of her heart monitor, I heard strange sounds—grunts and racquets hitting balls—and noticed the TV behind my head was tuned to a hard court tennis match. The women's semifinal match. I reached up and turned it off.

Standing at the head of the bed, a well-built, smart looking doctor in a white coat shouted out orders to two male interns as if they were the cause of the lady's respiratory arrest. After some difficulty, the doctor inserted a tube into the elderly woman's windpipe. Linda began squeezing a bag attached to the tube to deliver oxygen to the woman's lungs. I feared the two interns would exchange blows with the doctor as his shouts at them got louder. The interns, sweat beading on their foreheads, took turns doing chest compressions, which had obviously stopped working. The lady's pale body and blue lips had turned gray, and her body had ceased emitting heat. The heart monitor revealed a flat, green line, and the doctor ordered everyone to stop.

Linda saw my irritation and led me outside into the hallway where she explained that it was the doctor's job to shout like a bully. Confounded, I realized Americans had lost their civility and concern for one another because of some idea no doubt connected to legal Cogito. I also realized Linda was right that someone had to be in authority to run the code blue. I shook my head at Linda communicating I understood. But I was still upset and wondered why Americans had picked a bully persona.

At the next code blue, Linda acted as the bully. She tried to save a middle-aged man. She was more civil, and her English accent gave her shouted orders supreme authority. I was impressed. She passed the tube into the man's airway with the greatest of ease, but her multiple attempts to shock the poor man out of his cardiac arrhythmia failed. *Course fibrillation* I heard Linda tell the tall, newest arriving doctor with the emblem of a heart on his lab coat.

Linda approached me near the foot of the bed after relinquishing her role and whispered that the cardiology fellow needed to practice as the bully, so we left the dying man in good hands. The fellow shouted orders as we slipped out of the room, "All clear! All clear!"

I followed Linda to the nurse's station, and when she finished writing in a chart, I said, "Americans have an odd way of trying to save someone." Linda looked up and agreed with me that it was odd but said it worked sometimes. I'd not seen it work, but I believed her. Then I asked if she was American. She explained that she was not born in America, but she was American. I was curious about her accent but didn't want to embarrass her. I thought her voice was beautiful. She closed the chart and placed it in the rack.

Another code blue rang out, and we ran to the fourth floor. Another elderly lady had stopped breathing. All night long code blue alerts thundered through the hospital intercom. After midnight we'd stopped tracking them down; Linda said that the ICU doctors and cardiology fellow handled the code blues from midnight till eight in the morning. We stayed busy visiting the new admissions, patients admitted earlier through the ER, and then Linda finished some dictations in the medical records department regarding patients she'd discharged last week.

We were finally free, and I hoped I'd get a chance to talk to Linda about my concerns, what I'd observed in America. We walked to the medical wards to see if they were busy. The interns reported their night had been slow except for the code blues. We walked to the ER, and Linda explained to the medical admitting officer, or MAO, that it had been a bad night: twelve code blues and one code red so far.

"One of the patients was caught smoking cigarettes in the stairwell," Linda said.

The MAO shook his head from side to side in dismay and said he wanted to try to sleep while it was quiet.

I spoke up to get Linda's attention. "The code red, I meant to ask you about that."

Linda didn't say anything. She turned and smiled at me, like my mother's silly smile. We left the MAO in the ER and walked down the corridor toward the main elevators.

"Elevators are much more substantial than lifts," Linda explained. She preferred the word *elevator* because its meaning was a more substantial structure with more lift capacity compared to the word *lift*; its meaning was a smaller structure with less lift capacity.

"I thought *lift* was the word the British used and *elevator* was the word preferred by Americans. I didn't know there was a difference," I said.

Linda laughed. "It's okay to use the word *lift*. I still catch myself saying lift. It has taken me years. . . . Isn't that silly?"

I started to shake my head to disagree about it being silly, but I caught myself. The word *lift* was probably the word Linda had learned as a child, and she'd probably associated the word's meaning with its function, to lift. I didn't want to risk having to explain sensory causality and meaning making. I didn't want to talk about Sentio.

I changed the subject."Code blue is an odd thing to say because it can mean so many different things."

"You're right, Antonio. I always hope it means a mistake has been made." She waved her hand. "I'm going to take you on a tour since the ER looks dead. Come on."

We hurried through the lift doors as they were closing, and someone had already pushed the eleventh-floor button, which was where Linda wanted to take me. We lifted against gravity and rose slowly, stopping on every floor until we were finally on the eleventh. We followed an elderly couple who shuffled off the lift. Linda smiled at them as we passed by and led me down the hall to a big room, which was filled with carts and open cabinets loaded with plastic bags of water containing NaCl and dextrose. Some of the bags were tagged with red labels. There were syringes near little bottles on the counters. Granite counter tops in parallel, six by my count, served as worktops. We saw at least twenty staff members standing at the counters with their heads buried in computer screens, and some were injecting the bags of water with syringes filled with a yellow solution.

"They are adding vitamins to the IV fluids for selected patients," Linda explained.

She walked over to another worktop, called me over, and showed me how to access a computer. I caught on quickly as she let me search through the simulated pharmacology program, but soon the computer monitor was flashing so much memory at me that it overburdened my Sentio. Linda took over and found a program she wanted me to see.

Looking at the screen, I felt unnerved as it streamed 3-D images of endorphins—the molecules of pleasure and pain relief—interacting with larger endorphin receptor molecules on nerve cells in a simulated human neurophysiology module. The endorphin receptors also responded to opiate molecules like morphine and codeine. Interesting. Linda explained the 3-D program for several minutes and then complained that the images, endorphin and morphine molecules competing for the endorphin receptors, made her dizzy. I agreed about feeling dizzy, so she turned it off.

A short-haired, older man in a long, white coat approached and asked if we wanted a donut. Linda explained to him that she was giving me a tour.

He nodded at Linda and found my eyes. "This is our pharmacy and the central nervous system for the city's finest teaching hospital," he said. "Welcome to Harvard."

I could see and feel his pride in the facility. "Very interesting."

I didn't know what else to say as I looked around the room, taking in so many new things. Linda thanked him, and we declined the donuts and said goodbye. Then Linda whispered that she knew where we could get some healthy snacks. We left for the on-call room on the sixth floor.

14

"The faculty on-call room has the best snacks," said Linda as we hurried onto the lift.

She had a key to the on-call room because she was working in the sensory deprivation research center. Linda was a research fellow and a resident. Impressive. She explained her research as we walked down the shiny, white tile floor to the end of the hall. She unlocked the door, and we entered the lounge. She and Dr. Wolf worked on ways to increase memory using intimate human touch. Her research on something as simple and powerful as human touch intrigued me. I wanted to know more.

We sat at a table, and she explained. She talked and talked about her research. She seemed so serious when she spoke about precessing the hippocampus with a kiss. I had no idea what she was talking about, but I listened and nodded with a big internal smile. Next to Aunt Helen, Linda was the most interesting woman I'd ever met. She knew tiny details about matters I'd never thought to consider.

Linda finished talking, walked over to the counter, and picked up an apricot. "Want one?"

"Sure."

She delivered it with a perfect underhand toss and said apricots were her favorite. I told her they'd been my favorite since I was a baby.

"I think I'll get some carrots and celery from the fridge."

"We can share the apricot," I said.

"Oh, no. You enjoy. I like crunchy snacks."

We relaxed in reclining chairs, munching, and settled into a quiet, companionable time. I looked up at the clock: 5:00 a.m. Time passed so quickly when I was with her.

"The central nervous system of the hospital smells like jelly," I said, and leaned back in my chair.

Linda laughed and agreed.

"What is the smell in the hospital? It's everywhere."

"The medicinal smell is from the iodoform cleaners that they use to kill the microbes."

"There are microbes everywhere. I hope the smell is working," I said.

Linda laughed again and made a peculiar sound with her laugh. She smiled and apologized for making the funny noise. She was blushing.

A warm tingle spread from my chest to my head. I grinned at her. She'd looked so cute when she apologized for making the sound. And I liked her peculiar sound.

After a few seconds of silence, I asked Linda if she knew Andrew Wink. She said that she did and told me about the anal wink reflex and how Andrew got his nickname. I laughed at the thought of his mouth winking from a light touch, a feather rubbing over his cheek, like the anal reflex. Linda laughed too in fun. Then I told her about my conversations with Anal.

She understood my concerns about him, and her understanding gave me confidence that someone like her would soon be in charge, perhaps putting the attorneys in their place. The more we talked I realized I could talk to her about anything, and she seemed so forgiving of others' shortcomings, their human frailties. She made me feel safe and secure.

She and Anal would be finishing up their residencies

next year. Anal wanted to do cardiology, and she was going to continue her fellowship doing research in the sensory deprivation lab with Solomon Sol's group.

She talked and talked, delivering more scientific information about her research with her sophisticated British accent, her voice so sincere and civil. When she laughed, she made the funny sound again and tried to muffle it, the sound of a hiccup in her nose. I connected with her embarrassed eyes, smiled, and began talking about my homeland.

When I told Linda about Essence, she grew silent and still. I told her about being orphaned as a premature baby. I talked about Andorra, and her face glowed as she obviously enjoyed hearing about the mountains, the smell of pine trees, and the white-water rapids. Her eyes widened when I talked about the cedar and stone buildings at the orphanage and the cobblestone road into Pierre. She wanted to hear more. I told her about the sunsets over the mountains of Andorra and the fly-fishing in Pierre near Paradise. I told her about the Sisters of Freedom.

She smiled softly when I spoke of my love for my mother, Alex, Polly, Aunt Helen, Uncle Poulou, Javier, the orphans, and the Sisters of Freedom.

Linda's eyes had filled with tears. She sniffled and asked how I had gotten into Harvard. I explained my unusual preparation and circumstances as she wiped her tears, and when I told her my admission test scores, she looked into my eyes. "You are special."

She peered into my eyes as if trying to decipher a code. I felt a blush creeping up my neck.

"You're special, too," I told her.

She shook her head. "No, I mean you're so sensory aware, authentic, and genuine. You are the most unusual young man I have ever met."

I gave her a smile, tucked in my scrub top, and stretched out my arms and legs. For some reason I was nervous about her compliments. I think because she understood me and that scared me a little.

"Come here," she said.

My stomach flipped at her directness and soft voice. I got up from my recliner, and she stood from her chair. I walked over very close to her. She was fearless. She placed her lab coat and pager in the chair and gave me an embrace.

"I was born into existence just like you," she whispered into my ear.

Her hug and words made me feel warm and tingly all over. My Sentio had gained altitude, and my Intentio had rocketed toward a sunset at Essence. I savored the softness and warmth of Linda's body in my arms, the pleasure of her sensory. I hugged her back with all the love I could muster, trying not to squeeze too tightly.

I asked in a whisper how she'd developed into such a kind person. She pulled back, found my eyes, and said that she was blessed with a great family. Her parents came from England and had adopted her from an orphanage in Archangel, Russia, when she was four. Twelve years later she and her family moved from London, England, to Boston in America. Linda paused, looking down at the gray-white tile floor. After a long moment her eyes lifted to mine, and she appeared to force a smile at me and then said she had been orphaned as an infant, too.

A wave of sadness had washed over Linda's face just before she spoke about being orphaned as an infant like me. Behind her smile I sensed pain, most likely because she'd lived without a mother or father as a baby. I'd seen the look before in the eyes of the orphans at Essence.

I felt sad for her and shook my head in sorrow. I wanted to embrace her again. But she kept talking.

"I didn't learn language or how to talk until after I was adopted at age four," she said. "That's why I have such a strong English accent."

I stared at her, mesmerized. At that moment every-thing crystallized. I knew why she was different, special, and was aware of Sentio. I was not taught language until after my fourth birthday when my pure sensory consciousness was fully developed. That was why we'd connected when we first met. We'd formed a Sentio connection. Then it dawned on me. Linda was able to experience her attention in pure sensory consciousness. She was not addicted, enslaved to Cogito like the others.

"Antonio, why are you so quiet, staring at me?" Linda asked, tilting her head. When I hesitated to respond, she walked over and sat in a recliner.

"Oh, I was just enjoying your sensory presence," I said, turning toward her. I wasn't ready to tell her about Sentio, not yet.

"Come here and sit by me," she said in a soft voice.

15

My heart jumped in joy at her request. I loved being close to her. I approached and sat in the recliner next to her. We rocked and smiled at one another in silence. A few minutes later Linda looked at the clock and frowned. It was 6:40 a.m. Morning rounds would be starting in twenty minutes. She stood, put on her lab coat, pulled my hand, helping me out of the chair, and led me to the lift.

Reaching out, I caught the doors before they closed. I followed Linda into the lift and pushed the button for Ground Level 2. I gazed at her during our descent and noticed her hair had come loose from atop her head; she looked tired and spent. She told me she had to work the entire day before she could sleep. I furrowed my brow in concern and shook my head. I was baffled. What were Americans thinking, keeping medical residents from sleeping?

"It's been a busy night," she said.

The night had been busy, and she and I had spent the night together. I enjoyed the thought and told her.

She laughed. "We did spend the night together. Our third night together."

A pleasant sensation shot from my chest to between my eyes. A warm tingling glow. Linda had remembered it was our third night, and she looked rejuvenated after sharing the news. As the lift doors opened, I wanted to say something memorable about how much she'd helped me, but I couldn't find the right words.

We got off the lift and stood in the hallway, and I didn't want to say goodbye, hating the meaning of that word. But our time together had come to an end.

"I start medical school next week," I said, looking into her caring, brown eyes. I knew how demanding her residency and research was, and I believed I would be very busy in school. I wanted her to know how much she meant to me. "I'll never forget you."

"We'll see each other again."

"I want to see you again," I replied immediately.

Linda smiled and gave me a hug, pressing her body against mine. My nose rubbed against her soft hair, and I inhaled her lilac bouquet, wishing this moment would never end. After a long embrace, we relaxed.

"Don't let the bastards change you," she said, raised up, and kissed me on the mouth with her soft lips.

I closed my eyes, and the moment of bliss opened the gates of paradise for my mind's eye. Images of a gorgeous sunset at Essence appeared, and Linda was smiling, watching the sunset with me. I felt her Intentio flowing, beaming into my Sentio through her kiss, and then I experienced the softness of her presence against my chest. I wanted to stay connected to her lips as long as possible. Forever.

As she pulled away, the soft part of her tongue slid back and forth over my lower lip, spinning my mind. I looked directly into her sparkling, brown eyes for a long moment unable to speak, unable to find words. Finally I said, "I won't let them change me. You either."

Her relaxed face glowed. "I won't," she said softly, peering into my eyes.

Our eyes remained connected as Linda pushed the button to call the lift. I waited till her body rotated back toward me and embraced her again. Holding her close, I wanted to whisper that I loved her. But I remembered the first time I'd heard those words, when I was four years old, and how the words had frightened me. I remained silent, enjoying our intimate embrace.

Her bosom against my chest produced warm impressions, like hand prints, in my Sentio, which warmed my face and chest from the inside. When the doors opened, we released from our embrace, and Linda stepped into the lift. She looked up at me, and I detected sadness in her face for just a moment. Then her eyes twinkled, and she gave a smile as the doors closed.

I stared at the doors, enjoying the lingering sensations of my intimate encounter with Linda. When the X-ray tech appeared with an empty gurney, I pivoted with a smile and headed toward the on-call rooms, still spellbound by the touch of Linda's soft lips.

Then a light bulb went off in my head.

My Sentio had lit up as it did when I experienced the Compass of Freedom at age fourteen. I stopped, took a deep breath, and exhaled. Looking around, I appreciated the immediate sensory all around me: brown and black speckled tile floor, yellow and white walls, the colors and textures in the hall, more vivid and real than I'd ever experienced them. I walked slowly, enjoying my heightened sensitivity. My Compass of Freedom experience and this experience were the two highest Sentio sensitivity experiences in my life.

I walked even slower, asking myself why? Intentio waves began oscillating neurons all over my brain as I tried to figure out what had just happened.

Linda's words: *Don't let the bastards change you* played in my mind. She had delivered her intimate touch for a purpose—for my freedom so that I might live a true essence life.

I realized at that moment why my sensitivity had elevated. Linda had shared a very potent form of strange love, stronger than the strange love I'd experienced growing up at Essence, where we shared hugs, hand holding, kisses, and eye touching for freedom so that we could increase our Sentio sensitivity and live true essence lives.

I felt the urge to shout out in joy. I wanted to run to Essence, ring the Big Bell, and tell everyone. I wanted to call Alex and Polly and tell them I had just received the most powerful form of strange love ever—in America. I had to write a letter tonight to Polly and Alex because they were worried I wouldn't find strange love in America.

Adrenaline rushed through my veins, and I knew there was no chance of falling asleep after what I'd just experienced. I could still feel the pleasure of Linda in my arms, but it was waning while my Sentio sensitivity had gone through the roof, persisting. For some reason I thought about endorphin molecules and their receptors, remembering the module Linda had played for me on the computer. The feeling of pleasure and heightened Sentio sensitivity were different. I knew they were different and Linda's intimate touch had allowed me to experience them both.

Based on the immediacy, power, and duration of my Sentio response to Linda's strange love, I decided there must be a biomolecule stimulated by strange love that raised my Sentio sensitivity.

I walked into the on-call rooms, showered, put on my jeans and white shirt, and ate the last bite of a banana. I went to say goodbye to Anal and Dr. Bock, who were eating cereal at the table in the gathering room. I wrote a note on my menu, thanking Joe the chef and explaining I wouldn't need any more meals. I tossed my box of Raisin Bran to Dr. Bock.

"Anal, I'm leaving, but I hope to see you around."

"Yeah, me too," he said. "I'm going to read that book you gave me on intentialism. Thanks, Dasein."

I tried to give Anal some strange love through eye touching. He looked at me, cocked his head, and furrowed his brow. I believed he could sense my powerful Sentio. I caught his eyes for about two seconds, our longest eye touch ever. I waved goodbye to him and Dr. Bock. I would not forget them.

I ambled down the hall looking toward the lift, remembering where Linda and I had embraced. Smiling, I stopped to revisit that moment in my reflective Sentio, when I'd received Linda's powerful kiss there in the hallway. After reflecting for several moments, I decided to try the emergency exit door and jumped down the stairs to the ground floor. Linda had explained to me that the meaning of language changed depending upon how it was used, and it was okay to use the emergency door for non-emergencies.

Once outside I skipped over the bridge to the Director's office as if floating on a cloud. It dawned on me that Linda had delivered my first clue on my journey to free the Americans. Just as endorphins are biomolecules for pleasure, there had to be a biomolecule of freedom that raised Sentio sensitivity. There had to be a biomolecule of freedom connected to love. I smiled on the inside as I hurried inside the administration building.

CHAPTER

16

I pushed through the glass door of the Director's office, filled with new hope that I would lead the Americans to freedom soon, and approached the counter holding my head high.

A lady's voice called out in an Austrian twang. "Where is he? Where's Dasein, the German kid?" She sounded like Sister Phillips.

I heard her, but I couldn't see her. Glancing quickly to my left then right, I focused on the husky secretary behind the counter. "I'm Antonio Dasein. But I'm not German."

The secretary guided me with her eyes to another lady now standing to my left. I looked over and down at her round, pug face and found her brown eyes glaring at me. The lady rubbed against me, her bosom pushing against my abdomen.

"I'm Lisa, Harvard's best at finding great spaces for students and faculty. So, you're Antonio Dasein."

Lisa backed up and peered at my face, scrutinizing my eyes and hair for an uncomfortably long moment. "I expected you to be pale and blond. You look like a guy I once knew from Northern Italy. He was a soccer player, and I found him a great place."

"I'm from Andorra," I said, pulling my hair back with a tie that Linda had given me.

Lisa's close visual examination left me feeling uneasy, as did her overbearing presence and self-assurance. She looked me over again from top to bottom.

"You're a Spaniard," she declared. "You look more like a soccer player than a doctor."

"Thank you. But I'm not a Spaniard," I said calmly, hoping to finish this line of conversation and wondering what she wanted from me.

"Where is Andorra? Never mind. It's nice to meet you, Antonio. I hear that you have been living in the interns' quarters. Did you have a lot of fun with the interns? Are you ready to relocate to a great place?"

I'd wanted to respond about Andorra, but Lisa talked so fast, moving on to another question then another before I could say a word. I looked at her with my mouth agape.

"That was a rhetorical question. The Director asked me to find you a place, so let's get started. I have a long list of new vacancies."

Waving for me to follow, Lisa turned and walked toward the door. I trailed behind her short, quick stride, paying careful attention not to run up on her heels. Her little, red car was in the faculty-only parking area. I smiled to myself thinking about what Steely Eyes might say to Lisa for parking in the wrong lot. I imagined he'd be a good match for her. She unlocked my door, and I got in.

"I have some great new listings that have just become available. I can't wait. I think you'll really like them," Lisa said as she started her car.

I fastened my seat belt, and off we went. She drove on highways and byways to several of the finest neighborhoods in Boston. She described each neighborhood as perfect for me. The apartments she showed me were nice, but I had a hard time imagining living in them alone. Americans lived in lonely apartments, and I didn't want to live isolated in a box.

By early afternoon Lisa seemed upset that I didn't like her selections. As we drove away from another property, she put her foot down on the gas pedal and threw me back against the seat. I asked her to please slow down.

"Safety and stability are not for me," she said. "I like excitement."

I repeated my plea, and she slowed down. I think she was trying to excite me. She smiled and then began laughing as I tightened my seat belt. Her behavior seemed inappropriate. Lisa surprised me. I think she was coming on to me in a silly way, and I sensed behind her veneer of success was a lonely woman who needed love. I wished I could tell her about true love and freedom, but I knew that it wouldn't mean anything until she found Sentio.

Lisa told me she was a leader in the St. James Artillery and a spiritual crusader. She was going to lead a mission trip to Swaziland in the spring. I listened in silence to her oversharing. I felt sad for her. Lisa's Cogito dominated her beingness just like Anal's. She continued to sing her praises about another mission trip scheduled for the fall.

The Sisters at Essence would be upset at Lisa's holier-than-thou behavior of an institutionalized woman. But I didn't say anything to correct her. My mother had advised me that people have to discover on their own when they are self-righteous.

17

We stopped for lunch at the pier, ate fish cooked on a grill, and watched sailboats chasing the wind. Then we visited several row houses, a flat, and another basement apartment at the harbor. Getting back into the car after deciding against the basement rental, I noticed the corner of a white piece of paper sticking out from under my seat. I pulled it out, and it was a flyer for a new vacancy. I buckled up, and as Lisa steered the car onto the highway, I read the flyer aloud.

"The House of Essence has a loft apartment, a loft bedroom with a balcony, and a great room with a window seat for efficiency. It will go quickly. Call for price." I felt a pull inside me that told me to see this place. The word *essence* had triggered fond memories of my home in Andorra, and there was also something about the simplicity of the flyer, the directness of the offer. I turned to Lisa. "I would like to see this apartment. Could you take me there?"

Lisa scrunched up her nose and shook her head. "Oh no, that's a house of ill repute." She shifted gears, slowing down, and turned left onto Paul Revere Street.

"I would still like to see the vacancy."

Lisa began speeding down Paul Revere. I sat up in my seat and leaned forward, trying to put my face where Lisa would have to see me and pay attention to my request.

Suddenly, she slammed on the brakes and brought us to a complete stop.

"You can't block my vision while I'm driving. It's dangerous!"

"I'm sorry. I just wanted you to give me your attention."

Lisa frowned. "Fine, I'll show you."

I wasn't sure why she was so upset, but I could tell it was better not to ask. She made a quick U-turn in frustration and turned right onto Double Banger Street. After she parallel parked, we got out and continued on foot down an uneven sidewalk.

"This is where you want to live. Where it's unsafe to walk," mumbled Lisa.

She exaggerated her movements around the cracks in the sidewalk, drawing attention to every crevice. We advanced toward the large house at the end of the street where someone had created a flashing sign in a second-floor window.

"You can almost see the word *Essence* flashing green. The E is clear, but the other letters are hard to see," I said, squinting.

"Someone spelled out Essence with old Christmas lights," said Lisa, sounding exasperated. We stopped to catch our breath, and a few moments later Lisa seemed more composed. "Double Banger Street runs through the middle of Boston. The name came during the American Revolution when the Americans used a double barrel cannon against the Brits here. The people of Boston call this block of Double Banger, the Blue Light section," she explained, narrowing her eyes. "The city council declared the area unsafe for the citizens of Boston."

"Unsafe from what? What makes the area unsafe?"

Lisa did not respond and quickened her steps. I lengthened my stride so that each of my steps matched two of Lisa's. She scurried along, her legs moving so quickly and her arms pumping up and down in rhythm with her steps. I thought she might suddenly take off like an airplane. I smiled at the thought but suppressed my laugh. I knew that if I so much as giggled, Lisa might erupt. Over what, I didn't know.

"The neighbor watchers make me uneasy," Lisa said. "The visitors need to worry about the neighbors. It is just the opposite of a Neighborhood Watch." Then she gave a sideways glance to a man sitting on a step near the sidewalk.

Five other neighbors watched us, and they seemed harmless to me, relaxing, sitting on parked cars and old wrought iron porch furniture. They quickly turned their attention to a man running down the street and began cheering, but when two men in blue tackled the barefoot sprinter, the cheering stopped.

Lisa had turned to watch the excitement and got her heel caught in a crack on the sidewalk and gave a look of disgust. She refused my help, took off her shoes, stood in a huff, and proceeded up the steps to the House of Essence. She crossed the porch and knocked forcefully on the front door. I followed behind her and surveyed the surroundings.

The porch delivered a unique view of the neighborhood. A large fireplace sat between two stone pillars across from a swinging bench to our left. I walked around Lisa to look through the house windows. We heard no movement or sound from the other side of the door.

She knocked again, shaking the door. Finally, I heard a buzz and a click, and the door popped ajar. We entered a stairwell, and a silhouette appeared behind the screen door to my left.

Lisa looked away, holding her shoes in her hand. "We better get going."

"Just a moment. There's someone here." I approached the image behind the door.

18

The person behind the screen door was an older woman who said hello in a pleasant voice. When she opened the door, she resembled a picture of Sister Lena that hung in the Big Bell Chapel in Andorra. She was thin and pale with warm brown eyes and plump crimson lips; her wavy, salt-and-pepper hair brushed the top of her shoulders.

"You can call me Milly."

I introduced myself. I sensed her good nature and felt a sense of comfort and hope affecting me. I had a good feeling about this place.

"You must be here about the furnished efficiency," she said.

"Yes."

"We've three other people interested in that apartment," she said. "Come inside."

I followed her to the kitchen—everything nice and clean. Shiny granite counter tops and a sparkling steel sink. Sister Josephine had taught me that you could tell a lot about a person by the way they kept their kitchen.

Milly touched my arm with her soft hand and stared at me. "You have the prettiest hair and eyes."

She looked about the height of Aunt Helen, and I imagined she was around fifty. She made me feel warm and fuzzy. She moved closer and checked me over from head to toe as she provided details about the rental. "I listed the room two days ago, a fully furnished efficiency for $500 per month. The boys repainted it last week. Would you like to see? It's peach."

"No, that won't be necessary. I trust your description." Her way enchanted me. And the rock-bottom price pleased me. The other apartments we'd seen were renting for $1000 a month. "I'll take it," I said, hoping I was standing inside my new home.

We walked toward the screen door where Lisa was waiting.

"The apartment comes with a clause for your special consideration of my business, carried on at this facility."

"Oh," I said, and hesitated then asked about the consideration.

Milly explained that it would involve my cooperation with her business and that it was no big deal. She held out her hand. We shook hands, sealing the deal.

Lisa shot us an angry look. "Good luck; I'm leaving." She swiveled on her toes and ran barefoot all the way to her car. I followed to make sure she was okay. She unlocked the car door and thrust herself inside. If she wanted to leave, that was okay with me. I watched her speed away.

I returned to the porch where Milly was holding the door open as two handsome couples dressed for ballroom dancing were leaving the house. They laughed and frolicked out the door. The two young women smiled at me, interesting. Milly gave me another handshake and invited me to come in.

I entered her apartment and followed her to the kitchen.

"Would you like something to drink?"

"No, thank you," I said. "Do you think you could give me a ride to Harvard?"

She smiled, revealing a missing tooth, and said, "I'll take you."

We talked for a short while about Essence and Andorra, and then Milly drove me to Harvard so I could retrieve my belongings.

I was gathering my things from the closet near the Director's office and felt a hand tug on my right shoulder. When I turned, the Director stood grinning at me. "Lisa's in my office. I'll take care of her." He winked. "Enjoy your new place."

"Thanks. And thank Lisa." I hurried down the hall and down the stairs. I jumped into Milly's car out front.

When we got back to the House of Essence, Milly invited me to sit under an overhead light in her kitchen. I put my bags down and sat at her table.

"I need to check your hair." She removed my hair tie and then ran her fingers through my hair. My mother used to examine my hair for lice. The little crawling creatures in a new orphan's hair would give Sister Phillips the screams.

"You are clean. Go check out your new place," Milly said. "Oh, I almost forgot. I'm throwing a party tomorrow night, and I want you to attend so you can meet my girls."

"Sure." It sounded like fun. Milly made me feel welcome like Sister Josephine used to do for the new orphans arriving at Essence. She handed me the key to apartment 7B, and I gave her an embrace. "Thanks. I'll see you later."

I grabbed my bags off the floor and left to explore my new home.

CHAPTER

19

Eager to see my apartment, I hurried up the staircase to the top floor and opened the door to 7B. Immediately, a warm welcome from the sun affected me. I loved the high, white ceiling and the large bay window, filling the room with sunlight. The peach walls and hardwood floor pleased my Sentio. I climbed eight steps to my right, to the loft bedroom, which reminded me of the loft in the barn at Vichy. I put my things away in the closet and left my duffle bag and backpack on a thick white blanket over my bed. I stepped into a small adjacent bathroom with a walk-in shower and checked out my tired reflection in the mirror.

I walked out and stood on the landing at the top of the stairs and looked over the white balcony rail, eyeing the great room and kitchen. Smiling, I jumped down the steps, ran to the big window seat, and sat, looking out at the harbor against a clear blue sky where a beautiful, three-masted sailboat was docked, enjoying the view for several minutes. I got up and investigated the dining area and the cooking area behind an island counter containing a sink, like at the interns' quarters. I opened the kitchen window to let some fresh air in and the smell of paint out.

The kitchen had a dishwasher, fridge, wave cooker, electric grill, and garbage disposal—modern conveniences galore. The apartment was so neat. I couldn't believe it was all mine. And the furnishings—a beige, cloth-covered sofa, brown leather chair, and a rocker—were perfect. I pulled the mahogany rocking chair toward the window seat, plopped in the chair, kicked up my feet, and enjoyed my front row view of people at play on the water.

After writing a letter to Polly and Alex about experiencing Linda's powerful strange love, I wanted to mail it, and I needed to pick up some things at the store. I bounded down the stairs and outside to a beautiful blue sky. A busy neighborhood surrounded the House of Essence where several official-looking vehicles were parked along the street with their motors running. They seemed to function as taxis for reluctant passengers—the down and out people on the street. I walked around the block, mailed the letter, and then slipped into a local market to buy some groceries.

With bags in hand I exited the store, ambled down the sidewalk, and gazed at the official car parked across the street. I sensed the drivers' pride in his treatment of a barefoot man, as he helped the reluctant man into the back seat of the vehicle, carefully lowering his head, and then the driver jumped into the front seat and drove away.

A few feet ahead on my side of the street, another vehicle turned on a blue spinning light on top and sped away. I'd noticed each of the official vehicles carried the phrase: *Let none live in fear.* How interesting.

Oddly though, it appeared that most of my neighbors did live in fear. Steel bars protected their windows and doors. I remembered my residence did not have bars. Milly did not live in fear. I felt proud for a moment and recalled that the house was also a place of business. What business? Milly was a people person and fearless, so I figured her business had something to do with sales. She reminded me of my uncle Poulou, who sold women's undergarments, and he was the best salesperson in the world.

I was so busy thinking that I almost walked into a man in blue as I rounded the corner.

"Sorry," I said. "Please excuse me."

He put his hand on my chest and looked into my eyes. "Do you live at the House of Essence? I saw you coming out of the door a little while ago."

"Yes, that's where I live," I said, surprised he'd watched me but also proud because I liked my new home.

"Let me see some identification."

I put down my groceries and gave him my identification badge from Harvard, which he scrutinized. The man's countenance relaxed while he looked at my badge. I remembered the Director telling me how important the badge would be. The Director did know more than I did about America.

"Harvard, huh?"

"Yes," I said. "I'm enrolled to begin classes next week."

He handed me my badge and told me to watch my back. He seemed afraid for me. His concern made his eyes fill with fear. How strange. He warned me again as if there were a plot underway to attack my back.

Then he referred to the House of Essence as a blue-green cat house. I shook my head to disagree. I saw a beautiful, Paris-green, seven-story structure that stood alone at its grand location, a singularity overlooking older brownstone row houses on both sides of Double Banger Street.

"Watch your back," he repeated, turned, and walked away.

I returned to 7B and put my groceries away. I lay on my sofa, thinking about my wonderful morning with Linda, which seemed so long ago now, getting my first clue from her strange love, finding my apartment with Lisa and meeting Milly.

A siren blared from the street below. My attention returned to the men in blue—the civil servants—their reluctant passengers, the bars on my neighbors' windows, the reference about living in fear painted on the official vehicles, and the concern about being attacked from behind. America was in deep trouble. The citizens were living out their lives behind bars. Why?

My head ached. I sighed and sat up on the sofa, massaging my temples with the heels of my palms. How would I free the Americans from their self-imposed prisons? It seemed impossible. After a long moment, I realized helping them experience Sentio was their only chance. But how would I reach the masses? That might be impossible.

I stretched out on the sofa and visited Linda's image from this morning, still luminous in my Sentio, and drifted to sleep.

CHAPTER

20

The celebration for the Boston Red Sox fans at Fenway
Park brought sounds of cannon blasts echoing from the
harbor, and fireworks filled the twilight sky with bursts
of bright light: explosions of red, white, and blue sparkles. Milly's party was about to begin, so I got up from my
window seat and trotted downstairs. I helped move the vegetable plates, sausage balls, and dip from her kitchen to the
red, white, and blue tables on the porch.

Milly turned on the disc player, and fun music about
East and West Coast girls played. I rotated the two speakers
toward the concrete patio area, which was cordoned off for
a dance floor.

Two men in blue drove up to the house and waved from
their car. Milly told me the men in blue were police, and she
took them a tray of food. I recognized the officer who'd told
me to watch my back and waved at him. The men took the
food and drove away, and as Milly climbed the porch steps,
she asked me to bring out the drinks from her kitchen table.
I brought out two bottles of white wine and then a case of
Miller beer.

The party began on the porch and spilled onto the
patio and then Double Banger Street. The guests yelled for
more drinks, and Milly brought out some brandy, bottles
of scotch, vodka, and whiskey. Then she brought out five

new friends from Los Angeles and introduced the scantily dressed women and two young men, parading them on the porch. After their introductions the new friends kissed and touched the guests. Milly's friends greeted others, giving long, tight embraces and then holding hands like long-lost friends. It was different from the interns and students I'd met at Harvard. Interesting.

The atmosphere grew more relaxed and jovial, filled with joy, laughter, and loud conversation. The music grew louder as happy, upbeat songs played, and the guests danced. I walked around with Milly, who introduced me to my friendly neighbors and housemates—her girls. I met Danielle, Katrina, and Diana. They were welcoming and friendly. Then I met Pretty, Fancy, and Sassy. I liked them, too. They were a spicy flavor of American women who liked skimpy clothes and theatrical makeup.

"They just like to have fun," Milly said. "And they like to walk around with their backs straight and their heads held high feeling tall."

Interesting, I thought. Their shoes had long spikes, pushing them up towards the sky.

Sassy, a lean woman, jumped up on the patio and danced with gyrations around an older man, pivoting on her toes with incredible balance, an intriguing and erotic dance gathering everyone's attention. The party started rocking as Sassy continued her dance. The men cheered.

Diana approached and handed me a drink. I remembered I'd seen her and her friends stepping out of Milly's front door yesterday. I shared a brandy with her, and we talked for several minutes about Wales and Andorra. She wanted to dance with me, so we walked down to the patio. Diana was a beautiful, brown-eyed Welsh girl who pulled me onto the floor. We swayed and worked our way into the middle of the crowd. When her body rubbed against mine, her eyes widened. Thinking I was too close, I stepped back;

she pulled me in tighter. Wow. She'd sensed I was nervous, and she liked it. My nervousness had excited her.

A warm tingling sensation settled between my eyes. Diana turned her back to me and bumped me; her soft hips pushed against the hardness of my thighs. She bumped me again and again with her hips, encouraging me to return a bump. Her head turned, and her big, brown eyes glanced into mine. I think I was tickling her hips with my thighs because she'd given me a look like Polly used to do, and then she winked at me.

The music stopped, and Diana kissed my cheek and slipped away. The long-brown-haired Katrina approached and wanted me to dance. The soft music played, and I put my hands on her hips. As we swayed, she ran her hands over my chest. Her fingertips tickled me. She aroused me.

Katrina whispered in a sexy voice, "You have nice pecs."

"So do you," I said, staring at her nude breasts bulging above her lace-up vest.

As the music stopped, I let go of her hips, and she pulled my arms and led me up the steps to the porch where we shared one of Milly's brownies. After learning I was going to Harvard, Katrina wanted to know if I'd met Simone, who had a connection to the medical school. I shook my head no.

Danielle approached me as the music returned, and we slow danced. We held each other closely as we moved to and fro. I couldn't think of anything to say, so I asked Danielle about Simone. She said that Simone knew the chief of medicine at Harvard and that Simone was a beautiful blonde. I nodded and whispered into her ear that I was impressed with her slow dancing. When the music ended, she gave me a kiss on my cheek and smiled at me.

Danielle slipped way, so I looked for Simone but didn't see anyone who fit her description. Someone tugged on my hand, and I turned. It was the petite, blonde, blue-eyed

Fancy. She smiled at me and wanted to dance. I nodded. I couldn't say no. Sister Josephine had taught me never to say no to a girl who wanted to dance.

"Where is Simone?" I asked as Fancy and I stepped onto the dance floor.

"She's busy with clients," Fancy said, moving her hips to the beat of the music.

I swayed next to Fancy, gently giving her side bumps. For some reason, I wondered about Simone. Why was she still working? It was after midnight. The music slowed, and Fancy and I slow-danced.

Milly called for Fancy. She released me and hurried up the stairs into the arms of an older man who looked like her father. Odd.

I eased off the patio and walked toward the street where a small group of guests had gathered. I met an older gentleman, a professor at Harvard, who made some kind comments about his experience at the party, his sensory experience enjoyed earlier in the night. He and I walked to the porch and shared a brandy and then talked about existentialism and philosophy.

The professor said there were only three questions relevant to philosophy: Which phenomena exist? How do we know they exist? And are we prepared to act accordingly? An interesting proposition. I smiled, thinking my aunt would beg to differ.

Then the professor explained that death was not important because no one ever complained of being dead.

I responded, "Unconscious people don't complain, and they are important."

He agreed and then laughed, patting me on the back.

I asked him if he knew about intentialism: Intentio, Sentio, and Cogito.

He chuckled and said he understood. "Sentio, Cogito, and Bullio."

I laughed at his claim; I think he meant to say bullion. He was feeling the brandy.

Chatting with the professor, I heard a soft female voice address Milly, but I didn't look to see who she was. I listened to her voice while watching Sassy do a special dance on the lap of a happy young guy in a chair. The guy was so happy that he placed dollars in Sassy's underwear, and the professor cheered them on. The guy's pleasure tracks were firing on all cylinders as the scene reminded me of a time in Paris. I remembered seeing a man dance on the lap of a woman when I was in Paris with my uncle—

"Milly, who is that blue-eyed Spanish guy?"

The female's soft voice interrupted my thoughts; I listened in silence, wondering if Simone was speaking to Milly. I didn't want them to know I was listening.

"He is the new fellow renting the 7B efficiency," answered Milly.

"He seems very interesting."

"He is here from a place called Essence in Andorra," Milly explained. "He's starting medical school at Harvard next week. His name is Antonio Dasein."

"I'm going to meet him."

"You be nice to him, Simone."

Why did Milly need to tell Simone to be nice to me? My curiosity was piqued. Simone continued to converse with Milly while my eyes fixed on the movement of Sassy's hips, bumping the young guy in the chair. When Simone and Milly's conversation ended, I turned quickly to find Simone, but I didn't recognize any new faces. She'd disappeared.

21

Ambling toward the street, searching for a face that might belong to Simone, I gave up and headed back to the porch to get another one of Milly's famous brownies. I waved at Milly, who was standing in the doorway. I reached for a brownie. When I looked up from the table, the most desirous nipples I'd ever seen dangled before me. They were erect and firm with large, pink areolas, peeking through a white, silk blouse directly across from me. A goddess had bent over, peering at my brownie selection. I'd chosen one from the middle of the pan, and she pointed to a larger brownie in the corner and grinned at me.

"Hi, you must be Antonio. I'm Simone." She paused for several seconds, staring into my eyes. "Milly told me all about you."

My heart pounded, and I could feel its beats in my throat. I raised up and could not help gawking at the most beautiful blonde, blue-eyed woman who'd ever appeared in front of me. I worried she could see the pulsations in my neck. Then I realized I was salivating with a brownie in my hand moving toward my mouth. I put it down and swallowed fiercely, willing myself to calm down enough to speak with her.

Simone delivered a complete Sentio experience of wonder and bliss, a walking dream state of pleasurable consciousness. She smelled like fresh peaches. Her voice was exciting. Her eyes were sky blue. Her face was heart shaped with high cheekbones and downy skin, which I just knew would be soft to the touch. Her lips were large and succulent. Her pearly teeth were perfect. Her bosoms were like honey melons, and her hips curved like an hourglass. Her sexy, long legs shimmered under her sparkling skirt.

My heart continued to pound as the area in my brain between my eyes warmed and tingled in delight. Simone grinned, and I could tell she liked being the pleasure image projected in my Sentio. I focused on her eyes for a moment then snuck another look at her beautiful pink nipples. I hesitated. I didn't know what to say.

"I've been looking for you, Simone," I said. Simone furrowed her brow. I realized I shouldn't have said that. "I mean your friends suggested I meet you."

Simone smiled, and I produced an internal sigh.

"So you were named after the German word *Da sein*, there being. Martin Heidegger's word for *being there*, Dasein, the thinking, living, and feeling being: the care structure. How interesting," she said.

Her reply hit me like a physical force right between my eyes. No one had ever recognized the origin of my name; certainly, no one that looked like Simone. She'd transfixed me with her response. She moved in front of my face and kissed my lips, touching my tongue with hers, tickling me. My Sentio was spinning, and I felt giddy and staggered. I righted myself against the table. Simone withdrew her soft tongue and released her lips from mine. She met my eyes with her fathomless blue eyes. I couldn't find words; my Cogito had turned off. For a long moment, I tried to cover my inability to speak by smiling at Simone. Then I licked my lips and tasted her lingering presence.

"Peach," I said.

Simone smiled with her eyes, turned away, and walked

down the steps toward the party on the patio. I experienced the swing of her hips with every one of my sensory receptors, staring at her bouncy sequins—

Someone tapped my shoulder. Still reeling from Simone, I turned. It was Diana, and she asked me for a dance.

"Yes," I mumbled.

Diana grabbed my hand and pulled me down the steps and onto the dance floor. I tried to redirect my attention to her, but I still held and enjoyed the reflective Sentio experience of Simone. As I moved my arms and legs mirroring Diana's movements, I noticed Simone's kiss still gave me pleasure, but it was waning. I revisited Simone's reflective image, boosting the pleasure. I looked around at the other couples dancing nearby. My Sentio sensitivity had not spiked as it had with Linda at the hospital—

Diana punched my midsection, interrupting my thoughts, seizing my attention. I bent at the waist in reflex and gasped for air. She'd almost taken my breath away.

"Pay attention!" she said, and then rubbed my back with her hand in kindness.

She apologized. I raised up, looked into her eyes, and said I was okay. After a moment staring at her sad eyes, I apologized for ignoring her. Diana smiled and said that she understood why I was distracted. She said all the girls were goggling me. I wasn't sure what she meant by that, and I didn't ask. Diana scared me a little. She was fiery.

The music played, and I grasped Diana's right hand with my left, placed my right hand under her left shoulder blade, and looked into her brown eyes. She grinned and pulled me into her waltz-like sway. Wow! She was a ballroom dancer; Sister Josephine had taught me the style. Diana led with her novel moves then did a 360- followed by a 720-degree twirl.

"Diana, you're a great dancer," I whispered, embracing her.

She seemed to enjoy the encouragement, quickening her backward steps as we glided and twirled around the dance floor, garnering the attention of the crowd. I saw Simone out of the corner of my eye.

Images of Simone's beautiful nipples began intruding into my consciousness and triggered an avalanche of sense data. Every reflective sensory track my Intentio visited of Simone led to another Intentio that searched deeper for more pleasure connected to her, disrobing her. I couldn't get my attention away from my experience with Simone. When the music ended, I was able to direct my attention to Diana. I kissed her on the cheek in gratitude, and she turned quickly and sashayed away, holding her head high.

I saw Milly and walked over to thank her for inviting me. She said my invitation and participation were part of the deal, the consideration that required my involvement in her business. I'd somewhat figured it out by now.

"I understand, no problem. I see what's going on here. You're selling sensory experiences."

Milly returned a smile.

"By the way, who is Simone?" I asked. "What does she do?"

Milly looked at me with a serious gaze, and I sensed the warning from her eyes.

"Simone serves as one of my special girls for the faculty members from Harvard and occasionally some callers from Boston College. Her services are rendered for complicated men with troubled lives. You need to have fun; you're a young man. Besides, Simone prefers older minds, and your young mind will have more fun with my other girls. Did you meet Diana and Katrina?"

"Yes, they were very nice. Diana and I danced twice. She is Welsh and never knew her parents. I like Diana. And she can throw a punch," I said, amusing Milly.

She grinned at me, walked toward the porch swing,

and announced that she was lowering her prices on sensory experiences. She declared that the new personnel from Los Angeles had created an atmosphere of generosity and good will in the house. The plentiful supply of girls and young men allowed her to offer a summer sale. A few minutes after Milly's proclamation, everyone disappeared.

I went up to my apartment to enjoy my bed. After all the dancing, I was beat, and as soon as my head hit the pillow, I fell asleep.

22

The House of Essence was just a few blocks away from the byzantine structure that housed the Harvard teaching facility. On Monday, my first day of class, I got up early and sat in the window seat, thinking about all my years of study just to get into medical school. Chewing on the last bite of a cinnamon roll, I enjoyed the sunrise and finished my glass of milk. The sky above the harbor was clear. It was going to be a beautiful day. I headed up to my bedroom to get ready. After showering and drying my hair, I put on my jeans and white shirt, slipped into my brown loafers, and grabbed my backpack filled with my syllabuses. I eased down the loft steps then out the door and tip-toed down the stairs, trying not to disturb my neighbors.

Hurrying down Double Banger Street, pulling on my backpack straps, I paused for the stop light, crossed the street, and then walked north up Paul Revere. The bus stops were empty, and the streets nearly deserted save a couple of yellow cabs. Once on campus the walk to the teaching building was inspiring—so many historic buildings. I followed a brick road toward the oldest teaching facility in America. The inscription *Invicta Veritas*—the truth is unconquerable—was carved in stone over the entrance.

The ivy had grown high on the red bricks, reaching the copper dome. I traced the green-leafed vines around and up the three-story building and then surveyed the dome, wondering how it had been constructed. A few moments later I headed inside the rotunda where I found little monuments with inscriptions for Henry David Thoreau, Ralph Waldo Emerson, Margaret Fuller, and William James. Each name brought about memories of Aunt Helen's teachings. She knew all their names and their philosophies: transcendentalism and pragmatism.

I continued on a gray marble floor where a janitor was buffing.

"Excuse me," I said, and he turned off his buffer. "Could you tell me where the freshman medical lecture hall is?"

He looked at me. "Are you a medical student?"

"Yes."

"Come on," he said, and waved for me to follow. He led me outside and pointed to a large, gray-white building across from the hospital. "This is the undergraduate teaching facility. The medical teaching facility is in that building."

"Thank you, sir," I said to the kind gentleman, and hurried across the campus.

I entered the gray-white building and followed the signs. I pushed through the double doors that opened into a giant amphitheater with mahogany-paneled walls. To my left was a large sign: *Welcome Class of 1986.* I was in the right place. I counted sixteen rows and two hundred seats. The black leather seats had desktops made of polished wood. Each seat appeared to have a perfect view of the lectern down front. I'd read about such theaters used for education.

Ambling over, I stood at the podium looking up at the empty seats. I wanted to see what my professor would see: all two hundred seats without turning my head. For a few seconds I dreamed I belonged at the front of the classroom behind the panoptic lectern.

I took a seat in the seventh row near the middle aisle

and placed my backpack on the floor. Medical students—my classmates—trickled into the room. I attended their presence in silence and awe, watching and listening to them gab as they congregated near the entrance. They looked intelligent and talked with quick humor. Their eyes darted all around. Walking and gesturing with confidence, they were friendly toward each other. Many seemed to be old acquaintances, calling to one another by their first name.

A petite, young lady with curly, black hair and brown eyes approached and lifted her backpack from her shoulders. It was bigger than she was. She produced a sigh and sat next to me. Immediately she began talking as if I were her long-lost friend. She talked to me in such a strong voice for someone so little. She looked into my eyes for a split second; she looked away for a few seconds; she returned to my eyes for a split second, again and again, all the while talking about her troubles that ensued after her alarm clock had failed.

I felt a tickle in my chest and smiled. She didn't notice my amusement and continued talking about having to wait for a bus, missing her stop, and the long ride from Lexington that morning. I waited for a chance to tell her my name. She let out a deep breath and sunk into her seat. She was a cute and fearless young lady who'd brought a smile to my face.

I introduced myself, and she did the same. Her name was Barbara Weil. She reached out, and I shook her tiny hand. Barbara explained that most of the students were twenty-two years old and that she was only nineteen but that there was one other student in our class younger than her. She raised her bushy eyebrows at me. She seemed so proud of her age. I didn't want to mention I was the youngest student. She talked about her roommate, Izzie, and after she told me about her home in Baltimore, I told her about my home in Andorra. She grinned and didn't say anything for a long moment. Then she referred to me as a *Gentile*. Her biblical reference made me feel strange, but I liked little Barbara just the same. She was sensitive, petite, and spunky like my mother, and she'd become my friend in a matter of minutes.

Everyone took a seat, and the idle chatter grew quiet. When the dean of students entered, she welcomed us to Harvard and announced that we could expect ten percent of our class to drop out or flunk out during the first year. Her statement brought complete silence, and then some boos erupted. It bothered me too. I felt sad for my fellow students who might not make it through the program. I hoped little Barbara would make it. Then I realized the dean might be talking about me. My face flushed in anger. I shook my head. It seemed unfair to attack a student's Sentio that way. I didn't understand the purpose of sharing such a negative prediction.

The dean introduced Dr. Solomon Sol as our first lecturer. Or was it Dr. Sol Solomon? I wasn't sure because she'd introduced his name both ways and then laughed, suggesting either way would do. He oversaw the Department of Consciousness research, and I remembered that Linda had mentioned she was doing research with his group. He walked up to the podium with a serious look, and the dean took a seat.

When Doctor Sol spoke, it was as if someone had fired a starter's gun for our Intentios to begin a race. It was fascinating to watch everyone change. As I looked around the room, I sensed the competition and determination from every new face focused on his welcoming remarks.

Dr. Sol paused, looking around the auditorium, and said, "Let's begin. Buckle your seatbelts."

My stomach twisted into a knot. I pulled my desk top closer and leaned back in my seat. Dr. Sol's words introduced a topic I'd never studied. The knot in my stomach twisted, and I grew concerned. His detailed exposition of the limbic system, our emotional nervous system, was frightening. My three years of studying to get accepted at Harvard seemed of little value now. I wondered if medical school was going to be like my mother's philosophical dig. She'd told me the horror stories about reading Kant and many others for hours and hours without making progress toward her goal of finding a Cogito path to true freedom and finally concluding there is no Cogito path to freedom.

I looked around the room as the lights dimmed. My classmates stared at the slide of the limbic system on the big screen. Dr. Sol moved the red light pointer to a small structure and talked about the hypothalamus.

Then he talked about Candace Pert, a graduate student at Johns Hopkins who had discovered the first opiate receptor in the brain in 1972. Her discovery led to the revelation that the brain made molecules for pleasure, called endorphins. Hearing about the discovery of the brain's pleasure molecules reminded me of my last night on call with Linda when we'd watched the computer program: endorphin and morphine molecules competing for receptors. Closing my eyes, I remembered experiencing Linda's powerful strange love, leading to my moment of eureka. Then it dawned on me. Candace had made her discovery as a graduate student like me, and that realization lifted my mood, giving me hope that I might discover the brain's biomolecule of freedom. The knot in my stomach disappeared.

After the lecture several students congregated up front, talking about black bags and white lab coats. Listening to the students, I wanted to feel important too. I asked Barbara why we were not allowed to wear white coats to class.

Barbara responded, "You have to earn the privilege of wearing a white lab coat by squeezing your brain." She smiled. "You get a white lab coat at the end of the second year."

Frustrated, I wanted to say something, but the dean

flipped the lights, signaling the second lecture was beginning. I shook my head at little Barbara. It would be two
years before I could wear a white lab coat—the coat I'd seen
myself wearing in a lab during my vision of freedom experience at Essence. I didn't know if I could wait two more years.

The third lecture went on and on about biochemistry
and physiology. The fourth lecture addressed the most
important energy molecule for human life: adenosine tri-
phosphate or ATP. Waiting for the fifth lecture, a student
named Tinker—a small, nice-looking, brown-haired, and
green-eyed chap from Yale—explained to me that the professor's job was to make us feel bad for not squeezing our
brains and producing the best test scores compared to other
medical schools.

Tinker leaned forward from his seat behind me. "The
measure of how well or poorly you squeezed your brain,
compared with other schools, was the purpose of the education game of medicine."

Barbara agreed with Tinker.

I felt a fire ignite in my chest, blood rushing to my
cheeks. Outrage. This way of learning—squeezing information all over your brain so that the faculty could feel important—seemed inhumane. Medicine needed a person like
Aunt Helen or Uncle Poulou. Americans seemed too concerned about accumulating knowledge through language,
words, rather than experiencing and deriving knowledge
through sensory. I remembered my aunt saying that all positive knowledge must come through Sentio. *All knowledge must
come through experience.* Barbara looked at me with worry in
her eyes, and then she smiled, producing cute dimples. I
sensed she was trying to help me. I inhaled deeply and slowly
exhaled, calming myself.

Barbara grabbed her backpack and said goodbye; she
had to leave and could not attend the final lecture of the
day. Tinker too had something to do, and he and Barbara

left together. Feeling alone, I got up, grabbed my backpack, and walked toward the back of the auditorium.

I sat next to a young man who explained he was taking notes for those who couldn't stay for the late afternoon class. I wondered why so many students couldn't attend. The lecture hall was empty save for a handful of students.

"What is your name?" I asked the note-taker and offered, "I'm Antonio Dasein."

"My name is Lawrence Elias, but my friends call me Lar," he said, smiled, and shook my hand.

Lar was tall with brown hair as curly as a poodle and green eyes, and he and I became immediate friends. He'd come from Northwestern University. He said most of the students left early to watch a TV show. He'd already seen today's episode, several times in fact, so he was okay with missing it. The lights flipped off and then on, and Lar stopped talking.

Dr. Wall-Bird, a professor of anatomy, greeted the empty seats up front and began the lecture as if the hall were filled with students. Odd.

"The first cervical vertebra sits beneath the foramen magnum," Dr. Wall-Bird started. He went on and on, all the way to the hip. He showed slides for every bone and how they developed from the embryo to the adult form. It was fascinating, like hearing about tadpoles becoming frogs, which Sister Josephine had taught me in the fourth grade.

One of the students up front made a coughing sound disguising a strange word he'd uttered. I didn't recognize the word. At my look of confusion, Lar spelled the word out for me: *bohica*. Then another student coughed up the same word. They both got up and left. I looked at Lar.

He smiled and said, "I'll tell you later."

The professor paused for a couple of seconds, looking around the hall. Lar looked at me with a monkey face. "This is in last year's notes," he whispered. "He's going to share his philosophy. Every year this guy gives his annual words of warning about cause and effect, causality in medicine."

Dr. Wall-Bird continued, "In medicine one cannot take anything for granted. Did the fall cause the hip fracture or did the fracture cause the fall? The answer might never be clear. But remember that falls and hip fractures are drawn together by gravity. The little beggars are called gravitons, and they are out to get you and me."

According to Lar, Wall-Bird was the senior professor of anatomy. It was unsettling to find out on the first day of medical school that falls and hip fractures could be used for such a silly, circular argument. How could he say that a hip fracture could cause a fall? I didn't understand. Lar told me that the professor was trying to make a point about getting a good history to understand what happened first, and the professor was an old English guy, as if that somehow explained his strangeness.

"Everyone knows that falls cause hip fractures," I said, and asked, "What are gravitons?"

Lar didn't respond.

The lecture ended. Lar finished his notes, and then he found my eyes. "Dasein, anatomy class is a waste of time. It never changes; it's invicta veritas—there's nothing new. You simply have to memorize everything."

"What was that word?"

"Bohica? Bend over, here it comes again. Don't worry, Dasein; just memorize everything."

How odd. I didn't want to bend over—ever.

I acted as if I understood and nodded my head. Then I asked Lar how I should study, besides memorizing. He explained to me which classes were the most important to attend, and the best way to cram data into my brain was via notes and old tests. Lar's brother, Mark, was in his fourth year of medical school, and he had taught Lar, who was now teaching me. The way of medicine.

"What about anatomy lab?" I asked.

Lar shook his head no and explained. I didn't like the sound of smelling formaldehyde on my clothes for six months nor the images of carving on cadavers. I knew it wouldn't be good for my Sentio, and I could learn anatomy by the book since it was invicta veritas. I decided I'd skip anatomy lab after his wise words.

Lar told me where I could have a nice run; Chariot Hill was near the harbor and provided a beautiful view of sailboats and the morning sunrise. He said that the hill got its name from a nineteenth century Harvard student who believed that a chariot could pull the sun across the sky— sunrise to sunset—while riding around the hill. I wondered if the student was Thoreau.

Lar—a six-foot-seven fellow who'd played basketball in college—was really kind to me. I'd learned to play basketball at Essence and liked the game. I suggested to Lar we could play. He agreed, got up, and put his notes and book in his backpack.

Talking with him had relaxed me. I felt better about the possibility of a Sentio life at Harvard. I didn't come to Harvard to become addicted to Cogito as a student of medicine. That much I knew. But studying medicine was part of my vision for freedom, and I was grateful to have Lar as my friend to give me direction. He and I shook hands; we were the last students standing at the end of our first day of class. We said goodbye, and I headed for the House of Essence to begin my studies.

23

On the second day I found out my advisor would be Professor Solomon. Or Professor Sol. I still wasn't sure. I was thrilled he was my advisor because of his connection to Linda. His lab was in the Department of Sensory Deprivation building, the annex building with a connector to the city's finest teaching hospital. His laboratory took up the entire seventh floor. The rumor from Lar was that it was the quietest place on campus, and I looked forward to checking it out.

Two days later I went to meet with the professor. Large mattress pads lined the elevator walls and made the ride quiet all the way to the seventh floor. When the elevator doors opened, three beautiful young women with short white lab coats, dressed like Milly's girls, got on the elevator. I held the door open, and they giggled at me.

I heard one young lady say, "How about his buns?"

The blonde woman punched the eleventh-floor button. I touched her eyes, smiled, and slipped between the closing doors. I wondered why they had come from the seventh floor and where were they going on the eleventh floor? Were they working with Dr. Sol?

In the seventh-floor hallway, I saw a big sign two meters wide posted on the wall just outside the elevator.

Sound alert!

Please do not raise your voice above five decibels!

Turn off your pagers.
Animal and human studies are in progress.
Please, no loud noises!
Thank you, Sol.

Written in fine print at the bottom of the sign was one additional note:

The whispered word spoken at the end of exhalation is five decibels.

I practiced making a five-decibel sound. Then I walked with care on the foam-covered floor down a long corridor to a door marked with a sign: *Professor Solomon.*

The door was half open. Dr. Solomon was sitting at his desk staring off into space. I was afraid to knock because it might exceed five decibels, so I walked in and greeted him.

"I'm Antonio Dasein," I whispered as I exhaled.

He found my eyes, and said in a soft voice, "Yes, the German kid from Max Planck. I've been expecting you."

I'd given up correcting people about my nationality. "You're Dr. Sol Solomon, assigned to be my advisor."

"No, I'm Dr. Solomon Sol," he said with a hint of annoyance in his voice, but also warmth. "You know, I've been here for twenty years. They are still calling me Professor Solomon. But you can call me Dr. Sol."

It sounded like he said *Dr. Soul.* I nodded. "I like the vibe in here. I mean the quiet."

"You get used to it," he said, and closed the textbook on his desk.

Dr. Sol stood up in his long lab coat and approached. He was about six feet tall and bald with pointed ears, a thin professor type who looked to be about fifty-five. He looked different than the way he had appeared behind the podium in the lecture hall. He seemed gentle and sensitive now.

He leaned a bit closer, his pale, blue eyes peering into mine, and whispered, "My God, young man, your eyes are astounding. Come here."

I inched toward him, and he gave a closer look. Then he spoke quickly with excitement about my eyes but still maintained his practiced, soft tone. He touched my shoulder and patted my back while I kept my eyes as wide as I could for him to examine them.

"Have you ever been in a sensory deprivation booth? For visual or brain stem potentials? Have you ever had your hypothalamus stimulated?"

Each question followed the other without as much as a breath in between. His questions sounded almost erotic when whispered. I stepped back reflexively after his eye examination, leaning my head back and away from him.

"No, I have not been in a sensory deprivation booth," I whispered back.

"Well, come again around the first of the month. I'll be conducting a tour. I'd like you to see what our research is all about. I think you may find it interesting. With a name like Dasein, you may even want to do some student research with my group," he said. His hushed voice reflected a bit of fervor.

Dr. Sol's whispers had tickled my mind. Giving a nod, I smiled. Between his low voice and his enthusiasm, I was drawn in and intrigued by his proposal. I was very interested in student research in his lab.

For some reason my attention wandered to Linda and the time she'd given me strange love. I had a sense that Dr. Sol and Linda were part of my mission for freedom.

"When would you like me to come for the tour? What day, and what time?" I asked.

Dr. Sol did not hear me. His attention was focused on a letter his secretary had handed him. She'd slipped in and out without a sound. It was amazing. Dr. Sol returned to his desk.

I took out my pen and note card and wrote my request— *What day? Time?*—and placed it on his desk. Dr. Sol glanced at my card.

"Ask my secretary. She'll set it up."

He got up from his desk, still staring at the paper his secretary had handed him, and shook his head. The content of the letter captivated his attention as if I'd disappeared. It felt strange to go from having his undivided attention to suddenly not existing. He wadded the letter into a ball and threw it into the wastebasket and stepped toward the door. The words, the content of the communication, still seemed to possess his attention.

I hadn't talked to him to vent my frustrations from my first days of school, which Lar said was necessary to prove that I cared. As Dr. Sol passed by, I reached over and pulled on the tail of his lab coat. He turned, narrowing his eyes at me.

"Dr. Sol, I thought that you were supposed to hear me out. Ask how I'm doing. This is my first week of medical school, and you're my advisor."

It was hard to whisper my concern, but the pull on his coat seemed to snap Dr. Sol back into the present, once again aware of my existence. He seemed a bit confused and not as lucid as he'd been just minutes before.

"Quite right," he said. "Please, did I tell you that you can call me Dr. Sol?"

"Yes, you did."

"Dasein, what could be bothering your innocent, young brain?"

His pale-blue eyes focused on mine, and he seemed more like the man I'd met minutes before.

He walked back to his chair. "Sit down, sit down. Make yourself at home. Just push those periodicals off the chair."

I'd not noticed before, but his office was in complete disarray with books and journals spread everywhere. I didn't know which way to push the journals because either way, they'd land on top of other books and papers.

"Here, I'll put them on my desk," Dr. Sol said, seeming to sense my indecision.

I handed him the periodicals, and he placed them on the edge of his desk where they hung precariously and tilted a bit downward. It made me nervous. I watched as they started to slide from their perch. I reached up and caught them.

"Just lay them down on the floor," Dr. Sol said. "Sorry for the mess. I'm in the middle of a big push for a grant proposal."

I set them on the floor to my left and leaned back in my armchair, pondering what to say. I began to unravel inside. My stomach churned with discontent and unrest. I'd not had time to eat lunch, which only exacerbated the agitation through my midsection. I decided to just get to the point.

"This whole science of medicine has got my mind turned upside-down," I whispered.

He leaned back in his chair and crossed his arms. "Well, that is our job. We confuse you until the end. When you're forced to treat patients, then the learning begins."

Frustrated, I uncrossed my legs and arose from my chair.

"I need to stretch," I said, and paced back and forth in front of Dr. Sol's desk, searching for the right words to explain my concerns.

"But rarely do medical observations uncover the truth for the ages. I do not know what to think of untruthful medicine. Look at cardiac arrest resuscitation instruction. I learned yesterday that it's changed every five years since 1959. They still don't know the truth. The number of compressions and breaths to resuscitate a single fallen life seems so complicated and forever undone by the brightest minds in medicine. Only basic science can claim credit for DNA, genes, and the important things, the truths for the ages." I turned to Dr. Sol's gaze.

"I can't hear all your whispers, young man, when you're walking around like that. Why don't you sit down?"

I walked back to my chair and sat. "The science of

medicine?" I said with a questioning expression and shook my head.

Dr. Sol found my eyes. "It does seem like a lot of BS, the science of medicine. But the *art* of medicine will live on like a Monet of science. Human science is about motivations, and the science of nature is about causality. Never forget that."

I nodded. My aunt Helen had told me the same thing. "But it's frustrating not to be able to say something with certainty," I whispered.

"Well, you're just dealing with first-degree frustration, my son. Wait till you have to play the paper bureaucracy word games. You will be forced to say and write things that no man can do with conviction, and those statements will be compounded with greater uncertainty every day. You'll have to say these things to get treatment approved for your patients."

"But what if I refuse?"

"You'll have no choice. It will be in the best interest of your patients, who you've sworn to care for as best you can. You'll have to say it or else. I guess that you shouldn't think about that just yet. Don't worry; I'm here to help you," he said, and gave a reassuring smile.

"Thank you."

I knew that I was in the right place. I liked Dr. Sol's demeanor and his kindness, and he seemed to understand the threat of legal Cogito on the welfare of patients and doctors. I got up from my seat and whispered goodbye. I walked to his secretary's office and got info about the tour for students interested in doing research with him. With a lift in my step, I passed on taking the elevator and bounded down the stairs.

I stepped out of the sensory deprivation building into the sounds and smells of Harvard. I took a deep breath and smiled: the beans!

Enjoying the delicious smell, I walked toward the

harbor. Waiting for sunset, I enjoyed watching the sailboats, sails filled with wind as they crisscrossed over the sea. The shadow from Chariot Hill crept into view, and that was my cue. I found the path leading around and up the hill. Pondering what Lar had told me about a chariot pulling the sun, I trudged around, down, and up a steep winding path. The idea of a chariot pulling the sun across the sky did seem possible. I lowered my gaze a few meters from the top, and there on a small mound facing west stood the bronze statues of Thoreau, Emerson, and Fuller, and below was an inscription on a brown granite stone: *The Transcendentalists* and beneath in smaller letters, *The Consciousness of Nature.*

I paused in awe, thinking that Aunt Helen would be proud to see this monument.

I climbed a little farther to the top and found a field surrounded by trees with purple and white flowers. I took a seat on a bench, gazing at the beautiful green field, flowering trees, and pigeons searching for food, and then watched as a beautiful sunset ensued. During twilight I closed my eyes and for several moments experienced the Intentio of Providence, the Compass of Freedom.

In my reflective Sentio, I could see Dr. Sol, Linda, and me working together in a research lab. The powerful Intentio released, and my eyes and attention returned to the turquoise sky. A warm sensation spread throughout my chest, and adrenaline surged through my veins. Excited, I got to my feet, wanting to run to the hospital, find Linda, and tell her she was in my vision. We needed to do research together. We were going to free the minds of Americans.

Instead, I jumped several times trying to touch the sky. Everything was falling into place. The reason I'd been directed to Harvard by my Compass of Freedom experience four years ago seemed to be coming true. I smiled to myself skipping toward the House of Essence.

Waiting to cross Paul Revere Street at the traffic light,

I looked about at the citizens waiting to cross from the other side and realized that I still had no idea how I'd free the Americans. Walking as if the wind had been let out of my sails, I crossed and headed down Double Banger Street. How would I free them?

24

On Friday afternoon the psychiatry professor, who had long hair like me, played a song during class. I'd never heard the melody before. I closed my eyes. The tune played in my Sentio and directed my attention toward a vision: a field surrounded by buildings, like at the Harvard undergraduate campus, a green ball field where a large group of people cheered. A calmness came over me, and then waves of joy rushed through me. I leaned back in my seat. Someone had written a song about Sentio. The song was so freeing, and until that moment nothing in medical school had seemed even vaguely familiar to the philosophy I learned growing up. Then an Intentio in my reflective Sentio took me back to Essence and renewed my connection to my mother, Alex, Polly, and everyone back home as if they'd joined me for a sunset experience at that moment. It was as if my mother had sent the song to me through my professor. A tear ran down my cheek.

The tune was called "Imagine" by John Lennon. When class ended, I hurried down front and told my professor Dr. Schnapper that "Imagine" was the most freeing song I'd ever heard. He agreed and said he was glad that I'd enjoyed it. He told me to wait and responded to another student's question. He then pulled a disc of songs from his briefcase and handed it to me, telling me to enjoy. I produced a broad

smile, thanked him, and returned to my seat. Hearing the
song had given me hope, and I thought it might be a turning
point after a difficult week of basic science lectures—not for
its words but for the way the sounds affected my Sentio. And
I knew since my professor and fellow students liked the song
that there was hope for America.

I sat in the lecture hall and reflected long after class and
long after most of the students disappeared. I'd finished my
first week of school. On Fridays back home I would sometimes go with Alex to the river in Pierre and float on the
water with inner tubes. At times the water moved faster and
created turbulence and white water. Those parts of the river
where it was a challenge to stay on the tube—and we often
fell off—were the most fun. My first week in medical school
was like riding the white water rapids in Pierre. There was
a shallow end and a deep end and a lot of rocks in between,
and I'd remained on my tube throughout the first week.

Grateful to be in America at the Harvard School of
Medicine, I got up to leave the lecture hall, and Lar yelled
to me from the back of the auditorium, startling me.

"TGIF," he said in a happy voice.

"What does that mean?"

"Thank God it's Friday."

I laughed. He did not have to explain. The students
of Cogito existence at Harvard wanted Fridays to come
because it meant a reprieve from the squeezing of their
brains.

"TGIF," I yelled back, and waved as I left the lecture
hall.

On my way home I saw TGIF in the eyes of the people I
passed on the street. The sounds of conversation were louder
and more jubilant than they'd been all week. People had a
hop in their steps and greeted each other with eye contact.

I stopped at the grocery store to pick up a few things,
including a player for my disc. I carried my four grocery

bags two blocks and up six flights of stairs. My body felt shaky by the time I set the bags down in the hallway outside of my apartment.

I opened the door, then bent over to pick up my groceries when I felt a hand reach between my legs and give my testicles a gentle tap. I jerked upright and spun around, holding a bag of groceries and fighting to balance my carton of eggs. Simone stood behind me in a pink robe and platform shoes. I was taken aback by her beauty, her presence, and the fact that she'd just touched me—not to mention where.

"Nice ass, Dasein," she said.

"Excuse me; did you just slap me on my testicles?" I asked.

I was surprised by her behavior but so enthralled by her presence that it was all I could do to keep from smiling. I didn't want to encourage her. She'd known before she tapped me that her presence would quell any negative reaction I might have. Simone seemed so in control—calm and cool with a surplus of confidence.

She responded to my question with a smirk, and she walked away from me in silence, shaking her bottom while the sun's rays fell on a sliver of bare skin at the bottom edge of her hips. Her robe was so short and her walk so bouncy that the robe easily snuck up, and she clearly wasn't concerned. My neck blushed, and my heart pounded as when I'd first met Simone. I guessed that the rest of her body was bare under the robe as well. She sashayed into 7C, the apartment down the hall from mine.

Before I could get my groceries inside my apartment, Diana had popped out of apartment 7A.

"Hi, Antonio. Do you need a hand?" she asked.

"Oh, no thanks. I can get this myself."

"Okay, I'll see you later. I have a date across town at the Ritz."

A date. I now knew that this almost always meant work—sharing sensory in exchange for money. "Have fun."

Diana stopped on the landing at the top of the staircase. "Are you doing anything later tonight?"

"I have to study."

For a moment her eyes flashed with disappointment. Then she nodded, waved, and disappeared down the stairs. I wondered if perhaps I should spend time with her. She was my new neighbor after all.

Diana was pretty. Very pretty. Polly would be impressed at how little material she required for a dress. With her hair rolled into a bun and her glittery makeup, she was almost as pleasing a view as Simone. I liked Diana because she was honest, and I believed she had a strong Sentio waiting to be restored. But she didn't grab me like Simone. She didn't cause me to lose control over my limbs or jumble words in my brain. Simone was hard to get out of my consciousness, for I'd never met anyone like her.

I went inside, took off my shirt, and cooked an omelet with cheese and green peppers. Sitting at the kitchen table, preparing to dive into my omelet, I poured a glass of red wine and sipped. Enjoying my meal, I listened to the music my professor had given me on my new disc player. "Imagine" played. A few minutes later "Like a Rolling Stone" by Bob Dylan played. His voice reached out to me and immediately called forth my attention. Dylan's music pleased me, and I found myself singing along with him. I was like a rolling stone, and I was on my own. I smiled as he finished. Unlike the lyrics of the song, I did have a direction home. I would always have my true essence compass, the Compass of Freedom, through my Sentio.

Chewing on the last bite of my delicious omelet, I rinsed my plate in the sink. Grabbing my syllabus and glass of wine off the table, I headed to my chair and rocked in front of the window seat, reading *Biochemistry, the Chemistry of Living*

Cells as the songs replayed. About an hour later, I looked out at the harbor, thinking my mother would be quite surprised at my life in America. I'd called her before I began school, and she reminded me not to let things distract me. *You have a mission,* she'd said. I took a sip of wine and listened to "Imagine" again. My mind relaxed, and I focused on my mission. I had to get a research position in Dr. Sol's laboratory—

I heard a knock and turned the music down.

25

I'd never had a visitor before. I grabbed my shirt, buttoned it, and opened the door. Simone stood in her pink robe, her head cocked to the side. My pleasure tracks lit up, and I struggled to speak, stunned by her breasts, her nipples peeking at me as her robe had pulled apart.

"Can you come help me?" she asked with a hint of desperation, pulling her robe together.

Hmm, for once not calm and cool.

"What's wrong?" I asked.

Simone widened her eyes and raised her hand to her forehead. "I need some help moving my sofa. I tried, and I think I've hurt my back."

"Of course I'll help."

I stepped into the hall pulling my door closed. Simone walked slowly, cautiously, and allowed me to take the lead. I was wearing sandals and noticed that Simone was wearing high heels. It seemed odd that she would have been wearing high heels in her home alone, or that she would have chosen those shoes to put on to come to my door. I wondered if she owned other shoes.

She'd left the door to 7C wide open. I walked into her apartment and took a deep breath of her peach scent. Simone entered behind me. I wanted to say something, but I was nervous. Thinking of my mother earlier, I'd decided I needed to talk to Simone if given the opportunity. I turned to tell her that what she had done—tapping my testicles—was inappropriate.

Before I could say anything, Simone slammed her apartment door. She no longer looked hurt or distressed. Confused, I lost my resolve to bring up the testicle tap. She playfully pushed me onto the sofa and pulled off her robe. Just as I'd thought, her body was bare underneath. My head buzzed as if all my pleasure tracks had lit up. She ran her hands through my hair, tickling my scalp with her fingertips, making me dizzy. She leaned into me with her back straight and her head tilted upward and tickled my face with her gorgeous pink nipples. More pleasure tracks fired in delight, activated by Intentios from the touch of her nipples.

Simone unbuttoned my shirt. "Mmm, I love a flat, hard belly pushing against my soft pleasure. You are firm all over, and your shoulders . . . I love to feel big, rock-hard muscles like yours." She moved her index finger in tiny circles until reaching a ticklish area around my navel.

"Stop," I said jovially.

"*Shh!*"

Her presence completely captured me, and when her soft thighs straddled me, I stopped thinking. My Sentio seized in pleasure as I gazed at her scintillating blue eyes and plump, crimson lips. At that moment for some reason, the thought that I was Adam and she was Eve played in my mind.

She unbuckled my jeans and grabbed my maleness with her hand, pulling on it, and then rubbed my belly with her other.

"You have a big cock," she said, stretching my maleness and rubbing my belly harder. "I thought so. You're lucky. Most of my clients from Harvard have small dicks." She stared into my eyes. "You're mine."

Speechless, I couldn't respond; my Intentio was trapped

in her Sentio pleasure tracks. I moaned in more pleasure as she'd found the *allegro giusto* with her hand massage: up, down, and around. She gripped with just the right pressure at just the right tempo. My maleness grew large and hard, pulsing with my heartbeat and throbbing in pleasurable pain. A wave of heat moved through my neck into my face as if anger were readying me to explode.

Simone pulled my pants to the floor in a quick move. Straddling my left leg, she pressed and squeezed my thigh while moving up and down, arousing herself, her heat warming my thigh. I wanted her like Adam must have wanted Eve, and my desire to have her was impossible to stop. I wanted to dominate her, driven by a need for power over her, something I'd never experienced before.

She touched my nipples with her lips then straddled my thighs and placed my maleness inside of her. At that moment my eyes closed and my attention rocketed into another dimension as if I had jumped into the universe of warm, sensual surround pleasure.

Silence filled my mind; the air molecules moved against my eardrums in Simone's rhythm. I felt everything and nothing just beneath the ceiling of pure ecstasy, and all my attention was focused on Simone's softness, responding to my hardness. I'd never experienced the inside of a woman in my Sentio.

Excited, Simone rode me as if she were riding a horse, racing to the finish line. Her excitement grew. I moved in one rhythm as she squeezed in hers, preparing me to explode inside of her. I again felt the desire for power over her, to physically dominate her.

Simone pulled back and stopped riding me. I opened my eyes, and she slapped me hard across the face—then again even harder. My head turned with her slaps, and my cheeks burned. Her angry slaps left me dazed. What was happening? Strings of her hair dangled in front of her eyes, and she peered at me with complete disgust. In an instant she'd become a different person. She jumped up and grabbed her robe.

"You're trying to rape me, you impotent bastard! Get out of here!" Her voice had filled with anger and hatred. I'd never heard this voice before.

"What happened?" I asked. "Simone, what's wrong? What did I do?"

Bewildered, frozen in place, in shock, what had I done? I tried to look into her eyes for an explanation. She approached and slapped me again. Her eyes darted away. I couldn't touch them. If only I could touch them, I would understand what had happened.

"Get out of here before I call the police," Simone said harshly.

I'd never been talked to like that before, and it scared me. I stood, pulled up my pants, held my shirt together, and hurried back to my apartment. I heard Simone slam her door. I shut my door, locked it, and stepped into my great room, buttoning my shirt. The song about a rolling stone with no direction home was playing at a low volume. I turned it off.

Frightened of what Simone might do, I walked in circles, around and around, in my apartment with a horrible, empty feeling like a hole had formed in my chest. My whole body ached for my mother. What had just happened? Why had this happened? I wanted to leave, to run, but I made myself stay. I sat on my window seat, my chest aching, and the hole now seemed like an abyss. I stared at the heavens and watched twilight turn into darkness—no moon, no stars. The fact that I'd completed my first week of medical school was unimportant. I feared what was going to happen next. Why did Simone perceive that I'd tried to rape her?

I wanted to sleep hoping I'd awake from this nightmare, but I couldn't fall asleep. I got up from the sofa and walked. What had I done? My Sentio was raging, and Intentios were firing all over my mind searching for a language solution. I'd not intended to harm Simone in any way.

Had I?

Replaying her words in my mind convinced me I might have for a moment. When I thought about her calling me an impotent bastard, a hot wave of rage washed over me, which I'd never felt before. She had cheated me from exploding in ecstasy, and part of me wanted to hurt her, to physically dominate her and make her submit to my power.

I wasn't thinking clearly.

I lay on the sofa and used my selective attention to find Linda's Sentio reflections, but as soon as I stopped enjoying my memories of Linda, Simone's words intruded into my consciousness: *You're trying to rape me.*

What would Linda think about me? I tried to release my horrible feelings by stimulating my pleasure tracks, trying to get Simone out of my consciousness, but my mini ecstasies gave only a temporary reprieve. Exhausted, I gave up, closed my eyes, and dreamed of being in prison.

On Sunday afternoon I awoke and spent the rest of the day and night worrying about being arrested. Around midnight I found a pleasant memory of fishing at Paradise with Alex and Javier, which helped me relax and drift to sleep.

On Monday I sat in the freshman lecture hall and couldn't focus on the words of my professors. The only relief from my agony over Simone was enjoying reflections of Linda and her strange love. I knew I couldn't run from what I'd been accused of doing. I felt all alone with no clear direction of where to go from here. No direction home, just like the song. I sat next to Lar in silence. I didn't want to tell him. But he noticed there was something wrong with me. He suggested I run around the harbor to lift my spirits. I thanked him.

26

After my last class that Monday, I said goodbye to Lar and visited Chariot Hill, but the sunset was pale and dull, almost silvery. The color was gone. What had happened to my Sentio? Had I lost my sensitivity? I stood in the field and closed my eyes, trying to reflect on a sunset experienced in Andorra, but I couldn't conjure a memory of the images, the feelings, or the serenity that sunsets delivered to me. I sat on the bench and thought. My unrest over the incident with Simone had created disturbing thoughts about my guilt, which continued to intrude into my consciousness. Vile emotions attached to those thoughts incessantly intruded into my consciousness, which must be dulling my Sentio.

During twilight, I returned to my apartment and tried to relax on the window seat. My neck muscles tightened, and my shoulders felt heavy. My heart dangled on a string, beating erratically against my chest. What was happening to my Sentio?

I remembered the night before taking the medical school admission exam in Paris and how I'd found serenity on that night rocking in a chair in Uncle Poulou's friend's apartment. I needed to find that serenity again.

On that night when Intentio flowed in my Sentio as I looked at the yellow-painted windowsill in the cramped bedroom in Paris, I had used my agency of selective attention to experience my sense of being in Sentio, experiencing the color yellow. Then when I got really tired, I focused my attention on Intentio, and soon after I experienced the serenity of Intentio. I'd experienced my sense of being in Intentio, Intentio within Intentio, rejuvenating my Sentio on that night. I needed to do that now.

I walked around rubbing the back of my neck and then sat in the rocking chair. I rocked, and the to-and-fro movement relaxed me. I delivered my attention to the peach window seat, and soon after I found my Intentio and its nothingness, its serenity, and bliss, Intentio within Intentio. Rocking and meditating for about thirty minutes, I magically found peace. I got up from my chair and passed out on the sofa.

The next day in class Barbara asked me what was wrong. I faked a smile. "Nothing." I couldn't tell Barbara. She wouldn't understand.

I tried to focus on the lectures—first pathology, then anatomy, then biochemistry, and finally psychiatry—but nothing held my attention. It was as if Simone had trapped my Intentio with her accusations, taking priority for every Intentio that emerged in my mind. Her word files were attached to my reflective Sentio, and I'd lost my sensitivity to other sensory. I attempted to redirect my attention through the agency of free will then, but even as I tried to deliver my selective attention to safe areas in my reflective consciousness, new Intentios from the safe areas arose and found Simone's files. Her files were calling for my Intentios.

So I stayed in the present moment—in pre-reflective Sentio—to avoid my memory files as long as possible. I could not let my attention visit Simone's words or images, no matter what. During the final lecture, it took my total concentration to keep my attention on my professor's words and away from Simone's memories.

After my classes, I returned to 7B, and it dawned on

me I needed strange love, as my mother warned I would. I needed to find Linda, but I was too exhausted. I climbed the stairs to my bedroom and collapsed on the bed.

The next day after classes, I went to the on-call rooms at the hospital and asked Dr. Bock if he'd seen Linda. He explained that she was rotating at another hospital thirty miles away. I returned home disappointed and too upset to study. I fell asleep on the sofa, hoping I'd dream about Linda.

27

On Thursday classes were intense, and thoughts and feelings about Simone continued to intrude. I couldn't stop my Intentios from digging through my Sentio and Cogito memory files attached to her.

I remained greatly troubled that she'd accused me of trying to rape her. I replayed the incident repeatedly, trying to discern where things had gone wrong. No matter how I looked at it, Simone's actions and reaction did not add up. She'd pursued me; I was merely a passenger on the ride until the moment she turned on me—just after I'd experienced that wave of anger and the desire to dominate her. It was as if she'd known what I was experiencing at that moment, and she used it against me.

After classes that afternoon, I went for a run on the undergraduate campus, hoping to find the cheerleaders, but they'd gone.

I'd made it through the week, and on Friday night Milly was throwing a party. I ran into her on the porch. She was decorating the tables, and she asked me to attend. It was my duty; she reminded me. I went upstairs, showered, and ate some leftover spaghetti.

I showed up late for the party and stayed off to the side by myself, walking back and forth delivering food and drink from the kitchen to the porch. I didn't want to dance, and

Sassy flipped at me when I turned her down. Diana noticed my odd behavior and asked me what was wrong.

"Nothing, I just don't feel well," I lied.

"Would you like to go for coffee?"

"Sure, why not?" I wanted to get away before running into Simone.

We walked to the Majestic, a beautiful little restaurant built many years ago that I imagined was like the cafés Uncle Poulou and Aunt Helen used to visit in Paris. Diana and I shared some apple pie and coffee on the veranda. We munched, listening to the piano music drifting out from inside. I recognized Rachmaninoff's concerto.

"Thanks, Diana, for getting me out of there," I said. "I need a friend tonight."

She gave me a friendly smile. "I heard about your episode with Simone."

My stomach churned into a knot. I looked down at my pie. Diana did not mince words; she was as truthful as any orphan girl I'd ever known. I raised my eyes and met her gaze.

"What episode?" I knew it was irrational, but I hoped it was not the episode last Friday.

"Simone told everyone," Diana said, and sipped her coffee. Her twinkling eyes suggested to me she didn't believe what Simone had told her.

"Told everyone what?" I asked, even though I wasn't sure I wanted to hear.

Diana hesitated for a couple of seconds. She looked at her coffee, and her face became serious.

"Simone said that you tried to rape her," Diana said rapidly in one breath. "But you couldn't because you have a flaccid penis, and you're impotent."

Struggling not to react to the word rape, I took a deep breath, released it, and asked, "Do you believe that?" I shook my head in disbelief. "Simone is lying. She is a horrible liar."

Diana lifted the corners of her mouth, and her face relaxed. Her eyes told me that she believed me, and I breathed out a small sigh. Simone was a liar, but I didn't want to explain what had happened. It was too embarrassing.

"Antonio, leave Simone alone. I know what she can do to your mind. She plays mind games. Some of her clients are very weird. Simone has become weird, too. You want no part of her."

Suddenly my face had flushed in anger. Mind games, I thought. I was furious at Simone. I chewed on pie to keep from saying something I'd regret. At least I knew that I was angry, which was important. My mother had taught me that an angry disposition could lead my Intentios astray and make me less objective. And at this moment Simone was like a mythical siren calling out to me, inviting me to be angry—so my Intentios would search for a way to attack her, but I wouldn't give in to her any longer.

I looked at Diana, took a deep breath, and released. "What about Milly?" I asked.

As soon as I asked, I thought of Aunt Helen's words: self-consciousness is simply being conscious of what someone else thinks about you.

"Milly doesn't care; she is not judgmental as long as she gets paid."

"But I like Milly," I said. "I don't want her to think this about me." I could not help myself. I cared what she thought about me.

"She won't think differently about you," Diana said. "Milly knows Simone very well. She's had many problems with her. But Simone has a large customer base. Many old, rich guys have sold their souls to Dominatrix Simone, and Milly puts up with her weirdness because she brings in so much money."

"I dislike Simone more than anyone that I've ever met," I admitted.

Diana sat back into her seat and sighed. "She must like you or she wouldn't try to incite you. She is weaving her web. Be careful Antonio."

Our waitress appeared offering more pie and coffee. Diana refilled her cup, and I had another piece of pie. Warm apple pie smelled delicious. While chewing, I had an epiphany. "She's trying to condition my Sentio."

Diana's brow furrowed. "She might be trying to do more than that."

"I've never met anyone like Simone," I said. "What happened to make her want to control me?"

"You are a tall, strong, handsome young man. Simone is getting older. She's probably threatened by you."

This thought perplexed me. Why would Simone be threatened by me? She seemed so confident. She'd been in control each time we interacted. I crossed my arms in frustration.

"American women are very confusing," I said.

Diana looked surprised. "You mean German women aren't?"

"I'm not German. I'm from Andorra."

Diana grinned. "That's right. What are Andorra's women like?"

"They are like me. They are people. Their womanliness does not make them different. Polly is a little bit like American women, but the women I grew up around knew they were not born women. They knew they were human beings well before being defined by their gender."

Diana nodded. Then she gave me a questioning look. "I need to visit the little girl's room." She got up and went inside.

28

I twiddled my thumbs waiting for Diana to return. She seemed very interested in my upbringing. When she came back, she looked me in the eyes, taking her seat.

"Antonio, what do you mean when you say Sentio?"

I waited till she settled in her chair and said, "Sentio means *I feel* in Latin. It is your sense-processing consciousness that's separate from your Cogito or language-thinking consciousness. It plays our sensory experiences: smell, sound, color, taste, touch, pain, position, vibration, motion, and number. It's where pure sensory data and sensate causality data make meaning, nature's truths. It's where empathy and true love emerge. It provides our vision for freedom." I smiled. I'd gotten carried away.

Diana nodded, sipping on her coffee.

It felt good to talk about Sentio and Cogito even though I couldn't deliver Diana's Intentio to her Sentio, and she didn't know she was addicted to Cogito. I wasn't going to tell her.

She asked if I had a girlfriend, and I told her about Linda. She listened and then shook her head as if she understood why Linda was so special. She told me she'd met a young man once and felt the same way. His name was Fred.

I told her the story of my aunt's discovery of the Sentio Consciousness of Eden—the first consciousness before Cogito—and added, "Language may have an innate basis, but human language delivers man-made meaning, and the meaning of a word can change with use. The meaning of the words *love* and *freedom* are changing. Language meaning is susceptible to human motivations, time, context, and meaning drift."

Diana narrowed her eyes. "How can we communicate without language?"

"We can still use language but in a positive way; we need better ways to communicate based on the sensate causality of nature experienced in the data sphere of Sentio."

Diana's face had twisted into a question mark.

I added, "Language has a role to play in reasoning, but people driven by the will for power and pleasure use language as a weapon to control others.

"The great thinkers, starting with Aristotle, recognized that sensory data was the source of all truth. But then most of the great thinkers got tangled in the argument between rationalism, meaning knowledge comes through reason, and empiricism, meaning knowledge comes through sensory. Descartes pointed out that you cannot trust sensory, but he didn't know that the sensory he experienced was altered, sensory processed through his language filter, Cogito sensory. Locke argued for empiricism as the source of all knowledge and said we all started with a blank tablet in Cogito, but he didn't know about Sentio either. Then phenomenology made sensory data seem even less reliable, but again, it was sensory data processed in Cogito. Pre-reflective Sentio precedes the effects of phenomenology.

"My aunt Helen discovered Sentio—the first consciousness and the source of all truth—where sensory data is projected immediately into consciousness, revealing things as they truly are in the world and the causes of things, sensate causality."

Diana's brown eyes had grown dim, and I realized I'd gotten carried away again. She looked at her coffee cup, took a sip, and then asked me why I'd come to Harvard.

I told her about my mission to free the slaves of Cogito existence. I didn't think she understood my explanation, but she listened intently. Afterward, Diana's eyes twinkled at me with a caring look of concern, and she touched the top of my hand with her fingertips. My chest warmed on the inside. I looked at her hand and then smiled at her. She moved her hand away and looked at the couple at the table across from us.

After a long moment of silence, Diana talked about Fred, smiled at me again, and then asked about Polly. I told her Polly had decided that she and Alex were meant to be together for eternity. Diana said that she'd felt the same way about Fred. But then she clammed up, and we sat in silence.

The silence was calming, and being with Diana gave me pleasure; her brown eyes and green dress had lit up my Sentio tracks of pleasure. She then told me that my eyes were beautiful, and I had a cute dimpled chin. She wanted me to let my hair down, but I left it tied back.

"It's too curly," I said, and told her about my vow to let it grow until I could deliver the Americans to freedom.

Diana leaned forward, and her face grew serious. "Simone is dangerous," she said. "Leave her alone."

I believed she'd repeated this warning because she'd grown to care about me. She knew that Simone had lied about me, and she was worried what else she might do. I told Diana that I'd thought too much about Simone. I wanted to stop thinking, and I wanted her out of my consciousness for good.

Diana asked if we could go to my room. She thought

she could help me forget Simone. She winked at me; I winked back at her cute smile.

We walked back to Essence holding hands under the starry sky and saw that Milly's party had ended early. I led Diana to 7B, and we sat together in darkness on the window seat, looking toward the skyline above the harbor. The reflection of the moonlight shining on the water created a romantic mood. We embraced then kissed, touched, and tickled each other. We'd enjoyed intimate sensory for about an hour when Diana needed a break. I got some wine while she went to her apartment. She returned and played her music, a nice song by a lady named Carly Simon, and then I played my song "Imagine." Diana loved it. We played it again, hugged, and kissed on the sofa. When Diana's songs played again, we got up and laid our heads on sofa pillows in the window seat, looking up at the twinkling stars.

Diana turned, found my eyes, and said that she had never met anyone like me. She said that she felt I knew her better than she knew herself. I grinned and petted her soft brown hair.

A few minutes later the music stopped playing. "It's getting late," Diana said.

"I'll walk you to your apartment."

We got up and walked toward the door. She turned and thanked me for treating her like a Sentio being. I smiled on the inside at her use of the word and told her I'd enjoyed our kissing.

"I would like to do it again," I said.

She lifted the corners of her crimson lips, nodded, and then kissed my cheek. Diana left, and I walked into the kitchen enjoying the velvety texture of the peach walls. My Sentio sensitivity had heightened. It was not as intense a response as Linda had generated, but Diana had given me strange love too.

I walked upstairs, relaxed in my loft bed, and rolled onto my side asking myself how would I free the Americans? My experience with Simone had created doubt whether I could maintain my own Sentio freedom in America. Where would I be tonight if not for Diana? I sighed and turned over to protect my back, drifting to sleep, hoping the incident with Simone was behind me and then enjoying the reflective Sentio of Diana.

29

Three weeks had passed since my strange love experience with Diana. We'd become strange lover friends hugging and listening to music on weekends. Diana was tuning in to Sentio. I enjoyed the thought as I walked home from the store late on Friday afternoon, TGIF day. Being with Diana was great, but I longed to reunite with Linda, who I'd learned yesterday from Dr. Bock was now rotating far away at another hospital. I had to get that research position with Dr. Sol. It was the only way. I picked up my pace heading down Double Banger.

When I reached my apartment, Simone surprised me popping out of 7C, wearing a skimpy, black dress. It was odd that she seemed to know my routine. I was holding groceries when she approached me in the hallway. She smiled and stopped by my door. She said she wanted to apologize. I shared a half-smile, opened my door, and put my groceries inside. When I returned to the hallway to pick up my bottled water, Simone was still standing there, waiting for me.

"I want to apologize for the misunderstanding several weeks ago," she said.

I listened in disbelief. Misunderstanding? Then she blamed the sexual miscommunication on her line of work, an occupational hazard of her profession. She moved toward me, flashed her cleavage at me, and peered into my eyes.

"Sometimes teasing games go too far for my clients and me," she said.

"Yes, Simone. Way too far!" I shook my head in disgust.

"I regret the entire unfortunate matter. It was a big mistake—my fault," she said, and stroked my cheek with her fingers. "Will you forgive me, please?"

I walked away and then remembered what my mother had taught me. I was raised to forgive those who asked for it. I set the case of water on my kitchen counter and returned to the hall and found Simone's eyes.

"Yes, of course, I'll forgive you. But there are consequences for your actions."

Simone continued with her apology, primarily for sending a mixed message to me. But what about the slaps and all her lies about me? What about my weekend from hell when I worried about being accused of rape? I grew angry at her again. My insides churned at her apology.

The corners of her peach lips drooped; Simone looked genuinely sad. "I just want you to be my friend," she said as a tear rolled down her cheek.

I hesitated to say anything, and then Simone begged me to join her for tea. She wanted to explain in private. I looked into her sad eyes. She motioned with her hand, and I followed her to 7C—I had a soft spot for Simone. We sat down at her kitchen table where she'd placed tea cups and saucers. I rationalized that I had a good reason for being here with her. I still wanted to clarify what had happened that Friday night four weeks earlier.

Simone poured my tea and shared some cream and sugar, and after a long moment of silence, I jingled a tune by tapping my spoon nervously on the saucer the way Uncle Poulou used to do. I was about to ask Simone why she'd spread the cruel rumors about me when she excused herself to the bathroom, so I waited, holding my question for when she returned.

Several minutes later Simone slinked from the bathroom naked with a challenging stare. Wearing black vinyl platform shoes and a black vinyl collar around her neck, she approached me and stopped. Hands on her hips, she shifted her weight from side to side.

Shocked, my jaw dropped. Was this really happening? My eyes searched every inch of her bare body in less than a second, then her nipples transfixed me. My pleasure tracks fired at will at Intentios from her sensory. Simone's nakedness was real. She was a sexy goddess, and I was defenseless yet again.

I managed to ask why she'd spread the lies about me.

She said that she told everyone the rumors to protect me from the other girls and continued slinking toward me as I inhaled her peach bouquet.

"You were protecting me?" I asked incredulously as she ran her fingers through my hair.

"You are special, Antonio. The cheap sluts that work for Milly would ruin you."

She touched her peach flavored lips against mine and then kissed my cheek.

A wave of fear crept through me, tightening the muscles in my chest and quickening my breath. I remembered all too well how I'd felt after my first episode with Simone. My pre-reflective Sentio wanted me to stay. My heart pounded. My reflective Sentio urged me to get up out of this chair and run.

Simone kissed my mouth harder and deeper. Then she tickled my ear with her tongue. She rubbed my chest and lower abdomen with her fingertips.

My Sentio tracks flashed in pleasure. I decided to stay and investigate.

"Yum!" she said, and pulled me up by my arm.

She led me to her bedroom and jumped atop her black silk sheets with grace, barely making a sound. She lay naked

on her stomach with her arms stretched up towards the head-
board and began putting on wristbands. She looked over her
shoulder and asked me to fasten another set of bands around
her ankles.

I noticed a gadget attached to her bed. A crank hooked
to cables running through pulleys, like on Uncle Poulou's
sailboat.

"What are we doing, Simone?"

"Shut up, you pussy," she said with authority. "Fasten
me and turn that crank."

I fell under her spell then, and she toyed with me,
directing my Intentio to where she wanted me to focus
my attention. She was in complete control of my Intentio,
and her dominant way enthralled me. I fastened the bands
around her ankles. Then I turned the crank, hypnotized,
and intrigued as every click lifted Simone's body a little
higher. She lifted from the bed, first her arms and legs, then
the rest. She was suspended in the air as if being drawn and
quartered. Fascinated, I enjoyed seeing her struggle, wig-
gling in pain, and hearing her cries as I turned the crank,
tightening the nylon ropes fastened to her outstretched arms
and legs. Simone's beautiful body dangled in the air as she
squirmed and twisted. My Sentio arousal tracks lit up in
pleasure at seeing her in pain.

"Do you have that little dick hard? Come fuck my little
clit, you impotent bastard." Simone lifted and turned her
head, trying to make eye contact with me as she repeated
her demand, taunting me. I stared from the foot of the bed
at her suspended, naked body.

Her words incited me, ignited me. When she called
me an impotent bastard the third time, I wanted to hurt
her. I don't remember getting undressed, but I found myself
naked and wanting to hurt her with my maleness, erect and
hard. I climbed up on her bed, my maleness throbbing. I
pushed inside her dryness, and her body began to swing in

my rhythm. Her screams sounded far away in my head, like echoes. I rammed her as deep and as hard as I could, and the feeling of power and pleasure overwhelmed me, consumed me. I wanted Simone to feel more pain. Again and again, I rammed her and enjoyed her screams; the echoes got louder and louder in my head. My maleness was about to explode . . .

I awoke on her bed, panting as if I'd run for several miles, with a horrible feeling inside my chest; I must have blacked out. I rolled over, and Simone was hanging above me. She was suspended in the air, her head hanging below her shoulders like a rag doll, her body entirely flaccid, her breasts dangling, and she wasn't moving. I thought for a moment that I'd killed her. Her chest lifted. She was still breathing.

What had I done? I was exhausted and dripping with sweat. Rising and stepping back from the bed, I staggered and nearly fell. My left leg had fallen asleep. I righted myself and tried to release Simone. The crank was stuck. She coughed, lifted her head, and then opened her eyes.

"Thank God. Are you okay, Simone?"

"Let me down." She directed me like a child with her dominant voice again. She demanded I push the button on the side and release her. When I did, she fell and rolled over, glaring at me with her deceiving blue eyes. She looked disgusting, with threads of her blonde hair covering her right eye and her mouth pulled sideways into a conceited smile.

"How was that, Dasein? Did anyone ever do that for you in Andorra?"

Speechless, I stared at her. I was upset with myself for what I'd done to Simone, but in a strange way she acted as if she'd enjoyed it and as if she wanted me to enjoy what I'd done to her. I shook my head no. I stood up tall. I'd regained control of my attention, and I wouldn't let her control me ever again.

"Simone, I know what you're about. I know what you're doing, and my Sentio consciousness is hallowed ground."

I stood naked, looking for Simone's eyes, but after I'd confronted her, she hid them. She lay flat on her back on the bed, taunting me with her legs spread apart.

"Come on!" she said. "You are my slave now, you little pussy. You impotent bastard, you can only fuck me now when I say."

I shook my head. "No."

I explained to her my mission in life—how I would lead the American slaves to freedom like Spartacus. She erupted in hysterical laughter. I'd never heard such cackles.

"I want no part of being under your spell. I'm free," I said.

My resolution grew as I spoke. I'd come to the United States to bring freedom, and I wouldn't let this woman derail me. I could overcome her power over me, and I knew that now. I could use my Cogito to protect my Sentio from Simone. I would have to be vigilant and direct my Intentio to these Cogito memory files when around her. I found my underwear on the other side of the bed and dressed as fast as I could.

"Don't you know history, Dasein?" Simone asked, peering at me with her mouth curled into an evil smile. "Spartacus lost and was crucified with hundreds more just like him. You'll not free anyone. You'll end up a slave or dead just like the rest of them. I wanted to give you the pleasure of being my slave, you ungrateful bastard."

I pulled up my pants, turned, and met Simone's twisted face.

"No, Simone, you're wrong. I'll set you free someday."

She got up and put on her robe as I stepped toward her apartment door. "I hate you, Dasein!" Simone said loudly. Her voice boomed with supposed authority, but I heard the desperation underneath.

I hate you. I'd never heard those words before. I walked with honor out of her door and closed it shut.

Quickly buttoning my shirt, I looked up, and Diana was standing quietly near a vent in the hallway. I met her gaze, and she smiled at me with sparkles in her eyes.

"Good for you, Dasein."

"You heard what I said to Simone."

"Every word."

At that moment, a warm joyous wave washed over me, like euphoria. I glanced back toward 7C, closed my eyes, and almost cried. I was free, free from Simone's control over me.

I opened my eyes. "Thank you, Diana." I turned, walked into 7B, and shut the door.

I leaned against the door and took a couple of deep breaths, enjoying the feeling of freedom for a long moment. Strangely, then I felt sad for Simone because she represented the people that I wanted to free from their misery, their longing for freedom and love, a longing that cannot be appeased by power or pleasure.

I thought as I sat on my window seat looking out at the harbor. I wished there was a way to harness Simone's intimate power and direct it for goodness, love, and freedom. If only . . .

30

Turning on my disc player and moving to the rocking chair near the window seat, I took a deep breath, relaxed, and rocked, thinking I'd just survived the most serious threat to my Sentio in my entire life. Rocking slowly, I realized that because I was a Sentio being, I was vulnerable to the American way. I had to be careful.

The good news was by staying alert I could use the knowledge gained from this experience to prevent similar threats in the future. Simone represented what I was up against in America, and I realized then that television had paraded case after case. I'd seen them on the TV in the gathering area of the interns' quarters. Everything I'd been watching made sense to me now. The use of advanced conditioning to control others was rampant. Americans did not know they were slaves of Cogito nor did they know they were conditioning one another beyond repair in their search for power and pleasure. Perhaps Americans used power and pleasure in an attempt to assuage their despair over their loss of freedom.

I'd only been in the States for a few weeks, but I believed I understood. The citizens had lost their vision for freedom and true love and were pursuing their desire for pleasure and power. They sacrificed their present moments, the now, for the illusion that they would someday be free.

But they will never be able to buy their way out of their institutional bondage. They do not know their longing for goodness and freedom can never be appeased by power and pleasure. I wanted to tell them, but until they found the way to freedom through Sentio, I knew my words would fall on deaf ears.

For Spartacus, it had been easy. He shared his vision for freedom with his fellow gladiators; they did not have to perform in the ring, fighting each other as gladiators to the death. And after hearing Spartacus's message, the gladiator slaves realized they wanted to live free or die fighting for freedom. They fought to the death, side-by-side. Young, old, men, women, and children, they fought to the death for freedom rather than die as slaves in the ring under Roman rule.

Americans die in the ring every day—the institutional ring—while chasing the illusion that their efforts will gain a purse and the favor of Rome and then they'll be set free. I knew the truth; Americans were destined to die fighting within their institutions, in a competition for pseudo-freedom, and many citizens—Simone's customers—had already realized this and given up.

My mother once told me I had the same true essence ilk as Spartacus. I hoped the Americans would rally if they knew they had a choice to live free and happy lives enjoying the Sentio Consciousness of Eden while pursuing freedom, truth, and love.

They needed the opportunity. I had to deliver Sentio experientially and restore their vision for freedom so they could see that we have what we need to meet everyone's needs. The American founders had discovered Sentio when they first set out for freedom, and I believed Americans would pull together at the renewal of such awareness. They would help each other climb toward the mountaintop, like the Sisters of Freedom at Essence.

Returning to the window seat, lying with my hands folded under my head, I imagined working in Dr. Sol's laboratory and finding a way to restore Sentio, the pathway to the truth and freedom. Next week I'd get my chance to tour his lab and try to impress him, so he'd pick me as his student research assistant. One of twelve student applicants for a single spot, I had to get that position in his lab.

I got sleepy and closed my eyes. In my mind's eye, I saw a vision of a large group of people climbing a steep incline, helping each other with outstretched arms and with eyes of encouragement, climbing toward the ultimate freedom hidden on the mountaintop. That's when it dawned on me. As the will for meaning approaches infinity, meaning becomes the will for freedom, and then it becomes the will for the ultimate freedom from the misery of need and time. The will for meaning is the will for freedom, and our objective meaning for life is to pursue greater freedom for all until we experience the ecstasy of infinity. I wanted to call my mother and tell her that she was right. Years ago, I'd asked her what was on top of the mountain of freedom, and she responded: *Well, more freedom.*

The corners of my mouth lifted as I thought about what a cute and funny genius my mother was. I got up, grabbed a pillow and blanket from the closet, returned to the sofa, holding the pillow as if it were my mother cuddling beside me, and fell asleep.

CHAPTER

31

In khaki slacks and my lucky white shirt from Alex, I stepped off the lift onto the shiny concrete basement floor of the sensory deprivation building. I walked down the hallway toward a group of my peers, waiting to tour Dr. Sol's research labs in the hope of becoming the student selected as his research assistant.

"Hey Lar, Barbara, Tinker . . . fancy meeting you here," I said.

Tinker greeted me with a nod and leaned against the wall.

"Hey, Dasein," Lar said. "Glad you made it."

Lar knew I needed to do research with Dr. Sol. He knew about my vision of freedom, and he was pulling for me.

Barbara, my curly-headed friend from Baltimore, twirled from a huddle with two female students to find my eyes. "Hey, Antonio." The corners of her mouth formed a sweet smile with dimples.

She knew how much I wanted to do research. I shot a smile at her and leaned against the wall next to Tinker. We waited near the swinging doors for Dr. Sol to appear.

From an office at the other end of the hallway, Dr. Sol's slender frame emerged and approached, hidden under a long white lab coat, and there was no mistaking his bald head and pointed ears.

"Good afternoon! Is everyone here?" he asked, and made a quick head count. "Let's get going; follow me."

We passed through the swinging doors and ambled down a long hallway when Dr. Sol stopped and motioned for us to gather around him. He pointed at a large door to his left.

"This is our new primate section," he said. "I want you to see what's in the pipeline for our brain research."

He opened the door and ushered our group inside. Immediately, the shrill sounds of primal fear erupted: blood-curdling screams then spasmodic hiccupping sounds, like evil laughter. Egg crate foam covered the walls and ceiling, dampening the piercing cries of chimpanzees.

From his cage, one little chimpanzee grunted, found my eyes, and gestured as if to acknowledge my presence. I smiled at him in reply, and the chimp smacked his lips and shook his head at me. Our group gathered near the door of his cage and watched as a young female lab assistant reached inside, pulled the little chimp into her arms, cuddled him, and attached a bib around his neck.

"How cute," said Barbara.

The other two chimps looked on from their separate cages, producing a series of shrill cuckooing sounds interrupted with grunts. One did back flips while the other climbed up and shook the top of its cage.

"The baby chimps require bottle feeding," Dr. Sol said. "I thought you'd enjoy seeing them during their afternoon feeding."

The lab assistant leaned back in her rocking chair and grabbed a bottle of formula from the table. The chimp sucked on the nipple and soon after formula began dripping from the side of his mouth onto his bib.

"You'll get yours, don't worry," Dr. Sol said in a calming tone to the other two chimps.

I looked around at my fellow students who were all smiling then looked at the door as a male assistant entered.

"I came to draw blood," the male assistant said to Dr. Sol.

"Not now, give us about ten minutes," Dr. Sol replied, and absently rubbed the back of his bald head.

The feeding chimp watched Dr. Sol and patted the assistant on her head. It was hard not to laugh, watching the mimicry unfold.

"Baby chimps are so cute," said Barbara from up front, crouched with several other students, who took turns gently petting the chimp's head.

"The chimps are cute, but they are noisy creatures," Dr. Sol said.

"What do you do with them?" asked Barbara as she stood up, and found Dr. Sol's eyes.

"These chimps are special. We need their brain tissue to locate the rare receptor of our newest bio-molecular discovery," he said matter-of-factly.

My fellow students seemed stunned by the gruesome thought of using the chimp's brain tissue for research, their mouths agape.

"Oh, God!" Barbara exclaimed, "I know that you have to do it. I just don't think that I could work here."

She looked at the assistant feeding the little chimp. The assistant smiled at the satisfied face of the chimp, sucking on the oversized nipple. It dawned on me then that the chimps would have to be sacrificed to use their brain tissue.

"It's a small price to pay," Dr. Sol said with detached assurance, and added, "There's no pain involved. We inject them with our radiolabeled biomolecule, euthanize them, and collect their brain tissue."

A few of the students nodded and acted as if it were no big deal to use a chimp's brain in medical research. Many of the others had looks similar to Barbara's and were clearly disturbed. My chest ached. I looked at Barbara and then Dr. Sol with wide eyes. Dr. Sol led us back out into the hallway.

As we walked down the hall, I wanted to do something to save the chimps. I looked at Lar and Tinker, their heads hanging low. A student named Bob raised his hand. He was an interesting fellow who liked to talk about his 4.0-grade point average, which he attained as a Yale undergraduate.

"Yes?" Dr. Sol said, looking at Bob.

"What have you found? A new endorphin?"

I sensed Bob was trying to create a distraction with his question, sparing us from our thoughts about the dreadful fate of the chimps.

"We found a small peptide in the blood of human babies that disappears when the babies turn four years old," Dr. Sol answered. "It may have antidepressant properties. Oddly, the same peptide reappears in some depressed adults after successful electroconvulsive therapy."

"You mean shock treatment?" I asked in amazement.

"Yes," Dr. Sol said, finding my eyes. "We've been using ECT on humans for despair since the late 1930s."

My Intentio ran through my memory files making connections. I knew this peptide had something to do with Sentio. It is present in babies and patients like my aunt Helen, who received ECT years ago, and it disappears in children around the age of four.

The biomolecule of pleasure is an endorphin; the biomolecule of fight-or-flight is adrenalin. This peptide could be the biomolecule of freedom. This could be the molecule I sensed had elevated my Sentio sensitivity after sharing strange love with Linda.

"But why chimp brains?" asked Barbara.

"Chimps are the next best thing to humans," replied Dr. Sol.

"When will the chimps be sacrificed?" I asked.

Dr. Sol turned away from Barbara and spoke to me in

a low voice. "Sometime next semester. We have to figure a way to stabilize the radiolabeled peptide molecule before we can inject the chimps and isolate the receptor."

"Good," I blurted out.

Dr. Sol arched his brow and looked inquisitively at me.

"I mean it's good that you're close to finding the receptor," I offered. I didn't tell him that I was going to find a way to free the chimps.

"So, what is it? What's the biomolecule called?" asked another student.

"We've named the molecule baby specific protein, or BSP," Dr. Sol said.

"Will you try to make it into a pill?" asked Lar, who was always thinking ahead.

"No, it has to be injected," Dr. Sol said. "It is a small peptide, like insulin. Let's move along. We have a lot to see in a short time."

We pushed open the swinging hallway door and continued our walk until the scent of sawdust and urine filled the air. We stopped, and through the window of the lab door, I could see a hamster running on its wheel. Dr. Sol opened the door, and our group marched into the lab, which was furnished with metal stools, stainless steel sinks, wooden cabinetry, and black granite countertops. Test tubes, pipettes, flasks, beakers, microscopes, and gas burners with rubber tubing filled the countertop. Dr. Sol called them the tools of academic bench research.

A large spectroscopy instrument was being reconfigured by an odd-looking, bald technician. He looked up at me, and I recognized him as one of the German engineering students. He said hello, and I nodded to acknowledge him.

"Our entire basement floor is dedicated to animal research," Dr. Sol explained. "Our research involves small animal sensory deprivation of light and touch. We deprive them and measure their cortisol, growth hormone, glucose, and adrenaline responses. And on the seventh floor we carry out similar studies depriving the animals of sound and touch."

"Where do you do consciousness research?' I asked.

"Our metaphysics and ontological research center is

on the eleventh floor. We study human consciousness and selective attention there."

We walked into an observation office decorated with a long, black table and four nice leather chairs. At least a dozen monitors played video feed: infrared images of small mice and large rats housed in darkened glass containers, like aquariums.

The light deprivation and isolation seemed to have a profound effect on the little creatures. Their red eyes and bodies were upsetting to watch. They contorted their bodies and darted their eyes as if danger lurked all around. Light deprivation seemed cruel. I watched two rats as they tried to gnaw through their glass containers. They were trying to find a way to freedom.

As I continued watching the rats, a wave of sadness affected me as if the rats were human. The way they darted their eyes reminded me of Anal in a strange way.

"What happens to the rats deprived of light?" I asked Dr. Sol.

"Eventually they become agitated and exhibit paranoid behavior, and if they are housed together with other deprived animals, they will kill one another," he replied.

I gaped at Dr. Sol for a long moment. The fate of the sensory deprived rats seemed to be what was happening to Americans.

Dr. Sol waved. "We've got a lot more to see upstairs."

Lar held the door, and our group hurried out.

I had to get the assistant research position. I knew there was something here that I had to figure out to save America.

33

We marched into the hallway and waited for Lar to close the door of the sad, smelly, small animal laboratory.

"Sentio is everything," Dr. Sol said, then waved us onward toward the elevators.

Unbelievable, I smiled. His words were music to my ears and came at the perfect time to lift my mood. He sounded like my aunt Helen. I found his eyes as we gathered by the elevator and nodded. Dr. Sol had surprised me. He did know about Sentio.

We took the lift to the eleventh floor, and as we exited, I saw the big words fixed on the wall in large, gold letters: *Consciousness Research Laboratory*. I hoped it was the lab where I'd find a way to deliver Sentio to the Americans.

We entered a large, sterile room with pale green walls and stood on a shiny, white tile floor. I sensed this was the lab where my vision of freedom in Andorra four years ago and my recent experience on Chariot Hill had pointed me. I noticed the high ceiling, and my eyes followed a bundle of wires that twirled down from a hole in the ceiling to the top of a ten-foot-by-ten-foot, pale-blue vessel resting on a wood platform with a step, leading to an open door.

Dr. Sol called it a sensory deprivation chamber. He walked over and stood between the two, stainless steel stands positioned next to the chamber, garnering our attention.

"In the beginning, the sensory deprivation chamber was used to test the idea that one could shut down consciousness by depriving the brain of external sensory. Theoretically, the test subject would experience blank consciousness while remaining awake in the chamber. Of course, we know from our streaming consciousness studies that consciousness continues, viewing memory files powered by internal, intrinsic sensory. Here at Harvard, instead of using the chamber to study sensory deprivation, we use the chamber to study consciousness while limiting external sensory distractions."

Lar whispered, "The chamber looks like a submarine."

Dr. Sol smiled. "It does look like a sub," he said. "One of my associates named our sub Zeni. I first used Zeni two years ago when we discovered Sentio and Cogito, the two consciousnesses, and we are using Zeni to look for pure Intentio—the attention wave, the Zen—that binds us to our sensory, thoughts, and nothingness; the ghost who holds the key to the ecstasy of infinity. Aristotle began the journey to find Intentio, looking for what binds all modes of being."

I grinned at the familiar words, similar to Aunt Helen's philosophy.

Barbara asked, "Where is the hypertonic salt water that you float on inside the chamber?"

"We do not need water because we can average out random electrical activity, skin stimuli—the noise—that for years had hidden the small evoked potential changes in the brain, which we were unable to map until the advent of computers and digital technology."

I didn't understand, and several students—Bob and Tinker included—furrowed their brows.

"Repetition cancels out the random noise, signal averaging," Dr. Sol explained. "By repeating a stimulus over and over and acquiring voltage changes, signal information confined within a short, fixed-time interval after the stimulus, we allow the random electrical noise to zero itself out while amplifying the electrochemical signal of interest."

Ah, I understood.

Dr. Sol continued his explanation, the others nodding in understanding. He paused and scratched his head. "We are each of us institutional nothingness until Intentio, attention, emerges in Sentio as the director of freedom. And the ultimate freedom is, of course, freedom from time." He smiled at me.

I could not help myself. "I know this, Dr. Sol. Despite it all, Sentio consciousness has survived and continues to allow Intentio to find greater freedom."

Dr. Sol looked at me with a fixed gaze as if amazed, and said, "Yes, Sentio consciousness was where Aristotle's Intentio emerged to begin deductive reasoning, thinking without language, the observance of nature and causality, but then Aristotle asked the four questions[1]. And humankind has been lost ever since." He sighed. "It's not Aristotle's fault that we have perverted his questions with our answers driven by our selfish desires for power and pleasure, driving our Intentios deeper and deeper into the abyss of Cogito."

A warm sensation filled my chest and spread to my head. At that moment I realized Dr. Sol grasped the predicament of humankind. More than ever, I knew why I was here at Harvard.

He continued. "And just like Dasein says, Sentio has come to our rescue time and time again, delivering us to a new freedom."

Feeling another pleasant tingle in my head, I grinned and nodded.

Dr. Sol turned his eyes from me, looked at the submarine, and then at Barbara. "Sentio consciousness is measurable and occurs milliseconds after being evoked. Sentio arises twice as fast as Cogito consciousness," he said with

[1] What is a thing made of? What form is it? Who made it? What is it being made for?

pride. "We believe Sentio projects the true sensory data of things as they truly are. We published our findings in the journal *Nature*."

Barbara puckered her lips and nodded as if to concur. Lar whispered into my ear that Barbara probably had no idea what Dr. Sol was talking about. I'd forgotten to tell Lar that Dr. Sol had excellent hearing.

Dr. Sol turned, narrowed his eyes at Lar, and then looked at me. I knew he'd heard Lar's whisper. Silence filled the room.

Tinker looked at me and then asked Dr Sol, "Haven't we been searching for objectivity ever since Socrates?"

I released an internal sigh, winked at Tinker, and listened as Dr. Sol explained humankind's search for objectivity from Zarathustra, Socrates, Plato, and Aristotle till now.

"Are Sentio and Cogito names for right and left brain?" Tinker asked.

"No. That's a misconception. In a majority of humans, certain Cogito language functions are isolatable to the left brain hemisphere like Broca and Wernicke's areas. But our thalamo-cortical oscillation studies of consciousness, electrical studies, reveal bilateral brain participation in both Sentio and Cogito."

Dr. Sol's secretary appeared and called for him from the lab door. He joined her, and as they talked I thanked Tinker for distracting Dr. Sol and whispered to Lar about Dr. Sol's excellent hearing.

Dr. Sol returned and faced our group. "Dasein, what do you know about that?"

"About what?" I asked.

"Sentio consciousness arising twice as fast as Cogito consciousness—our research published in *Nature*."

"I agree with the speed of Sentio. I mean, it matches my experience. I've not read the article in *Nature*."

My peers had all turned their eyes toward me. My face flushed. I felt like the Sentio king. Dr. Sol seemed taken aback by my response. I was afraid to say more about Sentio.

Barbara smiled at me and broke the silence. She asked if consciousness was like watching a movie.

Dr. Sol responded. "Before Kant, consciousness was viewed as a cinema experience. Then we shifted our understanding to include that consciousness of the external environment unfolds through our capacity to view the world. Kant proposed that what we experience in our minds are phenomena, and the things as they exist in the world are noumena.

"Previous to Kant, Descartes had proposed that Cogito served to ground our existence in the world. *I think therefore I am*—language-thinking consciousness. But Descartes made a serious error in believing that Cogito was more truthful and reliable than Sentio. Descartes shackled our Intentio to Cogito, which took us away from the truth in nature, and away from *res cogitans*, the thing that thinks, what we are— the thing.

"Husserl came forth with the idea that Intentio pulls up a mosaic of our relevant experiences in our memory files and projects the memories as the background, a conceptual veil for our perception of new sensory data projecting into consciousness.

"Husserl said Intentio assists in bracketing the real world as we embrace and reach out to explore, by adding or removing our own color or impressions between those brackets. Husserl called his findings phenomenology—the phenomenon of consciousness. But again he did not understand the existence of Sentio as we have discovered, nor did he understand Intentio's duality. Intentio settles in consciousness and becomes attention, and we direct our attention through the agency of selective attention, the basis of our free will.

"We now know that Cogito's sensory is processed through inhibitory neurons that project from our frontal lobes. I call it the mendacity filter—"

I laughed out loud, interrupting Dr. Sol because my aunt knew there was an untruthful filter for Cogito. Dr. Sol and his team had found it.

I grinned. "Sorry. You found the filter."

Dr. Sol wrinkled his brow at me and continued to address Barbara who'd crossed her arms.

"The total consciousness of a thinking, feeling, and acting human being did not dawn until the existential movement of the twentieth century, the phenomenology of perception and body consciousness. What we've discovered here at Harvard will change the understanding of *being* forever. Prereflective consciousness is two events, Sentio and Cogito, measurable over the human scalp, heretofore recognized as one event. We can measure in microvolts the conscious firing neurons oscillating within the brain.

"And soon we will find the elusive Intentio, the ghost of our existence, as it interacts in Cogito and Sentio, after flying through our memory files—traveling twice as fast as Sentio and four times the speed of Cogito, then settling in consciousness frames delivering our sense of being."

Thinking about elusive Intentio, I almost spoke up. I thought I knew why Dr. Sol had not been able to find Intentio: most likely because its electrical signal was trapped and hidden in Cogito. He did not know that Americans were addicted to Cogito.

Dr. Sol continued. "Heidegger got close to our two-consciousness discovery with his observation of ready-to-hand consciousness. The master carpenter hammers nails without a thought, using streaming Sentio, while he can access his Cogito files with an Intentio directed by selective attention to find last night's ball game scores in reflective Cogito.

"Merleau-Ponty came even closer to our discovery with body consciousness. The body is an extension of Sentio. The disposition of the body and motor function can alter our perception, affirming that a healthy body feeding data to Sentio is important."

I wondered then that if the body is an extension of Sentio, then I should be able to experience my Intentio throughout my body. I wanted to ask about body consciousness, but I thought it might confuse my peers, so I remained silent.

After pausing for a moment, Dr. Sol added, "I would be remiss if I didn't mention a woman named Helen Moyen, who gave us a new philosophy of freedom and a new paradigm for being in the world: intentialism. I encourage everyone to read her book. Her propositions and assertions provided the scaffolding used by my group to discover Sentio and Cogito, and her work has encouraged us that we will find Intentio."

I froze as a tingle shot to the top of my head where a warm feeling emerged. Dr. Sol had mentioned my aunt Helen and credited her philosophy for assisting him in finding Sentio and Cogito. The glowing warmth spread all over me.

"Has anyone ever asked you to hold that thought?" Dr. Sol asked. "How about, hold that Sentio image?" He paused and looked slowly around the room at the blank faces of several of my peers. "Language meaning is always deferred to more language. But in Sentio, sense data has inherent meaning and causality meaning. Every sensory event you experience has causality data associated: a human pinch of your cheek, a hypodermic needle into your butt . . ."

My classmates and I looked at one another and smiled as Dr. Sol talked. He'd mesmerized us with his line about *language meaning* being deferred to more language, a futile cir-cular exercise. Language thinking seemed meaningless com-pared to Sentio. He went on deconstructing 2,400 years of Western thought. I only wished that Aunt Helen were here. I felt so proud of her.

Dr. Sol continued about modern consciousness. "Sentio memories—our files of pictures, songs, smells, etc.—and our Cogito memories, thoughts, and thoughts connected to feeling content provide our preconscious database. Intentio searches looking for relevant files for our viewing or reviewing for every Sentio and Cogito event.

"We call a language memory a *cogi* and a sensory memory a *senti*. A cogi and senti are stored together as an *emoti*. There's no sub-consciousness. There's nothing more to say. Sub-consciousness does not exist. It is nothing more than fading and emerging Intentios in our preconscious data bank."

Lar and the others seemed startled, but I'd heard this my entire life from my aunt. Dr. Sol's words about Freud were final. Freud's work was not useful. Id, ego, and superego—finished. The troop of students relaxed their brows as if Dr. Sol had lifted a burden from their minds as Freud's human psyche model died, right then and there.

He added, "It's a new dawn for beings to understand the enterprise of being and liberty. Our new, simple construct will lead humankind to greater freedom: Intentio, Sentio, and Cogito—Helen Moyen's paradigm."

The warm tingle shot through my body again. Dr. Sol had adopted the same construct used by my aunt. I knew then why my Compass experience had led me to Harvard— so I could work with Dr. Sol.

Standing in front of Zeni, Dr. Sol talked about converting analog signals to digital ones and how the human head acted as a volume conductor for voltage changes in the brain. I wondered how he had confirmed the two consciousnesses: two separate events of perception for a single stimulus, separated by milliseconds. That is the breakthrough my aunt Helen had made empirically after her ECT treatment in the 1940s.

Dr. Sol moved near the table next to the open door of the chamber, and we gathered close around him as he continued.

"Sentio consciousness is the feeling-processing consciousness: form, flow, and color, as well as smell, taste, sound, and touch. Other sensory includes temperature, pain, and position. Sentio provides an objective foundation for all knowledge and has no man-made language for its basis, but it can interpret pleasing or noxious stimuli. Sentio provides the vision to dodge a falling rock, bouncing down a mountain above one's head. It provides our confirmatory sensory understanding of quantum physics, thermodynamics, gravity, electromagnetism, and time. Sentio provides our vision of curvilinear motion, acceleration, and velocity. Galileo said the book of nature was written in the language of mathematics. I say the book of nature was written in the language of Sentio, the language of sensate causality."

My legs felt like jelly. Dr. Sol's explanation matched my understanding and experience. He knew how I experienced the world. I was compelled to raise my hand, but rather than wait to be called on after Barbara and Tinker's hands had gone up, I blurted out:

"How about people living today? Have some of them found Sentio?"

Dr. Sol was so smooth; he never missed a beat. He found my eyes and answered. "Yes, Dasein, many have. But most do not know what to do with it or what it means. Mundane existence dulls our senses and makes Sentio fade or disappear behind the blink of our mind's eye, becoming like a dream overwritten and inhibited by our dominant Cogito. You might say man's conditioning and institutionalization has taken the experience of Eden off our conscious radar screen."

Dr. Sol did understand that most had turned their attention away from Sentio, but he didn't seem to understand that Americans were addicted to Cogito. Dr. Sol believed Sentio had faded because of mundane existence, conditioning, and institutionalization.

I knew the truth, but I couldn't tell him. Not yet. I wasn't sure if Dr. Sol was addicted to Cogito. He seemed as if he might be, and I didn't want to upset him. I knew there was no way to free his Intentio from Cogito with language. Just as an alcoholic's mind drives his Intentio to find his next drink, Americans' Intentio was trapped, addicted to words and language-thinking Cogito. There was no language solution for Cogito addiction, just as there was no way to free an alcoholic from alcoholism with alcohol.

Dr. Sol added, "I believe that our discovery here at Harvard will change the plot of the human story. The search for meaning is really the search for freedom, ultimate freedom from the misery of need, through Sentio."

At that, Dr. Sol paused and gazed around the room,

making brief eye contact with each one of us, and Barbara and Tinker lowered their hands.

"Where are the men of freedom?" he asked. "The great Sentio leaders of the past, of Romanticism, are gone. Who will replace them?"

Barbara, Lar, and Tinker shook their heads and looked down at the shiny, white floor. I knew the answer. I'd come to Harvard to be a great Sentio leader.

"To a pure spirit, nature is everything, said Ralph Waldo Emerson," Dr. Sol offered with a look of dejection as if there were no more true spirits.

I'd heard Aunt Helen quote Emerson. He was a special man during his days at Harvard. My aunt had a similar experience as him; however, Emerson did not understand existentialism. He did understand Sentio, but he did not know how to maintain Sentio sensitivity while living among others. Aunt Helen had told me Emerson eventually lost his Sentio freedom living among others.

Dr. Sol asked again, "Where are the men of freedom?"

I wanted to say that I was the deliverer. I wanted to tell Dr. Sol how I was raised, how I was not exposed to language until I was four years old, long after I had a fully developed Sentio. My insides were shaking, and I wanted to say something, but I couldn't bring myself to declare.

I looked around at my fellow students. They listened intently as Dr. Sol continued, but most looked confused, the concept of Sentio and Cogito foreign.

"Sentio is the alpha and the omega of man's journey to freedom," Dr. Sol said. "The existentialists delivered the scaffolding to begin the journey back to Eden. Sensory consciousness is our essence, and it does precede Cogito existence. It is up to us to use our technology to guide man back to his destiny. But it won't be easy."

"How can one return to the Sentio of Eden?" asked Barbara.

"We do not have enough time for me to do justice to your question."

Now emotion welled up; I could not help myself. "Strange love!" I yelled.

Laughter erupted. When I saw that Dr. Sol and the other students were laughing, I smiled. But I was serious. I looked at Barbara, and she cocked her head and shot me a silly grin, and then I laughed along with them.

"Now, I want to show you how we found Sentio and Cogito," said Dr. Sol, dipping his head through Zeni's open door. He disappeared inside.

Several minutes later Dr. Sol emerged from Zeni pulling
out a cable with several short wires attached.

"Dasein, will you be our guinea pig? I want to demon-
strate how we mapped our two conscious moments from a
single stimulus," Dr. Sol said. "And for the doubters in the
audience, we confirmed our visual evoked potential mapping
with magnetic resonance technology."

"Sure, I'm glad to volunteer," I said.

My empty stomach grumbled, and my heart pounded
against my chest. When I stepped out of the group of students, I stumbled, and Lar caught me. Was I ready to join
Dr. Sol's team? Lar patted me on my back and pushed me
forward.

Cautiously, like a cat backing down a tree, I stepped
toward Dr. Sol. I had a flash thought that I might be
exposing myself to the faultfinders, the ones my mother
had warned me about. But Dr. Sol was like Aunt Helen; he
searched for truth and freedom, and his intention was not
to find my faults.

The students clapped for me. Lar gave a two-finger
whistle like Sister Phillips used to do.

Dr. Sol asked me to sit on a stool next to the chamber.
I took a seat and looked inside the submarine. I saw a large,
black leather chair in recline and a headrest with wires.

Earphones and a microphone lay on the chair. I saw a black-and-white checkerboard monitor screen, like the tile floor in the Director's office. I smiled then. The checkerboard tile that I'd stared at on my first day at Harvard held the secret to freeing the American slaves of Cogito existence.

Dr. Sol picked up electrodes off the lab table and attached them to my scalp, little needles about a half centimeter long fixed to gel stickers against my scalp.

"Dasein, you have some long, thick, curly hair. I'm going to undo your ponytail."

I felt the little needle pricks as he secured the electrodes. There were six in all: three on each side of my head. Then Dr. Sol helped me into the chamber chair and placed headphones on my ears. Sitting inside Zeni was like being in another dimension of stillness and silence: no windows and no internal sound. No smell. Just still air. As the heavy door shut, an eerie feeling came over me; silence surrounded me.

I sat in darkness until the monitor screen directly in my line of sight lit up with the word *blue* in black letters on a clear glass pane. The black and white checks had disappeared.

The word blue flashed at least one hundred times. I didn't know what I was expected to do, so I sat there observing. Then Dr. Sol's voice came through my headphones.

"That's good. Rest for a few moments, and we'll repeat."

"Rest from what?" I asked Dr. Sol through the microphone, "I haven't done anything except read the word blue."

"That's all you're supposed to do."

He repeated the flashing exercise twice. Then he showed a blue bar. No letters, just the color blue in the form of a rectangle. It flashed one hundred times over a couple of minutes. I rested then he repeated the exercise.

I noticed something that intrigued me. When the word blue had flashed in black letters, I thought of the word blue. But when the bar lit up, colored in blue, the little person in my brain wanted to reach out and immerse himself in blue. It was an odd feeling. Then I realized that the little person must've been my Intentio trying to figure out what blue represented in my Sentio. Wow! I'd just experienced my sense of being in my Sentio—Intentio within Sentio.

Then Dr. Sol flashed the word blue in blue-colored letters. It was amazing. I thought of the word blue and felt blue at the same time. He repeated this twice.

I noticed then, that I could not feel my Intentio as strongly with the blue-colored letters that spelled blue as I had with the blue bar. My Intentio felt weakened or split between Sentio and Cogito.

I asked Dr. Sol to try it again, and this time I focused on the color blue and not the letters. And my Intentio strengthened, feeling as strong as it had for the blue bar flashes. Just as I'd thought, I could overcome Cogito's control over my Intentio with selective attention. But I knew the key for me was that I could experience my attention in Sentio. I knew that Anal, Barbara, and the others wouldn't be able to experience their attention in Sentio. At least not until I found a way to free them. That was the dilemma: how to free their Intentio from Cogito so they could experience it in Sentio. How? I sighed. How will I free them?

37

Dr. Sol's chuckling sounds filtered through my headphones bringing me out of my reverie. He asked me if I was finished with my experiment.

"Yes."

He opened Zeni's door, leaned inside, and unhooked me. I stepped out of the chamber, and my classmates clapped.

Lar smiled at me with his encouraging green eyes. "Say something, Dasein."

I waited until Dr. Sol came out of Zeni. "I feel; therefore, I am. *Sentio ergo sum.*"

The students cheered. *Sentio! Sentio!*

"Yes, Dasein, you do have a feeling consciousness," said Dr. Sol. "P20 will verify your existential existence, Sentio. The P40 will reveal Descartes's existence, Cogito."

My expression made it clear I didn't understand. Dr. Sol assured me that he would explain P20 and P40 when my results printed. Dr. Sol and I stood in front of Zeni. He cleaned my scalp with alcohol wipes, which stung a little.

As we waited for the computer to process my results, he said, "The real breakthrough in brain research, enabling us to record evoked potentials, came when we recognized that we could cancel out the random background noise of the brain by merely repeating the same stimulus one hundred times. We discovered we could sum the neuron-generated electrochemical impulse from each signal until enough signals were recorded to generate voltage changes measurable on the scalp. You see, the brain is very busy. It's like a ship, and you're Captain Intentio, sitting in the Sentio chair on deck or the Cogito chair below the deck—"

The computer printer behind the chamber hummed and interrupted Dr. Sol.

I heard Tinker whisper to Lar. "Sounds like a dot matrix printer, like the one in *Three Days of the Condor.*" Lar grinned.

Dr. Sol retrieved my results and read them out loud. "Antonio Dasein, eighteen-year-old, left-handed male.

"Response to blue spelled in black letters (100 reps): Sentio consciousness mapping parietal cortex at 20 milliseconds (P20) produced a 400-microvolt wave peak.

"Cogito consciousness mapping parietal cortex at 40 milliseconds (P40) produced a 150-microvolt wave peak.

"Response to blue rectangle (100 reps): Sentio consciousness mapping parietal cortex at 20 milliseconds (P20) produced a 500-microvolt wave peak.

"Cogito consciousness mapping parietal cortex at 40 milliseconds (P40) produced a 50-microvolt wave peak.

"Response to the word blue in bold blue letters (100 reps): Sentio consciousness mapping parietal cortex at 20 milliseconds (P20) produced a 450-microvolt wave peak.

"Cogito consciousness mapping parietal cortex at 40 milliseconds (P40) produced a 100-microvolt wave peak.

"Dasein's experiment: Second trial, response to the word blue in bold blue letters (100 reps): Sentio consciousness mapping parietal cortex at 20 milliseconds (P20) produced 500-microvolt wave peak.

"Cogito consciousness mapping parietal cortex at 40 milliseconds (P40) produced a 50-microvolt wave peak."

When he finished reading, Dr. Sol said, "The results are quite remarkable."

"Why did my Sentio voltage increase for the word blue in bold blue letters during my experiment, the second trial?" I asked.

Dr. Sol shook his head, looking stunned. "I need to study your results."

I believed I understood. My Intentio was adding voltage to Sentio during the second trial. My second trial using the word blue in blue letters could prove the existence of Intentio, and my Intentio was 100 uv by my calculation using Dr. Sol's numbers.

I knew Dr. Sol had not found evidence for Intentio because most likely all his subjects' Intentios were trapped, addicted to Cogito. I thought for a moment. I bet he'd not studied Linda. I knew her Sentio was strong, and I believed her Intentio was free to dwell in Sentio even though it probably dwelled in Cogito.

Dr. Sol continued to review my results.

Lar spoke up, "I've heard that fighter pilots can recognize 255 frames a second and that they can remember things from a picture flashed at 1/300th of a second."

"What you're talking about is flash sensory memory, priming, subliminal," Dr. Sol responded, turning his attention from my results to Lar. "That is not true consciousness. True Sentio or Cogito consciousness is the projection of sense data so that we can explore and wrap our attention around the experience in time. The pictures of flash memory are like the words flowing out of the mouth of a man with a loose tongue and no thought or intention behind his words."

"What do the microvolts mean?" I asked.

"Well, you have one of the highest microvolt recordings that I have ever made for Sentio. That is what it means," said Dr. Sol.

The other students looked at me with astonishment.

Lar asked, "What is the next highest that you have ever recorded?"

"Well, it was 210 microvolts. The genius from MIT."

Lar looked at me with a big smile. "Dang, Dasein. You blew right through the Sentio record."

I shook my head from side-to-side with a big grin. I felt no different after the mapping, but everyone looked at me as if I were a genius.

Dr. Sol thanked us for attending his tour and connected with my eyes and asked me to stay. After he'd dismissed our group, several students including Bob remained and asked questions. Once the students left, Dr. Sol turned and told me I could begin research with him next semester if I passed the summary exams. Since I was a first-year student, I'd have to pass the exams or wait until the end of my second year to assist in research. He wanted to give me the opportunity.

My heart lifted in joy for a moment, and I almost reached to embrace him. Then I was concerned. "What are summary exams?"

"They are special exams that will qualify you to advance to clinical medicine studies and research. Don't worry if you don't pass them. I'll let you do research at the end of your second year."

I assured him that I'd pass them.

Dr. Sol wanted to map me again and motioned for me to sit on the stool. I took a seat, and he hooked the electrodes to my scalp and helped me back into Zeni. He repeated the mapping of my Sentio and Cogito consciousness. He asked me to repeat my experiment. I did, focusing my attention on the blue color of the blue letters that spelled blue. Afterward, I explained to Dr. Sol my experiment of using selective attention to redirect Intentio to Sentio.

I glanced at my results as Dr. Sol reviewed them. Sighing in relief, I'd produced the same results as during my first mapping, and I could tell Dr. Sol had figured out that my microvolt measures—the changes in my selective attention experiment—were indirect evidence of Intentio's effect and existence. I didn't say anything, but I knew he knew. He paused reviewing my results and mumbled that he wanted to see me first thing tomorrow at 8:00 a.m. He wanted to perform more tests. He walked toward Zeni and stopped, still reviewing my results.

I wiped my scalp and tied my hair back, thinking about my two mapping experiences. Trying to compare my two mapping experiences, I noticed something. During the second experience, I'd felt more aware of my Intentio and its interaction in Sentio. I had an idea then that Dr. Sol's mapping technique could deliver a mini experience of Intentio in Sentio. That could be the breakthrough, I thought. The Zeni mapping experience could be the Sentio bicycle experience that will free Intentio from Cogito.

My heart pounded in excitement. I looked at Dr. Sol standing near Zeni. I was too excited to tell him. I was more excited by this epiphany than when I got my acceptance letter from Harvard, but my demeanor remained serious.

As I turned to leave, Dr. Sol called my name and approached. He said if I passed my basic science summary exams, I would be joining Dr. Linda Hedrick, Dr. Susan Wolf, and two other researchers. They were working on the effects of intimate touch on working memory.

My heart pounded harder with more excitement. I was going to be with Linda and her team.

I couldn't wait to experience her presence in my pre-reflective Sentio consciousness again. I thanked Dr. Sol, wanting to hug him, but instead produced a broad smile and shook his hand for several seconds. He grinned and turned toward Zeni, looking at my second mapping results again.

I walked out of the lab, restraining my excitement, took the lift, and skipped out into the sunlight. My feet felt so light as I jumped to grab the daytime moon. I felt I might actually touch the sky. When I came back to earth, I walked in a circle, thinking about the summary exams. I needed to find out from Lar how to pass them.

I ran back to the House of Essence to tell Diana the great news.

38

I ran up the stairs and knocked on 7A; I wanted to celebrate my selection as Dr. Sol's student research assistant, even though it was not a done deal. No answer. I called Milly, who said Diana was busy with a customer across town. After waiting for an hour, I reached Diana by phone and told her I was desperate to see her and needed to tell her something very important. She said she was on her way back to the apartment and would stop by my place.

I had a glass of wine while waiting and listened to "Imagine." When I heard a gentle knock, I hurried to let her in.

"Are you desperate for me?" she asked, looking so tired, with lazy brown eyes shadowed in a purple haze. Her hair was disheveled, and her makeup had dripped.

I gave her a hug, and when I released and pulled back, her pretty, brown eyes sparkled. "I want to take you to the Majestic for dinner."

"I look awful," she contested.

"Diana, you're beautiful." I hugged her again and inhaled the fragrance that I'd come to know as Diana, her sweet presence.

She looked at me with a grin, shaking her head. "I'm going to change into my green sundress and wash my face."

"I'll wait right here," I said, motioning with my hands for her to hurry.

I stood in the hall for several minutes, hoping I wouldn't run into Simone.

"Hurry Diana," I yelled into her apartment. When she came out of 7A, I grabbed her in the hallway and picked her up, cradling her. She looked into my eyes. Her eyes twinkled, and I gave her a kiss on the cheek.

"What is it? What have you done?" she asked.

I set her down. "I'll tell you at the diner."

We practically ran the two blocks to the restaurant and were seated at a table outside without a wait. We ordered the vegetable plate special with broccoli soup. I was so excited I couldn't feel my hunger. Diana smiled at me as she handed the menu to the waitress.

"What is it? You have to tell me."

Her eyes beamed as her crimson lips spread over her pearly-white teeth again, waiting for me to tell her.

"Diana, what do you want most in life?" I asked in a serious tone.

She paused for a moment and then said, "I don't know what you're getting at." She peered into my eyes. "I want pretty clothes, shoes, a pretty figure, and someone to tell me how beautiful I am—what most girls want."

"What about meaning, freedom, and purpose?" I asked softly as I reached to hold her hands.

Diana's face tensed, and she squeezed my hands. "I don't mean to sound presumptuous, but, um . . . are you proposing to me?"

Blood rushed to my face as I stared speechlessly. For a long moment, I searched for a polite and caring reply. I looked away then back into Diana's gaze. "That wasn't my intention. Not that I wouldn't like to have that honor."

I felt like Alex trying to talk to Polly. I used my eye-touching technique to relax Diana, and she smiled but only slightly. I repeated my eye touching maneuver several times until Diana fluttered her eyelashes. I smiled at her then restated my question.

"What if you could see your connection to every living being and enjoy knowing that you're part of the reason they can be happy and share love on their journey to the mountaintop of freedom? Wouldn't you be happy?"

Diana puckered her lips then nodded. "I'm not sure what you mean, but I think I would be happy if I could make others happy."

"I'm just happy because I have a chance to make others happy on their journey to freedom. I'm going to be doing research with Dr. Sol in the sensory deprivation lab at Harvard—if I pass my summary exams."

My Sentio warmed as Diana's face lifted into a smile. It felt so good to share my news.

"That's wonderful, Antonio. You'll be a wonderful researcher," she said sincerely.

The waitress brought out our food, and we released our hands. Inhaling the aroma of my broccoli soup, I reached for the spoon. Diana reached over and softly touched my hand with her fingertips. Looking into her soft brown eyes, I felt a warm glow in my chest. She'd given me strange love. I thought once again how grateful I was to have Diana in my life. She smiled and turned her attention toward a warm wheat roll.

We ate the delicious meal and skipped back to the House of Essence under the starry sky. I kissed Diana on the porch swing. Sassy and Katrina came hurrying out the door, waved at us, and disappeared into the night. It was getting late. I needed to study, and Diana had another call to service across town. I gave her another long embrace and inhaled her bouquet before we parted.

I went upstairs and called Lar, and he explained how I should prepare for the summary exams. I told him how important it was for me to begin research, and he reassured me that he would help me pass.

A warm feeling emerged in my chest as he continued in support for me; Lar was going to help me take another major step on my journey to free the Americans from Cogito. I thanked him for his caring way, which had affected me. I said goodbye and hung up the phone.

Rocking, looking out toward the harbor lights, I thought for a long moment about Lar, then Barbara, then Tinker, and my other caring American friends. I had to succeed in setting them free.

39

After eight weeks of preparing for my summary exams, I sat down to write a letter to my mother and family in Andorra. I had so much to tell them.

> To Mother, Aunt Helen, Uncle Poulou, and my family at Essence and Vichy,
>
> I have a photographic memory according to my friend Lar, a fellow medical student. He obtained the class notes for the basic science courses from the last two years for me to study. I went through lecture by lecture, photographing all the information through my Sentio. Then I used my Cogito to make a memory file for retrieving information like physiology, pharmacology, etc. It only took about eight weeks.
>
> My professors are going to let me take summary exams next week. I'll have a chance to pass my first two years of medical school. I'm so excited because I'm close to figuring out how to free the Americans.
>
> I have helped Professor Sol identify Intentio. Sol—pronounced soul, is my advisor, and he knows all about Aunt Helen's research. He could

not believe that she helped raise me. He is a big fan of her intentialism philosophy, which he credits for his success in finding Sentio and Cogito.

I also saved the lives of three little chimps. It's a long story. You see, Dr. Sol and his group recently discovered BSP, which I call the biomolecule of freedom because I believe it is. I figured out that BSP could not have a receptor that would react to other similar molecules. While opiates like morphine can actuate natural endorphin receptors for pleasure and pain relief, surrogate molecules like morphine can also lead to addiction. I figured surrogate molecules could not provide the vision for freedom. I knew that would have been a design flaw, undermining one's freedom by circumventing the true pathway to freedom which is dependent upon strange love.

If BSP had a fixed receptor, then other molecules might actuate it. So I concluded that the biomolecule of freedom must act as a receptor for itself. Dr. Sol asked an associate professor of biochemistry to investigate my belief, and his group confirmed my theory about BSP. Dr. Sol also said it explained why his co-investigators at Johns Hopkins had not found a receptor for BSP. And that's how I saved the three little chimps.

The vision for freedom can only be restored by the special form of love that I learned about growing up at Essence, which I believe releases and increases the production of BSP, which concentrates, complexes, and raises Sentio sensitivity.

Mother, you taught me about Aunt Helen's discovery of strange love, and its special power to deliver Sentio sensitivity. I want to find a way for Americans to experience Sentio, and then I want to figure out a way that others can share strange love to stimulate BSP and deliver the vision of freedom through Sentio.

After my summary exams I'm going to begin research with Dr. Sol. I cannot believe it. He has confirmed everything Aunt Helen experienced. Plus, he found the Cogito filter. It is amazing, Mother. I'm exactly where my true essence compass, the Compass of Freedom, pointed me. I know that now.

I have learned a lot about life in America at the House of Essence. The young ladies here are like you as Anna Simmons. It's interesting. Diana, my best friend, favors you a little. Simone, well, she is like Reverend Mother Mary Elizabeth and you put together. In your former lives, that is. American women refer to Simone as a dominatrix.

I heard from Alex and Polly, and they are doing very well, spreading the idea of Sentio and giving strange love to their actor friends. They will debut in the musical CAMELOT on December 17 at the New London Theater.

NEVER LET IT BE FORGOT THAT THERE ONCE WAS A SPOT, AND FOR A BRIEF SHINING MOMENT IT WAS KNOWN AS CAMELOT. That is how I think about Essence—Esselot.

Polly is playing Guinevere—she is so excited—and Alex is Sir Lancelot. Perfect. I can't wait till we are together again. They want us to come see them in London during Christmas, and I promised I would come. I want us all to be together again.

I'm getting very close to my mission goal. I get a warm tingling sensation in my chest that shoots to the top of my head just thinking about it.

You are always warm in my Sentio, Mother, and I know Javier is giving you plenty of strange love. I'll see you both soon.

Oh, one more thing; I found my Sentiomate. I've fallen in love with a young lady doctor. Her name is Linda Hedrick. Once you meet her you'll understand why I'm in love with her. I say love because the power of her Sentio image is more luminous than the sun over Andorra, and reflecting on her image elevates my sensitivity, just like strange love.

Love, Antonio.

40

Christmas wreaths and garlands, wrapped with colored lights, decorated the porch and windows of Milly's kitchen. Two large evergreen trees adorned the house: one in the front yard and the other on the porch. I was on the stepladder hanging mistletoe over the main entrance, and Diana was helping me. Sassy, Katrina, Fancy, Pretty, and Danielle placed red tablecloths on four large tables on the porch. Sophia prepared the barbecue while Milly cooked some goodies in the kitchen. The girls sported their long eyelashes, which meant they were ready to do some serious eye touching. I could always tell when they were advertising sensory for sale. Other times they were just like regular girls.

Christmas tunes played on Milly's stereo, creating a cheerful holiday atmosphere. I came down from the ladder and got a kiss from Diana, who'd been sipping on eggnog. After we'd smooched, I licked my lips, and just as I'd thought, the eggnog was spiked with brandy.

"Antonio, let's go ahead and start the fire," Milly said as she walked onto the porch, carrying a rum cake and pecan pie. My mouth was already watering from the smell of turkey and duck.

The fireplace sat between two pillars with a nice large hearth. Diana said Simone had decorated the mantel, and it displayed a ceramic nativity scene. I still had bad memories connected to Simone, and whenever I heard her name the hair stood up on the back of my neck. On Thanksgiving, I'd forced myself to say hello to her, and she turned away without speaking. I wondered if she was going to attend the Christmas party. Diana thought Simone had gone to New York for the weekend. I hoped so.

We had plenty of wood left over from our Thanksgiving party stacked high on the patio. I grabbed a couple of logs and placed some kindling underneath them in the metal grate. Diana rolled up a newspaper and handed it to me. I soaked it with lighter fluid and placed it beneath the grate. I lit a match and threw it into the fireplace. It ignited with a *whoosh*, and a warm blast of air washed over my face.

Milly came back outside and kissed me as the fire started roaring. She seemed very jovial and smelled as if she'd been testing the brandy.

The heat grew intense for a few moments. Once the flames stopped roaring, the girls gathered near the hearth. They loved being warmed by the fire, and I felt more warmed by their presence than the flames. Their faces glowed with painted smiles, and they looked beautiful in their Christmas dresses. They smelled like a wonderful flower garden: roses, tulips, and daisies.

Milly went back inside, and a few minutes later she brought out a box containing vodka, Jack Daniel's Tennessee whiskey, and scotch. I helped Diana move a table near the fire. Milly placed the box on the table, and we set out the brandy and shot glasses for everyone to share.

When the Christmas jazz song played, two new girls, Sandra and Sonya, danced together. I joined Diana, Sassy, Fancy, and the others dancing together on the porch. Then the girls wanted me to judge a best-tasting-kiss contest. I took my time, savoring their flavored lipsticks, and my head was spinning when I finished kissing all the girls. Their kisses—watermelon, lemon, key lime—had tasted delicious.

I was glad none of the girls had worn peach. If I'd truly had to pick a winner, it would have been difficult although I think in the end I'd have picked Diana's cherry-flavored kiss.

I looked over at Milly, now sitting near the fireplace in her white, wrought iron rocking chair, and she smiled at me. Usually alert and taking care of business, she seemed quiet and relaxed, enjoying the evening. I went over and kissed her then declared Milly the winner of the sweetest kiss contest.

Diana came over, hugged me, and stood silently next to me, holding my hand. She had asked me yesterday if she could move in with me, and I'd said yes without a second thought. She was going to tell Milly that she was retiring from selling sensory. I thought it was a good decision.

Diana and I had been to Chariot Hill several times before she made her final decision to leave Milly's business and start a different chapter of her life. She'd confided she felt free for the first time in her life and had realized nurturing her Sentio consciousness was now more important than making money.

I turned and gave her a smile and Diana squeezed my hand and touched my eyes with her soft brown eyes. She'd helped me prepare for the summary exams, the hardest exams that I'd ever taken, and we'd grown close. Diana reminded me of Polly in many ways, and she had become my main source of strange love.

I knew Diana was a born-again woman, experiencing the world through Sentio, and I hoped to map her Sentio and Cogito using Zeni in Dr. Sol's lab someday. I'd told Diana about my idea that I might be able to deliver Sentio by using Zeni. We'd joked that I could free all of Milly's girls and then use them as cheerleaders for strange love. It was a funny idea to use them as strange-love cheerleaders, but for some reason I sensed it might lead to greater freedom for all.

"How do you think you did on your exams?" Diana asked.

"I won't know the results until the committee meets next semester. They'll compare my results to other students' scores over the last five years. Lar thinks they'll be reluctant to advance me because of my age."

I didn't want to seem cocky, but I believed I'd passed. During the exam, I photographed the test questions and my responses in my Sentio, and later in the day after my exams, I compared my responses to answers in my class notes.

"I bet you passed. You studied hard, Antonio," she said with pride in her eyes, warming me to my very core.

"Thanks to you, Diana. And Milly."

During the last three weeks of intense studying, Milly had done my laundry, and Diana had prepared my meals.

When I told Diana and Milly that their care for me reminded me of my mother and the Sisters of Freedom's loving care, they both grinned at my compliments.

I knew I'd made them feel special; plus, it was true, and they were special. The House of Essence was becoming more and more like Essence, Andorra, every day.

"I haven't forgotten about your class party tomorrow night," Diana said. "I'm going to buy a really conservative dress to wear. I had Milly press your pants, and I picked up your shirts from the laundry."

I patted Milly on the back to thank her.

"I think I'll wear my jeans to the dance," I whispered to Diana.

"Antonio, I'm going to wear a nice dress. You have to wear your nice slacks," Diana admonished.

She looked upset, so I touched her eyes to reassure her. If Diana didn't want me to wear jeans, I wouldn't wear jeans. Her face relaxed, and I didn't have to say a word. Her face was so soft and sweet after that. I understood that my willingness to let her decide my attire, as little a thing as it was to me, was meaningful to her, and Diana cared about clothes more than anyone I'd ever met.

I embraced her, and we kissed for a long moment. When I looked up, it seemed as though suddenly there were people everywhere. They spilled out from the porch onto the patio, terrace, and street. At Milly's request, I built a fire in a barrel on the street for the reluctant customers as they waited to decide whether to purchase sensory from the girls.

Returning to the porch, I tended bar. I looked around at the young men and wondered if their purchased sensory had raised their BSP levels. It would be an interesting study. Thinking about it while observing them for a few minutes, I realized the response of the customers after their purchases gave me the answer. They were not the same as the fishermen after the dinners at Essence, Andorra, on Saturday nights. Something was different about the men after their purchases here at the House of Essence. They seemed satisfied, but they didn't have hope in their eyes like the fishermen.

41

"One chocolate martini," said the gentleman in a blue, silk suit.

Waving my hand, I motioned for Diana. I needed to be relieved from tending bar. The men in suits were ordering complicated drinks, and I was not very skilled at mixing them. Diana took over for me, and I went around with Milly collecting money. She was like Aunt Helen when it came to money. Precise and attentive.

Several of the girls danced together, and Fancy pulled me onto the dance floor near the mistletoe. When she turned to embrace me, I saw a blur then felt a kiss. Someone had broken in between us and kissed me, taking my breath away. I'd barely seen the young woman's face as she released my lips and moved away quickly, but the unmistakable peachy scent and the peachy taste of her lips gave her away. I knew it was Simone. Once I found her face hiding behind Fancy's head, the hair stood up on the back of my neck. Mesmerized by her large, blue eyes, I was speechless.

"Merry Christmas," she said breathlessly.

"Merry Christmas, Simone," I replied kindly.

I tried to catch my breath without letting on how much she'd affected me. Then I noticed something unexpected. Simone looked sad. Her eyes drooped, and her lip pouted as she looked up at me with a long face.

"I know that I can't have you, Dasein. But I want you to free me from this." She turned her eyes from mine and gazed at the men in suits. For a long moment she looked at them and then found my eyes again as if she'd lost hope.

I'd never seen her so genuinely distraught. My heart melted as she reached and squeezed my hand. Her sad eyes pleaded for my help. I wanted nothing more than to comfort her at that moment. My aunt had taught me that I had an obligation to help others find freedom. And the reason I was here was because my aunt had felt the obligation to help me and others on her journey to freedom. The only way I could continue my journey to freedom was by embracing my obligation to help others.

"Simone, I promise that someday you and I will watch the sunset together through the Sentio of Eden," I said.

"I'm sorry for what I did," she replied earnestly. Tears streamed down her cheeks, and I could see her lip quivering.

We stood looking into each other's eyes for several seconds. Diana came up beside me and put her hand on my arm. Her touch seemed to be more supportive than protective. I knew she trusted my ability to use my Cogito to protect my Sentio around Simone.

"I forgive you, Simone," I said.

Simone looked at Diana, then back into my eyes. She seemed to be looking for something, perhaps hoping for instantaneous redemption. She turned, and Diana and I followed her through the front door into the stairwell, then she disappeared up the stairs. Simone was like so many orphans that I had grown up with. She needed a freeing Sentio experience, and she needed strange love.

Diana and I returned to the porch. Diana put on her party hat and danced with Fancy. I smiled at her freestyle dance as she twirled and gyrated on the porch.

As I watched Diana and Fancy, it occurred to me that if I helped Simone, she would be able to help others. I had enough money to buy her a ticket to go with me to visit Essence in Andorra. If she could meet my mother and the children at Essence, I felt it would be a wonderful experience that might free her. I tucked the thought away for now and rejoined the party.

By the early morning, the dancing had ceased, and the crowd had waned. The fire had turned into warm ashes. It was 3:00 a.m., and we were out of brandy. I was tired. I told Diana to go warm our bed, and I would join her. Then I said I was going to bring Simone to sleep with us. Diana smiled at me then hurried up the steps. I followed close behind.

I knocked on 7C. When Simone answered, I asked her to come with me. She rubbed her eyes. I told her I wanted to bring her to sleep between Diana and me. She didn't understand.

"Antonio, what time is it?"

"Around three in the morning." I scooped her into my arms like a young girl. Simone in her flannel pajamas was soft and light as a feather.

"What are you doing? Put me down."

I pulled her door closed. "I want you to sleep with Diana and me. It's almost Christmas. You can't sleep alone. At the Essence orphanage we all slept together as much as we could before Christmas."

With that Simone relaxed in my arms. I carried her to my loft bedroom. When she saw that Diana had pulled back the covers and placed three pillows for our heads, her eyes opened wider. Diana smiled, causing Simone to smile, and I laid her down gently on the bed.

I took off my shoes and jumped in between my two friends who'd just been hugging each other. I put my arms around them, and they laid their heads on my shoulders, Diana's cherry scent on my right and Simone's peach scent on my left. Diana wanted me to tell a bedtime story, so I began telling them my short version of Parma, a love story

Sister Josephine used to tell the orphan girls. When Diana's eyes drooped, I let my voice grow tired, forgetting my place in the story. Simone nudged me, wanting to hear more about Fabrizio. I pretended to doze off so I could watch them fall asleep. They soon drifted off one after the other, and I watched them both sleep like little angels.

The next morning Diana and Simone woke before me and had fixed scrambled eggs and toast for breakfast. I wanted to ask Simone to come with me to Essence, but I needed to talk to Diana first. I finished my eggs and juice and joined Diana and Simone on the window seat. We talked about Boston and Christmas. But I didn't get a chance to talk with Diana about Simone in private.

Later that morning, Diana and Simone decided to go shopping, and I decided to stay home and pack for my trip. I reminded Diana that we needed to leave by 8:00 p.m. for the freshman Christmas party. Diana looked at me with a friendly stare. It was like she was learning to talk with her Sentio.

"I'll be ready," she said. "You need to pack your jeans and warm shirts for your trip, Antonio."

"I will, and I'll be thinking about how much fun you and Simone are having."

I gave Diana and then Simone a long embrace. The girls were excited. They were giggling and jiggling. Diana slapped Simone on her fanny, saying, "Yes, you can wear one of my dresses. They're in Antonio's closet. Don't stay too long in the bathroom."

Simone hurried up the steps to the loft. I was going to mention my idea about taking Simone to Essence, but instead Diana and I waltzed around to the sounds of Carly Simon, practicing for our dance tonight. After a few minutes, Simone came down the steps, looking beautiful wearing Diana's green dress. Diana shook her head from side to side with a broad smile, then she went to put on her face.

I washed dishes as Simone rocked near the window seat.

"Come on, gal; we need to hurry," yelled Simone. "We'll miss the best stuff."

I smiled at Simone. It was so good to see her being real and happy.

42

Around eight that evening, getting dressed for the party, Diana confided in me that on their shopping trip, Simone had told her that she felt very alone. Hearing Diana's concern and considering my own concerns for Simone, I told Diana about my desire to take Simone to Essence for Christmas. Diana said that Simone would never leave Boston this time of year.

"Simone will make half her income for the year in the next three weeks," Diana explained.

"Still, after the freshman party I want to ask her to come with me to Essence."

Diana hugged me. "You can try, Antonio." Then she turned. "Please zip me."

I pulled the zipper up her back and hooked the snap at the nape of her neck. She looked beautiful in her fancy new black dress and heels. Her hair was atop her head, and the earrings that dangled from her ears matched her necklace, sparkling like real diamonds.

"Did you call for a taxi?" Diana asked, grabbing her coat from my bed.

"Yes. We need to get moving."

We hurried out of 7B and down the stairs to the patio, where the taxi had pulled up. I opened the cab door for Diana and slid in next to her. Diana explained to the driver where we were going, then reached, and held my hand. Her hand was cold, so I gave her a warm hug.

"How did Milly take the news about your decision not to sell sensitivity?"

Diana smiled. "She was very supportive."

"I knew she would be. See, you had no reason to worry."

Diana squeezed my hand, and a warm glow emerged in my Sentio. I squeezed her hand in kind and thought about how grateful I was for Diana and her strange love.

Our driver pulled up to the arboretum building on Harvard's undergraduate campus. "This it?"

"Yes." We got out on the sidewalk, and I handed him a twenty-dollar bill.

"Keep the change," I said.

"Gracias."

Excited, Diana and I hurried inside. On the second floor, a band played loud music on a stage between two trees that were growing inside the building. Diana checked our coats. My fellow students danced on the brick floor in front of the stage. I glanced at the eyes of some of my peers and saw blank stares of Cogito shock, no doubt caused by questions from the pharmacology exam taken earlier today, which I'd taken last week during my three-day summary exam. Lar had called me a few hours ago, and I consoled him. He was afraid he'd flunked the exam.

I waved at Tinker and his girlfriend, Mary. I knew by his darting eyes that the exam had rattled him too. I introduced them to Diana, and Tinker said something about succinylcholine and atropine. I grinned as he continued talking about his mother's mitochondria, his source of ATP. Mary smiled at Diana, and I shook my head at Tinker as he guzzled a large cup of beer. Diana and I said goodbye and mingled with Bob and his friend Enya from Yale until they decided to dance.

Looking around the floor, I noticed little Barbara had

fixed her curly black hair into a wave for the occasion. Diana and I approached. Barbara introduced me to her friend Izzie. She told Izzie that I was her friend, which made me feel special. I introduced Barbara and Izzie to Diana.

"We're all friends," I smiled.

Barbara and Izzie agreed then walked over to the bar to get something to drink. I escorted Diana across the dance floor to meet Lar, who was standing alone by the exit door. His eyes lit up when Diana and I approached. Introducing them, I realized Lar and Diana seemed to have Sentio chemistry. Lar stared at Diana with a smile on his face; Diana lifted the corners of her mouth at him. The music played louder.

"He's tall," Diana whispered into my ear.

"Ask Lar for a dance," I whispered back.

Lar glanced at Diana's leg. Her dress was made of black silk with a slit for dancing, and her black-silk-stocking-covered thigh was exposed.

"Lar, come on! Show me some moves," urged Diana.

Appearing happily surprised, Lar took Diana's hand and led her to the dance floor. He was at least two heads taller than her. As a new song played a fun beat, Lar found his rhythm and moved effortlessly, very graceful, like a giraffe. They danced apart at first, but soon Lar took the lead. He surprised me with his agility and moves, gliding, waltzing around the dance floor, leading Diana. How interesting they both liked ballroom dancing. My entire class had stopped dancing, all eyes focused on their graceful pivots and Diana's twirls. I could sense Diana loved being watched, and she seemed to be having the time of her life with Lar.

Tinker walked up to me, yelled *Yes!* toward Lar, and then handed me his can of Miller beer. Mary pulled Tinker's arm, and they began to dance. I popped the top, took a swig of beer, and walked around. I wanted to ask Barbara for a dance although I thought she might be reluctant. Looking around, I found her. Barbara stood alone, watching the others dance. I approached and whispered into her ear.

"I would love to!" she exclaimed with her big voice.

I put my beer on the table, and we danced near Lar and Diana. I could hear Barbara mumbling: *one, two, three . . . one, two three . . .* More couples joined in the waltz. I looked over at the band leader on stage and smiled. They'd begun playing a new tune, "The Second Waltz" by Shostakovich, Sister Josephine's favorite. With a lift in my step, I twirled little Barbara. As we danced round and round, I noticed she was very pretty in the dim light. She held her head differently with her new hairdo, which looked nice with gentle waves. A warm feeling emerged in my chest, and then Barbara looked up into my eyes with a twinkle in hers. The way Barbara was experimenting with her hair and loosening up around men reminded me of my orphan sisters at Essence. Barbara was a bit behind the curve, but I knew she would find her way. She was so determined for someone so little. I'd never met anyone like her.

As "The Second Waltz" ended, another started, and the music slowed. Lar and Barbara walked away, so Diana and I danced slowly together. She pulled me closer and swayed gently to the music. I looked over at Lar and then Barbara. I wanted them to experience this feeling someday, intimacy and the power of strange love, which Diana and I were sharing.

The lights came back on; a new happy beat played. Diana and I started milling around the party. The Director waved at me; he was with the husky secretary. I believed he wanted to meet Diana, the prettiest girl at the party.

I led Diana over, said hello to the Director, and introduced them. I smiled at the secretary, and she introduced herself as Robin. The Director's eyes moved up and down taking in Diana's eye-catching dress.

"Dasein, you've come a long way from the scared,

German kid that I met six months ago," said the Director, focusing his attention on Diana's bosom, then staring at her leg.

"Thank you," I said, and reached for Diana's hand. We said goodbye to the Director and Robin and headed toward the exit. I explained to Diana that the Director thought I was from Germany, and it was impossible to change his mind on the matter. She chuckled, and said she'd thought I was German for a long time also because of my name, *Dasein*.

We left the party and headed back toward Double Banger Street. We walked through the decorated Harvard campus strung with sparkling decorations. The white and yellow Christmas lights strung around the doors and windows of the Georgian-style buildings made everything look happy at night. For me, the walk was more fun than the party. I was intrigued by the phenomenology of Harvard brought on by Christmas lights and decorations. My perception of the campus changed as Diana and I walked holding hands. The green street lights with globes lit, wrapped with red ribbons and with garland, reminded me of the gas lights on the cobblestone road back home. Harvard's undergraduate campus reminded me of Pierre, France, during Christmas.

When we got back to the house, we hastened up the stairs. I wanted to ask Simone to come with me to visit my family in Andorra. Diana accompanied me, her hand on my shoulder in support. I knocked on 7C, and Simone answered the door with tears in her eyes.

"What's wrong?" asked Diana.

"Nothing," Simone said, and sniffled. "Nothing."

"I want you to come with me to Essence for Christmas," I blurted, hoping to cheer her up.

At first she didn't answer and just looked at me with her sad eyes.

"I'm all booked up, Antonio," she said.

I pressed for an answer to my invitation.

"I can't leave now. This is tip season," Simone whispered with a quick glance back into her apartment. She looked pointedly at Diana and seemed to be sending a signal that was not intended for me.

Then I heard a man's voice coming from inside, "This damn crank."

"Thanks for the offer," Simone said curtly.

I felt the door close in my face as if it physically hit me. Diana explained that Simone was with a customer. I already knew that after hearing the man's voice. My heart sank then. I shook my head. I felt heartbroken for Simone because she was trapped in the gladiator ring. I had to give her something to hope for.

Diana and I made a plan. We would surprise Simone tomorrow night before my flight. We wanted to share a sunset experience on Chariot Hill with her.

43

The next day, late in the afternoon, about thirty minutes before sunset by my estimate, Diana and I knocked on 7C to pick up Simone. After several knocks, she opened the door. Standing in the doorway, her blue eyes looked empty and sad.

"Diana and I want to take you to see something very special," I said.

Simone seemed reluctant to come with us. When I said I wasn't leaving without her, she began to cry. I picked her up and said I was taking her to watch the sunset. She didn't ask to be let down. I cradled her down all six flights, her tiny form weightless in my arms. Diana had hurried ahead and had a taxi waiting. I strode through the terrace, feeling a little winded, and placed Simone in the backseat between us. Diana put my jacket around Simone and directed our driver to Chariot Hill.

"Do you mean Sunset Hill?" the driver asked.

"Yes," I replied, closing my door.

It seemed everyone had a different name for the famous place.

Diana asked Simone why she was crying. Simone said that no one had ever reached out to her in this way. No one had ever given her love for her freedom, love with no strings attached.

I smiled at Simone. She was an orphan, and she'd created a great gig to disguise the longing in her heart for the freeing love, the love I'd grown up giving and receiving at Essence in Andorra—strange love.

"I want your Sentio to be healthy, and I want your Intentio free to dwell in Sentio," I told Simone, hugging her as she cried on my shoulder. Diana reached over and caressed her cheek. The cab slowed and came to a stop. I paid the driver as Simone composed herself.

We got out of the taxi, followed the running path to the top of Chariot Hill, and gathered near a spot surrounded by dogwood trees, engineered to bloom year round. We inhaled the perennial fishy bouquet from the white and purple flowering trees, curling our noses, and moved away from the scent. We walked holding hands and stood in the middle of the field where the grass was green—rye grass stayed green all year long—my favorite spot on the hill.

I'd learned a lot about Chariot Hill from Lar, who said this was the highest point in Boston. The three of us stood together as the beautiful sunset got underway. After a long moment I broke the silence and recited a version of my aunt Helen's blended words, hoping I could deliver the Sentio experience of Eden to Simone.

From the corner of my eye, I noticed Simone was listening intently. Then I looked at Diana, who was smiling at me. After I finished speaking, we watched as beautiful pinks and blues gleamed above the orange-blossom sky. Wispy white clouds and splashes of violet streamed high above the horizon where a turquoise sky had emerged.

The tension in Simone's face disappeared as the corners of her mouth lifted. We continued holding hands in silence until twilight faded. Then I pointed toward the mountaintops still visible directly ahead.

"Like clouds, the mountains shape themselves and then go," Simone said.

"Yes, and the mountains will remain even after we lose sight of them. They are still in our Sentio memory," I said. "They will always be there."

We all three hugged for several moments then in silence walked down the running path. I inexplicably guided us toward the Majestic. Simone grabbed my hand and talked with excitement, saying that she felt close to me on her new journey, the journey toward greater freedom for all.

Simone surprised me. She understood. She said that she had never felt this close to anyone. She had always felt alone. We stopped and embraced, and Simone cried in my arms again and thanked me. Diana stood to the side, supporting Simone, gently patting her on the shoulder. Simone turned from me and hugged Diana.

Following the Christmas lights into town, we became jovial sharing a laugh about the fishy smell of the dogwoods in bloom, and then Simone turned the conversation to existentialism and freedom. Simone discussed existence and essence, proving to me she already had the scaffolding of existentialism, and she knew about mysticism, metaphysics, and transcendentalism. I was amazed by her disclosure.

We walked through Harvard's campus talking about William James and Ralph Waldo Emerson. At one time Simone had wanted to be like Margaret Fuller. I listened to the dreams she'd had as a young lady and wondered why she'd not pursued them.

I held the door open as we walked into the Majestic. We grabbed a table and ordered coffee and apple pie, my favorite. Simone settled across from me, smiled at Diana, and explained that during the sunset for a few seconds, she saw tiny grid lines in the clouds, and then everything seemed to move in slow motion. She explained she'd never seen colors more gorgeous or more vivid than she'd experienced during the sunset. Nodding, Diana agreed about the slow motion and that the colors had seemed real and vivid to her as well.

I smiled at Diana, and said, "The colors were brilliant because Sentio projects true sensory, pure sensory. You both experienced Sentio for a moment, and you were experiencing the world at forty frames per second through Sentio, but you were still viewing Sentio frames at your slower mind's eye speed, which created the sense of slow motion. The Cogito mind's eye processes at twenty frames per second, and until your Intentio can dwell in Sentio, you will see the world at your Cogito mind's eye speed."

For a long moment they both stared at me. Simone's mouth gaped, but her eyes indicated she believed my explanation of her experience. Diana sipped on her coffee and then nodded but didn't acknowledge with her eyes.

After long hours of studying in Cogito, I'd experienced the same slow-motion effect many times when switching my attention from Cogito back to Sentio. When I kept my Intentio dwelling in Sentio, my mind's eye speed was at forty frames per second—Sentio speed—that I now believed was influenced by BSP. My aunt had taught me all about the mind's eye—how you see consciousness frames with your eyes open or closed.

After the waitress brought our pie, we ate in silence. The girls were hungry. As I chewed, I wished I could take Simone and Diana to Dr. Sol's eleventh-floor lab and run them through Sentio and Cogito mapping in Zeni. I believed the Zeni experience could help them understand Sentio, and I wanted to verify that they had indeed experienced Intentio in Sentio.

A warm tingle shot to the top of my head then. I'd had another neat idea. I wanted to do studies with Simone and Diana regarding correlating their blood BSP levels with their Sentio wave voltage amplitudes. If I could correlate Sentio wave amplitude with BSP levels, then I would have a way to measure the effects of strange love on BSP immediately and noninvasively by simply measuring Sentio wave amplitude changes after administering strange love. Eureka!

"Why are you smiling, Antonio?" asked Diana.

"What are you thinking?" asked Simone.

"I just figured out a major piece of the puzzle of how I'm going to lead Americans to freedom," I said. "Diana, Simone, you both have given me an idea."

"Please tell us," said Simone.

"I will very soon," I promised, and finished eating the delicious pie. I knew they were not ready to hear my idea—not yet.

Diana whispered to me that she wanted Simone to join us. Immediately I knew what she meant. Diana had quit working for Milly and moved in with me. She wanted Simone to move in with us. I smiled and nodded. Then Diana explained to Simone why she was so happy and how she wanted Simone to join us, to live with us. Simone stared at Diana, ignoring the last bite of her pie. I could see that Diana had the joy of human connection and freedom; her brown eyes sparkled. I thought I saw joy beginning to emerge in Simone's eyes; a twinkle that was growing bright as she reached for Diana's hand.

Simone looked at me and proclaimed that she had been born in a life raft like Diana, orphaned and forlorn. She no longer felt alone because of us. She wanted to follow us to the mountaintop of freedom. She no longer wanted to live as a slave of Cogito existence.

"You can bury the memories of Dominatrix Simone," said Diana.

Then suddenly Simone's face grew sad. "I'm too evil to join you. What was I thinking? My memories will haunt me for eternity."

"Simone, you're not evil. If you give in to the suggestion of others that you're evil, then you give up your freedom to be the person you truly are—a great, free, brilliant, and loving Sentio being. You are not the person that the world has defined and tagged as dominatrix, Simone. Your memories will remain irrelevant as long as you live for freedom with Intentio dwelling in Sentio. Your sense of being will be free from your negative memories. You will reconstitute yourself in each now moment going forward through Sentio, and you'll search for greater freedom for all in each now going forward."

"I understand, Antonio, but what about the modern therapists?" Simone asked. "They say that you have to understand and admit who you are before you can change. It's a great paradox."

"But the therapists believe that you are your Cogito memory files, a Cogito being. They do not understand Sentio or Intentio. Their view of you is not your true essence. Those Cogito memories are fodder for your human essence, institutional essence, nothingness. The therapists believe you should conform to their institutional beliefs about your essence for your own good." I smiled at Simone. "My aunt Helen is right, and for 2,400 years man has used language to obscure what it means to be and live a life of true essence." I gently squeezed Simone's hand.

She raised her beautiful blue eyes into my gaze and smiled. She appeared to surrender the idea that she was an evil being.

I continued. "You are the nothing being whose future is virgin. Everything is allowed to you through the Sentio of Eden."

After a moment Simone lit a candle on our table, and the three of us held hands. In my mind, the light from the candle represented the light for Simone's path to freedom through Sentio. Then Simone announced that she would quit her job and move in with Diana and me.

Diana looked at me with a soft, glowing face of an angel. "Simone, I'll take care of Milly."

Simone seemed overjoyed; her face glowed, and her eyes sparkled with hope. I think she was afraid that Milly would pressure her to work. It was so nice for Diana to offer to handle Milly for her. I knew what Diana was doing.

I paid the waitress, and Simone put out the candle. I needed to break away, or else I would be late for my flight. I walked the girls back to the House of Essence and grabbed my bag. Diana was going to help Simone move her things into 7B.

As we shared goodbyes, Simone hugged me and whispered, "Antonio, I love you. Thank you."

I hugged her back, hoping to fill her with strange love, raising her BSP, raising her Sentio sensitivity.

Diana gave me a long embrace. "I love you. Be careful. Give Marie, Polly, and Alex hugs for me. Aunt Helen, Uncle Poulou, and Javier, too."

I blew the girls a kiss and glided down the steps. My taxi arrived, and as soon as I got in and closed my door, the driver put his foot on the accelerator and raced toward the airport.

My insides churned in excitement over Simone and Diana. I couldn't wait to see my family in Andorra, and in only a couple more days, I'd get to reunite with Polly and Alex in London. I was living a charmed life leading others to freedom like my mother had dreamed I would. I smiled on the inside.

Feeling as if I'd already freed the Americans, I looked out my window at all the people at the airport. I realized then that I hadn't done anything yet, and if I couldn't start research soon, it might be too late. I had to get that research position, so I could begin immediately. The cab stopped at the international departure gate. I needed to focus on my journey back to Essence. I paid the driver, got out with my bag, and walked through the sliding glass doors.

CHAPTER

44

Our Airbus chased after the sun on the flight back to America. Once the sun dipped beneath the western horizon, a violet halo appeared for a moment, far above the fading orange glow of the sun where the white and pink cirrus clouds merged with the purple sky. As darkness crept toward the horizon, I leaned back in my window seat, closed my eyes, and remembered the moment one week ago when I'd gotten out of Uncle Poulou's car on the terrace at Essence. Immediately I'd turned and found my mother's eyes beneath her blue and white wimple and then gazed at the others standing on the balcony porch, sending smiles of love to me as they welcomed me home.

On that special day tears streamed down my mother's face, and at first I was worried that something sad had happened. I glanced over at Uncle Poulou, and he was smiling at Aunt Helen. Relieved by his smile, I walked up the stairs to the porch where I could appreciate the rejuvenated appearance of my mother, Javier, Sister Josephine, Reverend Mother Mary Elizabeth, Sister Phillips, and the others. Everyone looked so young and happy.

During my visit we shared some wonderful times in Andorra and then later in London. I'll never forget how happy my mother and Sister Josephine were when we surprised Alex and Polly backstage at the New London Theatre, after a performance of *Camelot*. Alex produced such a warm, happy smile when he saw us, and Polly ran to embrace Josephine and then my mother. Polly and Josephine cried for the longest time. Everyone was so happy. Then for two days in London, I had so much fun loving on Alex and Polly, telling them about America and learning about the Barbican performing arts center. Polly and Alex had made plans to visit me in Boston for their summer break. I couldn't wait to be with them again. My mother wanted to come and visit me too. She looked so young and beautiful in London, and Polly told her she looked like a young Audrey Hepburn, which made my mother so happy.

Before leaving Paris I'd discussed the rejuvenation of my mother and the others with Aunt Helen who believed she understood the process. It seemed to take between ten and twenty years, and was complicated.

I couldn't worry about that now. If I couldn't free Americans' Intentio from Cogito with a Sentio experience, then Americans would never find freedom nor have a chance at rejuvenation. I decided to worry about doing research with Dr. Sol. I needed to begin my research as soon as possible, so I could explore my ideas, which I'd been thinking about since the sunset experience with Diana and Simone.

First, I wanted to measure the effects of strange love on Sentio wave voltage and then correlate Sentio voltage with BSP blood levels. That was the idea Simone and Diana had given me.

Second, I wanted to develop the most powerful form of strange love ever known.

I placed a pillow behind my head and thought about all the positive things in America. I thought about Diana, Simone, Linda, Dr. Sol, the House of Essence, Lar, Barbara, Tinker, and my medical school class. What if I used Milly's girls and my classmates as cheerleaders to deliver strange love as Diana and I had joked? The thought amused me for a minute, and then the idea seemed more profound than it ever had. Perhaps I would build a specially trained army of strange love cheerleaders to lead the Americans to freedom. With that thought dancing through my brain, I drifted off to sleep.

When I awoke, I thought about the $100,000 my uncle had placed in a special account for me to use for strange love research. He said it was money he'd put away for my education, but since I won the Pasteur scholarship, I had not needed the money. I'd talked to him about my ideas, and he wanted me to have the funds for my future freedom research. I loved Uncle Poulou, the most generous man in the world. I reached into my pocket to feel my checkbook, and I remembered money has a strange power. I decided not to tell Simone about the money because it might trigger her will for power and pleasure. Money was tricky because it had a way of driving one's Intentio crazy. The Harvard professor of philosophy who substituted the word *Bullio* for Intentio was right about that. I'd seen money have a negative effect in gamblers and tavern-goers. I thought perhaps I'd tell Diana about the money, but then decided it was better to wait.

When I arrived by cab at the House of Essence, it was past midnight. I hurried up the six flights of stairs, put my bag down, and opened the door to 7B. Diana and Simone were waiting for me in the great room, and I embraced them both in a three-way hug. Simone grabbed my bag and placed it near the sofa. Diana brought me a glass of wine. We pulled chairs around the window seat and sipped on red wine, gazing out at the moonlight shimmering atop the cold, black harbor water. It was great to be with them. I shared the highlights of my trip, and the girls fell into a trance as I talked about my family's rejuvenation. Their eyes grew sleepy. Diana admitted she was very tired. I suggested they sleep in my room where it was warm, and they shuffled out together. I got up from the rocking chair, grabbed a blanket and pillow from the closet, and lay on the sofa, enjoying the cold air in the great room; it reminded me of Andorra. I closed my eyes and fell asleep.

The next morning I awoke to the clang of pots and pans and the smell of oatmeal as Simone prepared breakfast. I tried to go back to sleep, but it was no use. I got up and sat at the kitchen table, feeling groggy. Diana called my sleepy feeling jet lag and gave me a glass of orange juice. Then she grinned at me.

"You passed your summary exams!" she exclaimed, handing me a letter.

"What?" I said, seeing my name and address. Then I saw the single word which meant everything: *Congratulations!* I stood up from the table and let out a *woo-hoo*.

I embraced Diana and twirled her in the air. "When did the letter come?"

"On Christmas Eve. I didn't call because I didn't want to distract your attention from your family."

I lifted her and twirled again. "We did it. We are going to free the Americans and then the world," I said, letting her down.

"I'll help you," Diana said with a broad smile, her soft, brown eyes twinkling.

I looked over at Simone standing in front of the stove. She nodded as if she wanted to help too.

I hugged Diana again and murmured into her ear. "I'm glad you waited till I got back to share the news."

I walked over and embraced Simone. She looked into my eyes. "Thank you."

Her voice sounded so sweet and authentic. I whispered, "You are free."

Diana came over and hugged Simone and me.

"I need to meet with Dr. Sol," I announced.

"What about your oatmeal and eggs?" Simone asked.

"I'm too excited to eat. I'll eat later." I hurried upstairs to get ready.

"It's Saturday," yelled Diana.

"I know," I yelled down the stairs. "I need to hurry and catch Dr. Sol in his office."

I showered, shaved, and put on clean clothes. I hurried down the loft steps, kissed the girls goodbye, and rushed to the sensory deprivation research building. As the lift doors opened on the seventh floor, I strode quickly and quietly toward Dr. Sol's workplace. I peeked through the crack of his office door. His back was to me, and I could see he was signing onto his computer.

"Hello, Dr. Sol," I whispered.

"Hello, Dasein," he answered gruffly without even turning to look at me. "What was the name of your first wife? What was the name of your second wife?"

"What?"

"A computer geek must have been having a laugh when he developed these security questions for me, and I was foolish enough to provide the answers years ago. Every day I have to visit these reminders of my failed personal life to log on my computer."

I didn't know what to say, so I stood in silence, waiting for my moment to share my good news.

When Dr. Sol logged on, I whispered, "I have some great news."

"Yes, I suppose you do." He swiveled in his chair to face me.

"I passed my summary exams; I can begin doing research."

He peered into my eyes. "I was on the committee that reviewed your scores."

So he already knew.

"How did I pass? Lar said that I was too young to pass."

"The committee had no choice. They had to pass you.

Your scores were perfect, and I told them how you'd helped us discover the BSP receptor and that I needed you for my Intentio research."

I wanted to reach down and pull Dr. Sol into an embrace, but instead I reached and shook his hand in gratitude for several seconds. We talked about my ideas for research and my strategy, which I'd developed on my flight yesterday. He smiled and said I would be doing research in Zeni and would be starting the following Monday at 9:00 a.m. My heart pounded with excitement. I knew that meant I'd be doing consciousness research.

Then Dr. Sol asked me to attend grand rounds on Friday because Dr. Linda Hedrick and Dr. Susan Wolf would be presenting their data. "It will be good for you to attend and hear about their research," he said.

I almost screamed in joy. "I can't wait! I'll be there!"

Dr. Sol grinned and swiveled toward his computer.

I whispered farewell, exited the office, and skipped down the hall. When I realized how loud my skips were, I tip-toed. I took the lift to the ground floor and walked outside where I shouted, "Sentio!" I ran back to Double Banger Street to tell Diana and Simone the greatest news ever. The revolution to free Intentio from Cogito and restore Sentio would start next Monday.

45

They entered through the double doors down front as singles, twos, and threes to attend the first medical grand rounds of the semester. Lar, Tinker, Barbara, and I watched from the very last row of the freshman lecture hall as the long white coats strolled in, greeting each other with hand waves, head nods, and gentle slaps on the back. The auditorium filled with attending physicians, department heads, researchers, fellows, residents, interns, and medical students.

At noon on this glorious Friday, Dr. Sol walked up to the podium. "Good afternoon," he said, and paused.

Fascinated, I gazed around the room at the brilliant leaders of medicine, sitting among my fellow freshman medical students. I figured that most in attendance would drive their attention deep within their Cogitos as soon as Dr. Sol began his presentation, but for the moment their attention seemed devoted to settling into their seats and getting comfortable.

Dr. Sol looked about the auditorium, holding the microphone in his right hand. The lights dimmed, and he showed a slide of two elephants on a big screen behind him. Their pose suggested they were trying to kiss; one elephant had turned sideways, and the other lifted his trunk so that their mouths could touch. Below the picture read:

Do elephants kiss?

Laughter erupted. I guess like me everyone wondered what this had to do with the presentation.

After the amusing moment, he began. "Welcome, I'm Dr. Solomon Sol. I head the Sensory Deprivation Research Department here at Harvard, and I hold the William James Chair for consciousness research. I want to welcome our new students and interns and wish you all the best during these important training years at Harvard." He paused for a long moment and looked around at the faces of my classmates. "We've been waiting for you."

A tingle ran down my spine. Dr. Sol and the other professors had been waiting for us. He said that we'd finished our first semester and were now part of the family of medicine. I thought to myself that my class would be known as the deliverers. Feeling proud, I gave a fist pump at Lar, who pulled my fist down as if he was embarrassed by my reaction. On my right Tinker and Barbara leaned forward, turning toward me with smiles.

I whispered a hooray.

"*Shh!*" said Barbara.

Dr. Sol continued, "I'm going to deliver the first part of the presentation, and then I'll turn things over to Doctor Linda Hedrick and Doctor Susan Wolf, two of our new stars in sensory research. Thank you all for coming. You're in for a real treat. For the students who have not attended my lectures, what I'll present is about one-quarter theory and three-quarters hard science from our own consciousness research." He paused for a long moment. "We've narrowed the consciousness brain gap here at Harvard. . . . The memory function locales we discovered by lesion experiences, advanced imaging, signal-averaged EEG, and consciousness related potentials.

"I could talk about Wernicke's area, Broca's area, the temporal lobes, the thalamus, or the frontal lobes of the brain, but where does consciousness reside? Is it a left or right brain phenomenon? Or is it just a state of the brain like a great orchestra playing a movement with waves that sweep front to back at 100 cycles per second, oscillating neurons all over your brain? Or can it exist in the body? We cannot put our finger on a specific place for consciousness. What we have found are the electrical waves that appear at specific latencies that correspond to the moments of consciousness arising after an external stimulus."

Dr. Sol went on in his methodical but bland fashion. He looked portentous with his pointed ears and bald, cone-shaped head. At least that's what Barbara whispered in my ear. I turned and smiled at her use of funny, descriptive language while Dr. Sol explained his Sentio consciousness discovery.

"It takes two nanoseconds for light emitted from your computer screen to reach your retina, and then millions of nanoseconds later, the light is projected into your consciousness window. But what if I told you that there are two consciousness windows and two moments of consciousness separated by a few milliseconds, by a blink of your mind's eye, for every single stimulus? Would you be surprised?"

Silence filled the room then Dr. Sol said, "I'll present my findings published in *Nature*."

He began his slide show, presenting the latencies for Sentio consciousness and Cogito consciousness, but they were hard to relate to as most people experienced consciousness in streams and not after a single event as a single frame. If only everyone could experience the process in Zeni as I'd done in Dr. Sol's lab, then they would understand. If only they could experience Sentio and Cogito in Zeni and correlate the experience with their latencies and voltage amplitudes, then after repeating the same measures several times, they could focus their Intentio on the color blue instead of the letters that spelled the word blue as I had done. They would experience their Intentio and understand the differences between Sentio and Cogito. My face and head warmed from the inside. I realized then that the Zeni experience needed to be exploited to free Intentio from Cogito. The Zeni experience had kept playing in my mind ever since my experience.

Applause followed Dr. Sol's slide show.

"Linda, could you come forward?" Dr. Sol asked. "Dr. Linda Hedrick is a senior resident and research fellow here at Harvard and a graduate of Stanford Medical School."

Linda stood up and approached, and Dr. Sol turned the microphone over to her.

What a beautiful sight she was. She was wearing a short, black dress underneath her white lab coat and was wearing heels that made her taller. She walked around the auditorium's gray marble floor, making eye contact, connecting with her audience.

I looked at Lar who grinned. "Wow!" he whispered.

Linda was the most elegant and genteel person I'd ever met. She moved with such dignity and grace. She'd captured everyone's attention without uttering a word, and she'd communicated more sensory to my Sentio than everything Dr. Sol had said before.

"Thank you, Dr. Sol," she said. "I want to give a special welcome to the students and interns. We have been waiting on you. We need you."

When Linda spoke with her English accent, the lilt of her syllables physically affected me as her sounds passed through my Sentio and formed words in my Cogito.

"I want to remind all the students to sign up for Intimate Touch Week, the first week after exams in late spring. I promise you will not regret it, so please sign up after grand rounds today. The sign-ups are here on the front table. I'm going to turn things over to Dr. Susan Wolf, who trained at Johns Hopkins and runs the intimate touch and memory research lab here at Harvard. I'll see you in a bit."

I whispered to Lar, "Have you signed up for Intimate Touch Week?"

"Yes, I'm in Dr. Hedrick's group. You better sign up fast. Last time I looked, there was only one slot left in her group."

"What? Why didn't you tell me?"

Lar shrugged.

Dr. Susan Wolf stepped forward in her long, white lab coat and pivoted to face the audience. She was beautiful: tall, athletic, and graceful with long, brown hair and soft facial features. She fastened the microphone around her neck and settled in behind the podium.

I was worried. I guessed I'd missed the announcement about Intimate Touch Week because I was studying for my summary exams. I had to be in Linda's group; that last spot belonged to me.

CHAPTER

46

"Welcome. My name is Dr. Susan Wolf, and I work with Dr. Hedrick and Dr. Sol in the sensory deprivation laboratory here at Harvard. Thank you, Dr. Sol, for your thorough review of consciousness and thank you, Dr. Hedrick, for my introduction."

Dr. Wolf cleared her throat, glanced toward Linda, and smiled. "Dr. Hedrick and I have spent the last year investigating the power of human touch. Specifically, how intimate human touch affects the working memory of the toucher and the touched. I want to talk about sex for a moment since I'm sure it's on your mind after hearing the words *intimate touch*—the private or personal touch associated with sex."

Laughter erupted from the audience.

Dr. Wolf smiled. "But before we go any further, I would like to make one large point: there is no sub-consciousness."

The front section of the audience grumbled at the suggestion.

"What about Freudian slips?" someone asked, and laughter erupted again.

"They are preconscious foibles," said Dr. Wolf with authority.

I could tell by her swift response that she knew her stuff, and the laughter was silenced.

"What are preconscious foibles?" I whispered to Lar.

He leaned and murmured into my ear, "They're like Freudian slips."

I nodded as if his circular explanation made sense. Then I smiled to myself remembering Dr. Sol's words: language meaning is deferred to more language.

Barbara looked at me with her lips puckered. "What about intuition?"

I whispered, "Sentio!"

Barbara smiled. "Ahh."

Dr. Wolf continued. "My first slide shows two African elephants having sex in the wild supported by trees on one side and a large formation of rocks on the other. Sex is no doubt the reason we are all here. But is pleasure the only thing driving these two elephants to have sex?"

She paused as silence filled the room. "If you said yes, then you were right."

Lar whispered, "I was going to say yes, but I thought it was a trick question. You know elephants supposedly have good memories, and I thought perhaps that is why they like sex."

"No, I didn't know that. How could memory have anything to do with sex?"

Lar shook his head and shrugged again.

"Second slide," Dr. Wolf requested. "You can see that sex is below thirst, hunger, and sleep on the survival priority chain for the Mammalia class.

"Third slide. The limbic system is shown here in a three-dimensional drawing. The blue shows the hippocampus, and the green shows the cingulate gyrus. There's one on each side, the right and left hemispheres of the brain."

"They look like a ram's horns on the inside of the brain to me," I murmured to Lar.

Dr. Wolf continued, "The sex pathways are stored deep within our brain to ensure our survival, and the act of sex is connected to our pleasure centers to ensure its priority.

The neurons originate within our limbic system and are connected to the experience of pleasure through the hypothalamus and the septum pellucidum.

"The sex tracts light up in Sentio and give rise to more Intentios that connect to a variety of sensory experiences through memory; then as the arousal alarms go off, Intentio becomes selective attention for sex, which begets the intention for stimulation. Sexual stimulation produces pleasure, and as if riding on a merry-go-round, Intentio follows the pleasure paths round and round until the hypothalamus releases its stash of endorphins, the biomolecules of pleasure that serve as a reward for our sexual organ stimulation used in reproduction.

"But what about working memory?" she asked the audience. "How is it related to intimate touch?"

I thought Dr. Wolf's entire discussion was confusing. I looked at little Barbara and saw a frown on her face. I whispered to her, "I think Dr. Wolf wants to clarify that intimate touch can produce other effects than just the desire of sex for pleasure. Sort of like my idea about the intimate touch of strange love producing the vision for freedom."

Barbara smiled at me and touched the back of my hand with her finger, as if she were playing around, creating a tingle sensation in my chest that shot to the top of my head. I had explained to Barbara, Lar, and Tinker my idea about strange love and BSP, and Barbara just tickled me. I wanted to tickle her.

"Fourth slide," Dr. Wolf said. "What is memory? Once a language thought is experienced, or sense data is experienced, the two are stored separately or in combination in memory. Some researchers, like Dr. Sol and Dr. Hedrick, believe that our experienced sense data is actually processed sense data, fogged data experienced in Cogito."

A warm sensation spread from my chest to the top of my head then. I stared at Dr. Wolf's slide, thinking Linda has experienced Sentio. She knows the difference between Cogito sensory and true sensory in Sentio. I will be able to confide in her about my belief that American Intentio is addicted to Cogito, which is where Americans experience their sense data. Linda will understand.

I wanted to scream for joy.

"Next slide," Dr. Wolf said, bringing me out of my reverie.

A thought is stored as a cogi.

Sensory data is stored as a senti.

When a cogi is linked to a senti, we call the stored memory an emoti.

I read her slide realizing Americans experience sensory data in Cogito, which is actually stored in Cogito as a *cogi.*

"Our permanent memories are stored in neuron circuits under inhibitory control, and of course all our memories are time-stamped by the cerebellum," Dr. Wolf continued. "To re-experience a cogi, a senti, or an emoti, one has to free the inhibition of the blocking neurons by stimulating neurons from different areas in our brain, releasing the inhibition with Intentio or selective attention.

"All memories start as part of our working memory and later get covered with cobwebs of inhibition and become permanent memory files. Instead of saying you have forgotten something or someone's name, you might reply that their name is in storage," she said, eliciting some chuckles.

"Why can't we say that when taking exams?" asked a student, and more laughter erupted.

"Good point!" Dr. Wolf smiled. "Working memory is our short-term memory. We know that working memory is processed and played in the hippocampus in conjunction with our frontal lobes, the gatekeepers of our brain. The hippocampus is deep within our brain and is part of the limbic system.

"Working memory is always up and running, waiting

for Intentio to do a search, scanning old circuits for relevance. Intentio flashes and sweeps through our memories, lighting up familiar files or files relevant to our real-time phenomenon experience, which form a mosaic or background for our perception.

"I like to think of *Name That Tune* as a way to understand the role of Intentio. *I can name that tune in four notes . . .*

"We have found that the working memory organ, the hippocampus, performs in a peculiar way under certain conditions. It can be made to wobble. When wobbling occurs, it's said to precess. The formation of inhibitory connections to our new memories, which are transitioning to permanent memories, shuts down. Also during the wobble old memories in working memory are temporarily unavailable. The precessing or wobbling of the hippocampus is a singular event, but there are two primary kinds of stimuli that can produce precessing.

"The first is the fight-or-flight stimulus, and the second is an intimate-human-touch stimulus. The former signals a serious threat, and the latter signals a gesture for friendship or love, though not necessarily sexual—my point earlier. These opposite stimuli capable of producing similar effects might seem odd to you. But both stimuli result in precessing of the hippocampus, only to have the working memory reset at a higher functioning capacity after said precessing terminates, meaning easier recovery of new memories formed during and after the wobbling event."

A hand went up from the audience. "Yes?" Dr. Wolf said as she pointed.

The resident stood, and I recognized Anal. "So, what you're saying is that after working memory wobbles or precesses, when it turns back on it confers a super memory state."

"Yes, exactly," Dr. Wolf said. "What happens after precessing is rather remarkable. The memories of the event that caused the wobbling are placed in an important memory file with no inhibition. And for a short time after precessing, there is an overall heightened memory for the experiences that follow around the time of the wobbling event. These subsequent memories are stored with less inhibition, making them easier to recall. Sometimes these subsequent memories have no inhibition at all. They can intrude into our consciousness after being sympathetically discharged by roving Intentios—for days, weeks, months, or a lifetime— even though they are no longer relevant. For example, as in a patient with PTSD . . ."

My mind whirred, processing the lecture and drinking in the new information. It all made sense. Simone had precessed my brain with her intimate touch and then her slaps to my face. She had created thoughts and feeling memories that were free to intrude into my consciousness and caused me to obsess about her. Now I understood what had happened to me after my episode with Simone.

But I knew that Simone's intimate touch and slaps had lowered my Sentio sensitivity. Why? I sighed. Then it dawned on me: intentionality—the reason for the intimate touch—and the tracts used in the giver's Sentio are recognized in the Sentio of the receiver, which must produce sensory data and sensory causality data effecting the production and release of BSP.

I thought with the right intention, intimate touch could increase memory and Sentio sensitivity—like the super powerful form of strange love I'd experienced from Linda.

I then remembered the sensation of being precessed when Linda kissed me, after she'd said *Don't let the bastards change you.* She knew she was going to precess me with her kiss, and her intention was to share love for my freedom, and she knew I would never forget her words.

Then I thought how awful it was that someone's intimate touch for the wrong reasons might cause one to obsess about something bad while suppressing BSP and Sentio sensitivity, as Simone's touch had done to me. Intimate touch could also be the enemy. I wondered how many people think they are getting strange love when in fact they are getting intimacy with the wrong or dark intentions, the intention to control another person. How horrible it would be to get caught in such an intimate touch trap.

My heart pounded, and my chest felt heavy as if someone were standing on it. Americans had fallen into the dark intimacy trap. The world needs strange love, the intimate touch given freely with the intention to restore Sentio sensitivity and to restore the vision for freedom.

After several deep breaths my heart slowed, and the pressure in my chest released. I reflected oblivious to Dr. Wolf's words as if I were on the balcony porch of Essence in Andorra, and the sun was about to set. Endorphins are for pleasure, and soon Dr. Sol and I would reveal that BSP is for Sentio sensitivity and freedom. Then I closed my eyes and had a vision of freedom with my new American friends. I would use my medical school class and Milly's girls as strange love cheerleaders to raise BSP levels and increase sensitivity; I could see my army of lovers marching toward a field filled with people cheering.

Barbara got my attention by touching my hand. I'd completely zoned-out during my Compass of Freedom vision.

Dr. Wolf continued. "After precessing we find a remarkable opportunity to store new working memory at a much higher recovery capability. Let me give the example Dr. Hedrick uses of how precessing increases memory. Let's say that your neighbor has a dog, and when you arrive home after work and jump out of your car, you reach over the fence and pet your neighbor's barking dog. Fido calms, wagging his tail. Every day when you come home after work, you do the same. Then one day you reach to pet Fido, and for some reason, he bites you on the hand and draws blood. Your hippocampus begins precessing in fight-or-flight response mode.

"After the experience you never forget about the moment when Fido bit you, and you're unlikely to reach out to pet your neighbor's dog ever again, or if you do, you will do so with the memory of the bite intruding into your consciousness. The dog bite experience becomes a permanent working memory. There's no inhibition of the memory, and it may intrude into your consciousness triggered by a roving Intentio, arising from a relevant or similar Sentio experience, like seeing your neighbor petting his dog.

"So, we posed the question: can the same precessing and hyper-memory state be achieved by intimate human touch? That is, can we create uninhibited working memory by precessing the hippocampus with intimate human touch? I'll turn the presentation over to Dr. Hedrick who has some interesting results to report from a recent study."

Linda came forward, took the microphone, and fastened it around her neck. She walked around the auditorium, making eye contact with her audience, and I thought she was trying to precess us. Linda turned a lot of heads as she moved around. By the time she spoke, she'd garnered silence and everyone's attention.

"Thank you, Susan, for that lead-in. I would like to add that while intimate touch and life-threatening events are ways to precess one's hippocampus, there are also other ways to deliver mini-precessing: naked photos, erotica, and romance novels, for examples. Shaking an old acquaintance's hand and not being able to recall his name may result from the brief little precess from human touch, which we've all experienced. But after the brief precess and lapse of working memory, we never forget the fact that we forgot our friend's name, do we? No, because the new memory formed immediately after precessing is uninhibited."

Linda paused and smiled, giving us a chance to digest. She taught like Aunt Helen.

"Remorse, comfort, consideration, praise, recognition, or kindness expressed to another may induce mini-precessing for the giver and the receiver, conferring rebound hyper-memory of the event. But these little precesses are of very short duration and do not lead to the same hyper-memory response level after fight-or-flight or intimate touch.

Dr. Hedrick walked around looking in the eyes of those up front. The audience became very still. She continued.

"Please put up the next slide."

The French Kiss and Memory Study.

The audience chuckled. Linda's face remained serious, her eyes scanning the front rows. "Our study group consisted of thirty male and thirty female medical students and was further divided into two sub-groups. Group 1, which I call the unfortunate lot of thirty, was not allowed to touch or talk for forty-eight hours. During the first two hours of seclusion, they were given six tasks to perform using Lego toys and were trained by video on how to perform the tasks. Then they were asked to remember the tasks and given the rest of the two hours to practice.

"Group 2, the other thirty students, were divided randomly into couples instructed to either French kiss for fifteen seconds or hug for thirty seconds. Then they were given the same six Lego tasks to perform and remember, and they were provided the same video support and time for practice as was given to Group 1.

"Each student was given equal time to practice the memory tasks. All the students in Group 2 remained in solitude and were not allowed to talk or communicate after their initial intimate contact. They were kept isolated until after the final exam, given at the forty-eight-hour mark.

"What do you think we found?"

The audience grew excited. Several students up front burst out with *Group 2*.

"The results confirmed our hypothesis. The French kiss group had superior memory capability. We believe intimate touch-induced precessing from a French kiss resulted in hyper-memory. All twenty participants who consented and shared intimate touch in the form of a fifteen-second French kiss were able to repeat the six tasks at the end of forty-eight hours, and again at fifty-four hours, demonstrating that hyper-memory persisted."

Dr. Sol stood. "It is important to note we gave explicit instructions on how to share a French kiss, and we monitored the time, allowing only fifteen seconds for the kisses."

"Yes, good point. Thank you, Dr. Sol.

"We did a follow-up memory test one week later with all

the student volunteers, and the results were the same. The group performing the fifteen-second French kisses had by far the highest retention. Six out of six tasks compared with four out of six for the hug group, and three out of six for the non-touch group at forty-eight hours, fifty-four hours, and one week." Linda walked around, and said, "We have time for questions."

I smiled as my brain processed. Dr. Wolf and Linda had already found a powerful form of intimate touch for memory. I simply needed to combine consent to give love freely with the intention for greater freedom for all with their French kisses, and then I could measure and correlate BSP and Sentio voltage amplitude changes.

At that moment the dawn of a new era of freedom opened in front of me, like the sun rising above the French mountains, shining through my bedroom window at Essence in Andorra, waking me. We could introduce strange love in America as a way to improve productivity in the work-place by increasing working memory. Productivity in the workplace was a concept I wouldn't have to introduce to the Americans; it was already at the core of their value system. We could take down the intimacy barrier in the workplace and set humans free at the same time! I almost laughed out loud. I was so tickled at the idea.

Little Barbara gave me an inquisitive look and whispered that she'd been in the French Kiss and Memory Study this past summer. She wrinkled her nose. "But I was unfortunate." She explained she'd been picked for the non-touch group and spent the weekend all alone for forty-eight hours and then forgot her memory tasks of how to make the complicated Lego toys.

I smiled at Barbara and gently touched the back of her hand. Her brown eyes twinkled at me as she smiled. I wanted to hug her because I knew what a lonely weekend felt like, thanks to my weekend all alone after Simone's spell.

Tinker grinned at Barbara. "How many tasks did you remember?" he asked.

Barbara replied, "Don't ask. I was happy I got paid $400. That's all I remember."

An older professor stood, and asked Linda, "What about simulated touch?"

"Our studies show that simulated touch does not work. Hippocampal precessing through touch requires genuine intimate human touch."

Her response made sense because simulated touch cannot simulate intention, which I believed was critical for the BSP response—intimate touch with the right intention.

Linda added, "We believe that it's perhaps physical chemical signaling that generates precessing from human touch. Hence we are excited with Dr. Sol's discovery of BSP."

I knew BSP was related to sensitivity, and I knew from my different post-wobbling experiences with Linda and then Simone that BSP could not be the cause of precessing. I wanted to say something, but I thought it might embarrass Linda, so once again, I kept my mouth shut.

Linda continued, "Sham touch is when one or both people involved with intimate human touch are ambivalent or not receptive. Sham touch does not lead to precessing or the hyper-memory response. Most real-life hugs are in fact sham hugs. Inhibited hugs are when people slap you on the back or talk while they hug. People know when they have experienced a real precessing, an uninhibited hug with intentionality." Linda looked at the back of the auditorium toward Lar and me.

I felt a wave of heat run through my body with her attention on me.

Dr. Sol stood up again. "We have time for a few more questions."

After a moment of silence, Linda said, "Susan and I have been trying to bring down the intimacy barrier in the workplace. We've done several studies about the benefits of brief, thirty-second intimate touch experiences while working a nine-to-five job. Our critics point to the fact that touch will lead to sexual relations and impropriety. We've found that, in fact, two people who have an intimate, healthy relationship may or may not have the chemistry for sex. If the couples in the workplace stimulate their sex pleasure centers as they precess, then they can delay the gratification of sex until they're off-duty. Some may not partake at all. And most professionals have a significant other as their sex partner. Precessing on the job is purely to help work performance among highly disciplined professional subjects. In fact, the cues for sexual intercourse become more obvious and easily discriminated."

Lar whispered to me that he thought Dr. Hedrick would be a lot of fun in the workplace.

"She's awesome," I replied with a broad smile.

Linda had the audience so quiet that her words seemed to hang in the air above our heads. Her ideas were so novel, yet made so much sense. We thirsted for more.

"What our studies suggest is that touch that leads to precessing will also lead to improved focus during complex tasks. In Dr. Sol's lab, we have already recognized this advantage and have incorporated intimate touch sessions into our daily work routine."

Yahoo! I screamed inside my brain. I could not wait to start doing research next week.

Dr. Sol stood and moved next to Linda. "We've time for one more question."

I raised my hand.

"Yes, you in the back," said Dr. Sol.

He couldn't see that it was me. I stood and spoke loudly. "Dr. Hedrick, does it seem that strangeness is necessary to precess?"

"That's a very good question. We are currently studying the loss of strangeness, so I do not have an answer for your question right now. My guess is that repetition will diminish the effect, but I remind you that frequent kisses are not necessary for memory gains."

"That is a very good question to end on. Thank you," said Dr. Sol, and shot me a warm, knowing smile.

I felt about ten feet tall. Barbara said that I'd asked a very good question. The audience all stood at once, and the group of white coats quickly dispersed. I walked down the auditorium steps to the front, near the podium, and listened to several students ask Linda and Dr. Wolf questions.

I looked at the signup sheets. Linda's group was full; someone else got the last space. So, I signed up for Dr. Wolf's group for Intimate Touch Week, hoping I could trade with Lar and be in Linda's class.

I caught Linda's eyes, and we exchanged smiles. She

approached and stood near me. She answered a question from Bob, my student friend from Yale. I wanted to engage Linda for a personal question, so when Bob turned away, I took a chance.

"Linda—I mean Dr. Hedrick."

"Antonio, since when did my on-call shadow—and my soon-to-be fellow research assistant—become so formal?" She smiled. "You can call me Linda."

My heart jumped for joy at her response. Our reunion was just as I'd dreamed.

"Would you ever consider going on a date with me?"

After I blurted out the question, my insides quivered. A tall male intern moved in front of me and asked Linda a question. I shouldn't have asked her here, like this, I thought. It seemed like an eternity as Linda talked and talked in response to his question. I continued tiptoeing and leaning to keep my eyes on her face, waiting for her response to my question. Finally the intern seemed satisfied and walked away.

Linda found my eyes and smiled. "Yes, of course, Antonio. I would love to go out with you."

A warm glow filled my chest then and shot to the center of my head. My Sentio lit up as if the gates of heaven had opened in front of me. Linda's eyes twinkled, and echoes of her voice saying yes played in my head. Staring at her angelic face, precessing, speechless, I glanced toward the door, searching for Lar as if he could help me respond.

"Antonio, did you have a time and place in mind?"

Linda's soft voice pulled me back toward her. Gazing down into her beautiful brown eyes, I found what I wanted to say. "What would you like to do?"

"Well, there's a visiting conductor performing at the Meyerhof next weekend," she suggested.

"Sure, let's do it."

"Are you sure?"

"Absolutely."

"I already have tickets," she said. "Can you pick me up?"

I was shaking on the inside with excitement. "Sure! Awesome!"

How would I pick her up?

She wrote down her parents' address on a business card and handed it to me. The card smelled like her. I took a whiff and put it in my shirt pocket.

"I'll see you Monday in the eleventh-floor lab for consciousness research," she said.

"Okay, I'll see you then."

I saw Linda grin as she turned toward Dr. Wolf. Ambling toward the door, I looked up and saw Lar standing at the back of the auditorium. He appeared taller and more vivid now. Linda's powerful strange love, I thought, and smiled to myself.

"Hey Lar, wait up!" I yelled.

I ran up the steps in excitement and told him about my date with Linda. Lar grinned and gave me a high five.

"Dasein, you'll need a tux, and I know where we can pick one up. What are you, about six feet two?"

I nodded. "But how will I pick Linda up?"

"My brother has a friend who drives a limo. But you have to get me a date with your roommate Diana."

"I'll do it," I said without hesitation. "I know you two have Sentio chemistry; Diana said she had a lot of fun dancing with you."

"We've got a deal," Lar said, grinning, and shook my hand.

I said goodbye to him as he exited out the back to meet his brother. I hurried down the steps and out of the auditorium. I ran into Anal in the hall near the door leading outside. He looked different; his eyes did not dart around as much.

I gave Anal a hug and noticed he gave a reciprocal squeeze, not a sham hug as I'd expected. He said that he was doing a basic science research elective this semester, and he would be working with Dr. Wolf and Dr. Hedrick.

"Good!" I said. "I'll also be doing research with Dr. Hedrick and Dr. Wolf. I look forward to working with you."

"You helped me," he said. "Dr. Hedrick told me what you'd said about me being addicted to legal-language thinking." Anal peered into my eyes for a long moment before turning his eyes away. "You were right, so I thought about your way and decided to read your aunt's book."

Wow, I thought. I was glad for him and proud of Linda for approaching him.

"Thanks, Anal." Maybe my eye touches had helped him, and he'd read my aunt's book. I didn't want to get his Cogito started, so I didn't say anything more. He appeared serene as we said goodbye.

49

The limo pulled into Mount Vernon where Linda's parents lived, and we turned onto their street. After we'd rolled to a stop in front of the house, my heart pounded, and my hands were shaking.

The driver opened my door, and I stepped out. I tightened my red tie and straightened my dove-tailed, black coat. A quiver of uncertainty pulsed from my chest. I loosened my tie, and the sensation passed. I was nervous. After a few seconds I crossed the street, strolled down the concrete walkway toward the four-story, red brick apartment building, and stopped in front of the steps to rehearse introducing myself.

I was meeting Linda's parents, and thinking about meeting them had produced a knot in my stomach. I knew why; I loved Linda and wanted her family to like me. Wanting to calm myself, I redirected my attention to the beautiful, tree-lined street and nineteenth-century row houses set aglow by tall, black street-lights—beautiful Sentio images. The lights reminded me of the gas lights at home on the cobblestone road that led from Essence to Pierre. I enjoyed the memory for several moments.

Another deep breath later I walked up the marble steps and pressed the button under the Hedrick name plate labeled Apt A. The door released with a buzz. I pushed into the entry area and stood opposite a stairwell. I followed the barking sounds to the right and peered through a screen door. A cute little silky tried to jump through the screen door to greet me. The small ball of energy reminded me of Javier's silky named Teak, his watchdog at Paradise. I inhaled Linda's fragrance and knew I was in the right place.

I knocked gently, and a nice older couple answered, inviting me inside. They introduced themselves as Jon and Barbara Hedrick and informed me that Linda was finalizing her attire. Linda's father had picked up their dog, and her mother offered me something to drink. I was not thirsty, so I declined. I asked about their dog, and Jon smiled at me. Barbara said Linda had adopted her from the pound and named her Eliza.

I heard Linda call out, "I'll be right there."

Linda's stunning silhouette appeared and paused on the landing at the top of the staircase, adjusting her brown locks atop her shoulders. She wore a black dress with thin straps exposing her sleekly muscled arms. Wow! She moved with the grace of a princess in a slow descent down the steps. When she reached the foyer, Eliza jumped from Jon's arms, barking up a storm and leaping with excitement.

When Linda turned toward me, her powerful attention beamed from her beautiful, brown eyes and enthralled me. "Hello, Antonio," she said, and smiled.

My heart jumped for joy. She'd said my name like an angel, and she appeared more genteel now than when she gave her lecture. I was in awe in her presence and couldn't speak. I just smiled, overwhelmed by her sensory—my Sentiomate.

She warmed her mother and father with embraces. Then she gave me a gentle hug and touched my cheek with her soft skin. Holding her touch in my consciousness, I turned my other cheek and touched her soft skin once more. I was still too excited to speak. My Intentio swirling in my

Sentio, attending to Linda's presence. Finally, I managed to push out a single word.

"Gorgeous."

Her father looked at me and smiled with pride. Jon and Barbara seemed very proud of their daughter, and I sensed their deep love for her. We exchanged farewell embraces. I kissed Barbara and then Eliza on her nose, and we were off. Linda grabbed her coat, and I led her down the stairs, then on the last step twirled her into an embrace, and lifted her to the sidewalk. I was so happy. After I'd put her down, she wiped her mother's lipstick from my face, straightened my tie, and said that I looked gorgeous. I touched her soft eyes with my own and conveyed that I was proud to be with her. We crossed the street holding hands as our driver got out and directed us to enter from the sidewalk side of the vehicle.

Linda stopped, staring at our driver and the shiny black Mercedes, and squeezed my hand. "You got a limo," she whispered.

"My friend Lar had his brother set us up."

The driver opened our door and made sure we were secure and comfortable, and then drove us out of Mount Vernon and cruised toward downtown Boston. Linda's eyes sparkled with excitement. She grinned and reached to hold my hand. She seemed to thrive on human contact, and I enjoyed holding her soft hand. She talked about her parents and the circumstances of her adoption from Archangel, Russia. I listened, looking at her sparkling eyes.

"Children were given up for adoption with the provision that their names never be changed," she explained. "But Barbara and Jon changed my name anyway."

A wave of sadness affected me. I wondered why they'd changed her name.

"Why did they change your name?"

"Barbara was afraid children in school would make fun of my name."

"What was your name before your adoption?"

"Sophia Lubov," she said with a grin.

I opened my mouth in surprise. "*Lubov* means love in Russian. That's you—your true essence name."

Linda touched my eyes softly with hers and caressed the back of my hand with her fingertips. She'd tickled my Sentio and captured my attention, hypnotizing me. When she rubbed my cheek with the back of her hand, I wanted more sensual pleasure. I could not stop the longing gaze I sent her way as she continued.

"Barbara and Jon supported me through my undergraduate education at Harvard, my medical school at Stanford, and now my residency and research here at Harvard. They have been incredibly generous to me. Their love and support have been remarkable, and I'm forever grateful to have joined their family."

The limo slowed to a creep, and I snapped out of Linda's spell. "Barbara and Jon sound a lot like my aunt and uncle. They paid for my education."

"I told Barbara about your family. She says your aunt is a well-known French feminist leader, and that she runs the best orphanage in the world." Linda's eyes were lit with curiosity.

I glanced out my window, thinking of my family back home. My chest swelled with pride. I looked back at Linda.

"Thank you. I know that to be true." Staring into her eyes, I added, "The future will prove what you just said about my aunt. She is a social theorist and a great philosopher, and she does not like tag titles like *feminist woman*. She prefers to be called a Sentio being."

Linda's face tensed at my response. I didn't mean to diminish her compliment or to be critical. I searched for something to say, then realized I just wanted to enjoy the sensory of Linda in my Sentio. I wanted my Intentio dwelling in my Sentio in Linda's presence.

After a moment her face relaxed. She said she liked my tux and complimented my hair. She stroked my cheek with the back of her hand again and found my dimple with her thumb. She peered deep into my eyes. "Where are you, Antonio? Where is your Intentio playing at this moment?"

I was going to say that my Intentio was following her thumb, but I found myself experiencing Linda's eyes in a warm and joyous way. At that moment I experienced her powerful attention joined with my beingness, beyond the veil of human reality as if we were one dwelling above our Sentio and Cogito existence.

I felt her softness, her warmth. Her eyes had warmed and tingled me. The moment created a reality of ecstasy that I couldn't explain, an ineffable experience, and after a long moment I realized we'd not been physically touching, yet our Intentios had merged into one. Our eyes relaxed, we embraced, and I inhaled her bouquet.

I wanted to be with her for eternity.

The driver stopped near the front door of the Meyerhof and requested we exit on the right. Linda got out first then I followed and reached for her hand. She showed me how a gentleman is supposed to offer his elbow to escort a lady, which I already knew but played along. We strolled on the red carpet through the double glass doors into a dome-shaped hall.

"You're just in time," the usher said, handing us a program and pointing toward our balcony seats. Linda took the lead down a side aisle. We stepped up through a doorway and settled in our front row seats, looking out at the ornately decorated hall, the beautiful red velvet curtains and seat covers, with ivory trim and marble everywhere.

"We'd never have made it without the limo," I whispered.

Linda agreed. "Good call.

"I left my coat in the limo. I might need your jacket if I get cold."

"No problem. Let me know."

The orchestra was tuning up, with the violins and horns producing dissonant sounds. I heard someone say allegro giusto. After a few moments the hall had filled with silence.

Then the Boston Philharmonic, joined by the Royal Youth Choir of Great Britain, opened Mahler's second,

Resurrection, with a bang. The violins tickled my Sentio. I thought I'd heard the music before, perhaps in the background of a movie, but I couldn't remember for sure.

"Wow, Antonio, this is going to be wonderful," Linda gushed into my ear. She tugged on my arm and guided my eyes toward the intricate details of the symphony hall, including the ornate gold-trimmed molding around the ceiling.

"This is my favorite piece of music," she added. "Thank you, Antonio."

"Of course. I feel honored to be here with you."

"*Shh!*" admonished a lady behind us.

I turned to apologize. "I forgot to whisper," I said.

The lady glared at me.

Then Linda whispered, "Quiet."

I relaxed and reflected on the music. The piece told an emotional story of life and death and a hope for either an end to the nothingness or for the joy of eternal life in a resurrection. I knew what the music was trying to do. Mahler was trying to deliver sensitivity to my Sentio for freedom. Then I read about his intent in my program. I thought it was interesting how he'd integrated the sounds of nature into his beautiful piece of music. I felt connected to Mahler because he'd tried to carry the torch for freedom in his day.

Linda reached for my hand, and we held hands again, exchanging glances. Later her attention seemed so focused and consumed by the piece. She triggered memories of living with my mother in Villa #4 as a child. My mother liked to listen to music.

At intermission we walked to the lobby where Linda saw several of her friends and embraced some friendly attractive ladies from the hospital. They smiled at me and giggled, whispering something to Linda. She turned to look at me and let out a giggle of her own. Walking back toward the balcony, Linda explained that her friends had laughed in excitement because they thought I was handsome. I chuckled in appreciation, and Linda lightly punched my shoulder in play.

Returning to our seats, I wanted to tell Linda about strange love and my idea for her research. As I opened my mouth and turned to speak, the music began, so I closed it but not quickly enough.

"*Shh!*" said the lady behind me.

I hadn't said anything! Linda glanced at me with a grin. I settled back in my seat.

The music drew us in with each movement, and soon Linda and I were floating on a cloud as if overlooking heaven. As the glorious finale neared its end, Linda and I had a firm grasp of each other's hands. Tears rolled down my face. I felt her clench my hand, and she released her own tears. We were a mess by the end of the performance. A happy, funny mess.

The music had lit up my Sentio tracts, and Linda's physical presence had aroused me. My Intentio wanted to engage her for pleasure of the erotic kind, but I wanted her to want me too. I watched out of the corner of my eye as she composed herself.

She sniffled and wiped her tears with a lacy handkerchief pulled from her purse. She had come prepared. How interesting: it was as if she knew she was going to cry, and she probably knew she would experience heightened sensitivity. That explained why she was so excited for the performance.

A warm, pleasurable sensation emerged in my head; our date had been Sentio-orchestrated by Linda. She touched the back of my hand with her fingertips, calling my attention back to her beautiful sensory. We got up from our seats and followed the line of people down the stairs. Linda wanted to thank the conductor, Lenny, but a mob of several hundred were waving their arms overhead trying to get his attention near the front entrance. So, we went out the side exit, where our driver was watching for us.

We got in the limo, and after a moment of silence, I suggested to Linda that we go to the Majestic for a late snack. I still had strange love on my mind and was anxious to talk to her about my plans. She nodded and looked down as if something else held her attention. I wondered if she had felt what I felt inside the symphony hall. I hoped her Sentio tracts had lit up like mine and that her Intentio experienced erotic pleasure from my sensory. I looked over at her, unsure of where her attention was at the moment.

"*Mon amour, nous ne serons dehors pour pendant une courte period.*" I told her in French we'd only be out a short while.

"*Je sais;* I know," said Linda.

She moved closer and curled up against me. She told me she liked listening to men speak French and that it was sexy. I explained that Aunt Helen had made the orphans at Essence learn English for freedom and that as a teen I surmised that French was useful for attracting the sexy women at the tavern in Pierre. She laughed and reminded me that spoken language has both Sentio (sound) and Cogito (information content).

We decided to talk in the back of the limo and gaze at the stars through the sunroof and forgo dinner, so I had the driver just cruise around Boston. We discussed BSP and my ideas about correlating BSP with Sentio wave voltage amplitude. I told her all about Diana and Simone. I wanted to bring them into our research, as well as Lar, Tinker, and Barbara. I explained about Simone in a nice way because I had wanted Linda to experience the new Simone before I told her about Simone's former life and our conflict.

Linda was so accepting of others. She agreed with my plan and said something funny. "I think Simone and Anal might be a perfect match."

I laughed so hard just thinking about the two of them together.

"I'll talk with Dr. Sol and Dr. Wolf," Linda said. "I think they'll agree, and we can begin your correlation studies next week."

"Awesome!"

We kissed for a long time then stretched out on the black leather seat.

The driver asked, "Where to next?"

Linda sat up, looked at the clock above the minibar, and straightened her dress. "I better get home. It's after 1:00 a.m."

"Mount Vernon," I told the driver.

Ten minutes later we arrived and parked. I escorted Linda out of the limo. We shared a long embrace on the sidewalk a few paces from her door. When we relaxed, I looked into her eyes, holding her in my arms, and said, "This is the most romantic night I've ever had."

Linda's large, brown eyes twinkled like stars. She gave me a sweet look and then a long kiss.

After our kiss, I struggled to say goodnight.

Linda grinned. She seemed unable to speak too. Finally, she said, "Goodnight."

Then I was able to say goodnight. We'd precessed each other. Linda's grin had grown into a broad smile. She turned, ascending the steps, and opened the front door, disappearing inside. I twirled and skipped back to the limo. I thanked my driver, and he looked at my reflection in the mirror and smiled. I asked if he could play the romantic station on the BBC. I listened to "You, My Love," and reflected on my kiss with Linda. We drove through the tree-lined streets of Mount Vernon and headed toward Double Banger Street.

CHAPTER

51

On Friday night the large, green street lights lit up the Harvard campus. Linda and I strode out the entrance gate and turned onto Paul Revere Street on our way back to the House of Essence. It had been a long day of research. We'd prepped thirty students and measured their Sentio voltage amplitudes in Zeni. We'd measured thirty new students every day over the past week, and we had accomplished the first step in freeing Intentio from Cogito for most of the students. Even if only for a moment, the students had ridden the Sentio 'bicycle,' experiencing their Intentio in Sentio for the first time in their lives.

But it had not been easy. We had to coach the students and repeat the measures of Sentio and Cogito using Zeni for the word blue in bold blue letters twenty times on average before the students could redirect Intentio from the word blue in Cogito to the color blue in Sentio. Linda and I had enjoyed their amazed expressions, the twinkle in their eyes, as they stepped out of Zeni describing what the true sensory of blue felt like. My fellow students had tuned into the Sentio consciousness of primal blue for the first time, and that had meant everything to me.

I reached for Linda's hand and gave a little squeeze. I felt so much love for her. She'd worked so hard to free the students. She produced a smile and said we were almost home. Linda had moved in with me because we were practically living in the research building, and my place was much closer to campus than hers.

"TGIF!" I exclaimed as we walked down Double Banger Street, approaching the House of Essence just ahead.

Linda tried to smile again but said she was too tired. I was exhausted, but being around Linda helped my tiredness for some reason. I led her up the porch steps and held the front door open. "After you, Dr. Hedrick, my Sentiomate."

Producing a half smile, she agreed that we were Sentiomates. We embraced and kissed in the stairwell, and after a brief rest in each other's arms, we dragged ourselves up the six flights of stairs to 7B. Once inside Linda collapsed on the sofa. I guzzled down a glass of water at the sink, pulled out some leftover pizza from the fridge, and reminded Linda that it was our night to sleep downstairs.

"Oh yeah, good. I'm too tired to climb any more stairs," she said.

It sounded like Diana and Simone were already asleep in my bedroom; they were not making a sound. After pulling the pizza from the microwave, I joined Linda at the table, where she'd poured some wine. We sipped and ate in silence, which was neat about being around Linda—she was not a talker. She was like Aunt Helen.

After eating she retreated to the sofa, and I joined her with a pillow and a blanket from the closet.

"You are really tired," I said.

"I'm too tired to get ready for bed."

We fell asleep, with me cradling her in my arms. I slept soundly through the night until Linda got up to shower. It was 7:00 a.m. by the clock in the kitchen. Unable to go back to sleep, I lay thinking on the sofa. Now that we had a way to free Intentio from Cogito, we needed to focus on Sentio sensitivity. I had an idea about expanding our research, growing our number of lovers.

Linda looked beautiful and refreshed when she came down the steps brushing her hair, dressed in jeans and a white blouse—her casual attire. I embraced her and told her about my idea to expand our research from the eleventh floor to the House of Essence. She agreed immediately before I could explain the details. When I expounded, she said she'd had the same idea while showering.

Wasting no time, I ran up to the bedroom, showered, changed, and wrote a check from the account I'd opened with the money from Uncle Poulou. I looked over at Simone and Diana; they'd rolled into an embrace and were still sound asleep.

Returning to the kitchen, I phoned Milly and requested a special meeting. "We need more room and more strange lovers," I said to her. "I have a proposition for you."

Milly said, "I'll come up, and we'll talk."

As I hung up the phone, Simone and Diana made their way into the kitchen.

"Good morning, sleepy girls," I said.

"Morning, Antonio. Morning, Linda," said Diana.

Simone smiled at me, and said, "Hello, Linda."

Linda shared an embrace with Diana and Simone then I shared embraces with them.

A knock on the door startled the girls. I ran to open it, and Milly entered with a smile. Diana and Simone raced to greet her and shared hugs. I hugged Milly and introduced her to Linda, who gave Milly a hug. We all sat at the kitchen table. Diana got up and poured coffee, while Linda and I told Milly about our research. Simone listened with enthusiasm, and I could tell Linda and Milly had connected on a Sentio level—they were holding hands as I talked.

Finally, I asked Milly if she would consider letting us take over the House of Essence for six months. She would have to close her business of selling sensitivity, and the girls would have to take in medical students as roommates for strange love research. I knew that Tinker, Barbara, Lar, Anal, Bob, and several others wanted to move in with us.

Milly's eyes widened in a look of surprise, then she stared at Simone for a long moment, turned, and smiled at Diana. "Yes, you can," she said with encouragement.

"Yes!" replied Simone with excitement.

I pulled Milly into an embrace and kissed her on the cheek. She looked into my eyes with a cute, girlish grin.

I pulled out a check written for half of what Uncle Poulou had given me and handed it to her. Tears welled in her eyes. I loved her and was glad to make her happy. She had agreed to my plan without the money, which made it even more special.

Linda hugged her again. I think Milly had been getting strange love from Diana and Simone. She was a different person than the Milly I'd met about seven months earlier.

Simone wanted to begin training the other girls immediately on how to give strange love. She told us that she had talked to Sassy and Fancy, and they wanted to join our group.

That evening we joined Milly and the other girls on the porch, and Milly made the announcement. I looked at Diana, Simone, and then Linda. They were all smiling. Sassy and Fancy cheered, and the girls started dancing in celebration. We were going to begin strange love research at the House of Essence.

52

The following week Simone brought all the girls to our research lab for BSP measures, and we discovered most of them had BSP levels less than 10 ug/100 ml. Then we used Zeni to free their Intentios for the Sentio experience of the color blue, as we'd done with the medical students, and measured their baseline Sentio amplitudes, correlating with their BSP measures. Most of their Sentio amplitudes were less than 50 uv, which indicated to me we had a lot of work to do since my Sentio amplitude was 400 uv.

So the next week, I brought a troop of my medical school classmates to the House of Essence after classes every day so Milly's girls could give and receive strange love in the form of hugs and kisses. Lar, Tinker, Bob, Barbara, Izzie, Joe, and Vinay had already moved into the House with us the week before, and we'd already begun experimenting with strange love hugs and kisses and recording the girls and their progress with measurements in Zeni. Everyone had pitched in to help, experimenting to find the most effective strange love.

On Saturday night, we had a little dinner party for the girls and students in Milly's large apartment dining room, a launch party for our strange love research. After the party Linda and I retreated to 7B, and we lay on the window seat listening to romantic songs. After helping Milly with the dishes, Simone and Diana came in and joined us. They listened to our music and lay on the sofa, looking sleepy.

It was 2:00 a.m. by the kitchen clock when Linda got up filled with new energy. I believe she'd been inspired by my tickling her ribs. She asked for everyone's attention and began to explain how to deliver a precessing French kiss. I smiled as Simone stood up beside Linda, engaging her in play as if she knew how to give the best French kiss in the world. But Linda surprised Simone with details about the history of the famous kiss, which the French women had shared with American and British troops during WWI. Linda explained how her research had led her to discover a magical variation of the French kiss, which caused precessing. As Linda explained precessing, Diana sat up giving her full attention.

"After you have engaged your lips with the strange love recipient, making sure your lower lip is just below their lower lip, open your mouth giving them a chance to enter your mouth with their tongue. After a few seconds enter their mouth and use your tongue to tickle their tongue for four to five seconds. When you get ready to withdraw your tongue, make sure that you slide the under surface of your tongue in a sweeping motion over the entire top of their lower lip at least two times but quickly. The entire kiss needs to last approximately fifteen seconds."

Smiling with her eyes, Simone grabbed Linda and kissed her, for probably thirty seconds. Wow. I smiled at Diana.

"You mean like that?" asked Simone, pulling back from their embrace.

I could see Linda was precessing as Simone released her. Linda staggered, raised up wide-eyed, and grinned at me, trying to speak. "Yes! Yes! That's it."

Diana stood up and approached, and I practiced on her. Then Linda practiced on me. She slid the bottom of her soft tongue over the top of my lower lip, back and forth several times then several more times.

A pleasurable sensation shot through my head, and I couldn't find any words to say.

Acting silly, Simone and Diana kissed for a long moment, and releasing they were speechless. Diana gaped at me as Simone pulled her arm. They waved goodnight and left.

I grabbed Linda and pulled her onto the sofa. My entire brain had lit with warm pleasure, still spinning as we lay together, and with Linda in my arms, we cuddled and shared erotic pleasure till our minds filled with ecstasy. I drifted toward sleep knowing I would never forget this night.

The following week all the girls learned how to deliver Linda's special French kiss, and we followed the girls' and my classmates' progress with Zeni. We immediately saw positive results in the Sentio uv amplitudes for the girls and my classmates. Their amplitudes had increased in response to strange love in the form of a French kiss.

Simone and Diana had joined our team as research associates at Harvard and were placed in charge of the students and girls from the House of Essence. They also attended our research conferences in the lab every Friday, wearing their long white lab coats with pride. Simone frequently contributed, asking great questions and causing Dr. Sol to grin and shake his head over her novel ideas for improving our results.

A month passed, and I met with Simone and Anal in the lab to discuss the progress. Things had slowed, and our early positive results had plateaued. Simone told me she was concerned. She believed the Intentio to share strange love needed to be experienced in Sentio and Cogito. She explained if the girls tried to share strange love simply through an Intentio that came solely from Cogito consciousness—language thought—then their kisses would have little effect on the Sentio uv amplitude of the student recipients.

I reviewed her results. Simone had made an important observation, and she and Anal had confirmed her theory with an experiment on ten students' Sentio amplitude measures in Zeni. A powerful Intentio that arose from immediate sensory stimulation of Sentio and then redirected with the right intention in Cogito had improved the effectiveness of strange love.

Later that night Linda and I worked with Simone to firm up the Cogito part of strange love that we could control. Linda suggested to Simone to prime the girls on why they were giving strange love. Then I presented the language-thinking that Linda and I wanted everyone to adopt as our cogi for delivering strange love: *strange love is the sensory share or intimate touch given freely to enhance another person's Sentio sensitivity so that they might find greater freedom for all.*

The following day I watched as Simone met with the students and girls in our lab, teaching them and helping them perfect their delivery of eye touching embraces and French kisses as they learned to direct their Intentio from Sentio to visit my suggested strange-love-cogi and then to redirect their Intentios back to the French kiss moment in Sentio. Smiling to myself and filled with joy, I continued watching as twenty of my classmates got to receive a French kiss from Simone. How awesome!

By the end of the day, my classmates were so good that they could deliver the fifteen-second kisses without looking at a watch. Then Simone explained to me that she and Anal had figured out that eye touching for about five seconds without talking seemed to be the key to initiating a strong Intentio from Sentio for the most effective strange love. Anal had suggested eye touching.

I warmed on the inside because Anal had benefited from my eye touching, which my mother had taught me growing up at Essence, and now he was using the technique to help others.

After Simone and Anal experimented with the longer eye touches on several students, I reviewed the students Sentio results and concurred with their conclusion. I gave my approval for the use of longer eye touching and not talking before administering strange love. Simone and Anal grinned at each other. I sensed they'd developed a strong Sentio connection.

53

During spring break, Linda and I had 7B all to ourselves. Simone, Anal, Tinker, and Sassy had moved into 7C. Lar, Diana, Barbara, and Bob had moved into 7A. Fancy and Dr. Sol were considering moving into 7B with Linda and me, but for now we were all alone.

Late on Friday night Linda and I lay together on the window seat looking out at the starry sky.

"Linda, how did you get interested in touch?"

She turned to face me and twirled the hair on my chest with her finger. She looked at me with the eyes of a great, humanistic doctor, and I could tell she was getting ready to share a great story.

"I became interested in the power of touch while doing pediatrics. The little children who faced death from leukemia introduced me to the power of touch. It took me a few months to understand what their touches were doing to me. Several children had affected me, profoundly. Then I realized many of the children continued to fight leukemia not so much for their lives, but for we the living."

"The children who were dying fought death for us?"

"Yes, they suffered through the horrible treatments and multiple relapses for us. Several of the children confided in me they knew they were going to die, yet they fought to live to free us. They touched my heart. Their touches during their moments of agony . . . I'll never forget their tiny hands reaching and touching me as I tried to start IVs in their scarred, little veins."

Linda hesitated and struggled to get out her words. Her description brought tears to my eyes.

"There was a little girl I'd grown very fond of with recurrent lymphocytic leukemia. One night she got very sick and couldn't breathe—"

Linda broke down in tears, and I understood her sadness, without her saying a word. She sobbed in my arms for several minutes before composing herself.

"The little girl's name was Jaclyn. She was a cute blue-eyed, sandy-haired orphan. She had just turned six when her disease went into blast crisis. I was part of her treatment team, and for six weeks we blasted her body with the strongest chemicals known. She got better—or at least we thought her cell count numbers were better—and we discharged her to the orphanage with the plan to check her cell counts the following week in the pediatric clinic.

"Two days later, I was called to admit her through the ER. I rushed to be with her because I knew how serious such an early relapse was. I made it just in time. She grasped my hand, gave a gentle squeeze, and said goodbye with her eyes. Then she let out her last breath. Her death came like a thief in the night. And I believe she held on till I arrived in the ER so that she could set me free with the touch of her sweet little hand. I'll never forget her eyes as she reached to free me. Her panic had disappeared, and her eyes had filled with love. After she touched my hand, she let out her last breath. I tried to save her, but it was no use.

"It has taken me a long time to understand what she was doing. I felt her strange love then; I just didn't understand what it was. Jaci and I were like sisters. I'd only known her for six weeks, yet I knew her better than anyone I'd ever known and she, me. When she gave me her farewell squeeze, I felt a freedom that I'd never experienced before that moment, and I know now that Jaclyn is free."

I looked at Linda, and her face glowed. I felt like crying for her, for her loss of Jaci.

"Jaci was a beautiful little girl," I said, holding back my emotions. She was just like Linda.

Linda and I held each other, looking up at the stars flickering above the harbor on the heavenly canopy. I pointed out Polaris, the North Star, which had begun humankind's journey to external freedom.

Linda smiled. "Jaci's there."

CHAPTER

54

I sat reviewing the results at Linda's desk in the eleventh-floor research laboratory while she looked over my shoulder. It turned out that BSP did not completely disappear in children four years of age and older or adults. The blood levels dropped below the laboratory's ability to measure at age four, the 10ug/100ml threshold. That was good news, according to Dr. Sol, because the genes used for BSP's production were still turned on, which made it easier to stimulate production of the molecule.

Linda's baseline BSP level was 50 ug/100 ml, and her baseline Sentio amplitude was 200 uv. I knew her baselines would be high. My baseline BSP level and my baseline Sentio amplitude were twice as high as Linda's, and oddly my BSP measure was the same as most newborn babies. I read our results out loud, and Linda reached for my hand and squeezed. I looked at the other results and correlations, which Linda and Dr. Wolf had made.

Most of the student volunteers fell into the <10 ug/100 ml category for BSP, with low Sentio amplitudes, around 50uv–100uv. The measures of Milly's girls, the student volunteers, and our own results had allowed them to correlate BSP levels with Sentio wave uv amplitudes, producing a curve—Sentio uv versus BSP ug/ml—which would allow us to predict BSP levels by knowing the Sentio uv measure.

Dr. Wolf brought the latest results from her office and laid them on Linda's desk. The results of my classmates after visiting the House of Essence and receiving strange love were interesting. Sentio amplitude increased immediately after strange love as measured in Zeni, but increases in blood BSP levels lagged by a couple of hours. Dr. Sol had told Dr. Wolf he believed the blood-brain barrier contibuted to the lag. Dr. Wolf expressed her agreement with his explanation. I agreed. It made sense.

The other important finding was that BSP levels had increased in both the giver and receiver of Linda's precessing kiss and continued to increase with more strange love; however, Linda had given the girls and students memory tests, and the memory gains seen initially in week one did wane for Milly's girls—the givers of the precessing kiss—in week two, suggesting the loss of strangeness did have an effect on memory gains. Linda didn't seem upset by the results. The BSP increases and Sentio amplitude gains were far more important.

I laughed when Linda pointed to the next page of results. It had taken four weeks to boost Anal, Lar, and Tinker's BSP levels to Linda's baseline level.

"I think the guys enjoyed their slow response because they got to receive more strange love," I said.

"Yes, but we worked hard to increase their levels," Linda said, "Which boosted our own levels too. Look." She pointed to the bottom of the page at the most recent BSP measures for her, Simone, and Diana. Their results were the same: 75 ug/100 ml.

I caressed Linda's hand on my shoulder. "I love Diana and Simone."

Diana and Simone were extra special to me because they had responded to my strange love early on, which gave me hope that strange love alone might deliver a freeing Sentio experience to the masses.

Linda leaned over my shoulder and kissed my cheek. "They're amazing young women. I love them too. They really helped Lar."

"Yes, they did. I have to admit I felt envious of Lar when you, Diana, Simone, and Dr. Wolf teamed up, giving him kisses and hugs and then petting him as if he were a baby." I smiled at Dr. Wolf, who smiled at me with her eyes. I was truly happy for Lar; he was a different man now and Sentiomate with Diana.

Linda turned the next page of the results and read aloud. "After two weeks of strange love, Barbara and Dr. Wolf elevated their BSPs to 50 ug/100 ml and Sentios to 200 uv."

"Because I administered their strange love," I joked, knowing they had both started with higher baselines than Lar, Tinker, and Anal, who'd required four weeks to reach the same levels.

"Let's get back to work," Dr. Wolf said. "We've thirty new students coming for testing this morning."

CHAPTER

55

Linda and I enjoyed the sounds of romantic music on Sunday night. Smetana's "The Moldau" played on my disc player. I sat in the rocking chair, looking out at the small lights on boats in the harbor, deep in thought, while Linda hummed the magical flowing sounds of the Vltava River, cleaning our kitchen.

Three months had passed, and our research was progressing better than expected. Simone and Diana had become the most powerful strange lovers for our new student volunteers. Anal had fallen in love with Simone just as Linda had predicted. Anal and Simone had perfected the use of eye touching as a way of connecting and generating the most effective form of strange love. I could not have been more proud of them and how they both had changed after finding their sense of being in Sentio. Anal and I frequently shared embraces for strange love now, which never would have happened six months ago.

All my classmates had participated in Intimate Touch Week after exams. Dr. Wolf and Linda allowed Simone, Anal, and Milly's girls to participate as well. Simone and Anal had taught all of Milly's girls—now about thirty throughout the city of Boston—and my classmates how to give strange love, and they all continued to administer hugs and French kisses to one another during strange-love parties held after Intimate Touch Week.

For several weeks after Touch Week, we played music, danced, and shared beer and wine on Friday nights at the arboretum and then retreated to the House of Essence for what Lar called the after-hours party for strange love. We'd started the parties because Lar and Tinker thought they'd be fun, and they were. I'd also studied my classmates after the parties, and they'd had positive Sentio responses, measured in Zeni. Simone had invited some of her old faculty friends to the parties, and their pre and post responses had been encouraging as well.

Linda finished in the kitchen and joined me in the rocker, sitting in my lap, hugging my neck, telling me how much she loved me. I knew her Intentio was enjoying her romantic tracts for pleasure. I massaged her shoulders hoping to light up her erotic tracts. We rocked in silence rubbing on each other for several minutes before heading to the loft bedroom for our rendezvous with erotic pleasure.

▲ ▲ ▲

We spent all day Monday in the eleventh-floor lab working with second-year medical students, freeing their Intentios with the blue Sentio experience in Zeni. Anal and Simone worked with us and left around 9:00 p.m. Linda and I stayed late looking at new mathematical, geometric, and physics test results from the previous week. We compared the results of the first-year students: their Sentio amplitudes for weeks four and twelve with their mathematical, geometric, and physics test scores for the same weeks, four and twelve. The students' test scores had improved in conjunction with higher Sentio amplitudes. There was definitely a strong positive correlation.

"Woohoo!" I said, looking over Linda's shoulder. "This means as Sentio amplitude increases Intentio is dwelling in Sentio."

Linda turned her head and found my eyes. "I think you're right."

I thought about how my fellow students had changed over the last two months after Zeni and strange love as Anal had changed. Their eyes no longer darted around, and they were so tuned in to Sentio.

Then it hit me like a ton of bricks. I felt woozy. I looked at Linda. "Come with me. You're not going to believe this."

I grabbed her by the hand.

"What? Wait; I've got to turn out the lights and lock the door."

"The sensory deprived rats in the basement. I've got to show you."

We locked up and hurried to the lift. We dropped down to the basement floor. I pulled Linda by the arm, running down the hallway through the double doors. The smell of sawdust and urine filled the air. I pushed open the lab door, flipped on the lights, and led Linda to the observation room. The TV monitors were on. I took a seat and rolled the chair toward the far monitor on the left. Where were the rats?

"Oh, I get queasy watching these large gopher rats," said Linda, taking a seat.

"Where are they?" I said.

"They must be sleeping."

I slapped the counter twice, and the rats awoke. Their eyes darted all around just like Anal's eyes used to dart.

Linda stood up, her eyes glued to the far monitor screen.

"You see, don't you?" I said, and looked at Linda, who remained mesmerized staring at the monitor screen. "Sentio deprivation is a form of sensory deprivation."

Linda continued to stare, transfixed by the large rat with darting eyes.

"Anal and my classmates," I said.

Linda moved her head slowly from side to side, again and again.

"This is what's happening in America, the reason for the missing Y and everything else I told you about."

"Oh my God," Linda whispered. "Americans are agitated, paranoid, and depressed, and they are killing one another. The senseless acts of violence and all the trauma cases in America. They are sensory deprived? I mean Sentio deprived."

"Yes. Sentio deprivation produces the same effects on humans as sensory deprivation does to Dr. Sol's rats. Sentio deprivation is a form of sensory deprivation."

"Americans are behaving like Dr. Sol's sensory-deprived rats," Linda said.

"The citizens don't know, and telling them won't help."

"We've got to tell Dr. Sol."

"No, not yet," I said. "I have an idea. It's something big. It's part of my last vision for freedom experience."

I'd explained about my vision of seeing Milly's girls and my classmates on a field sharing strange love with a large crowd of people.

Linda's face grew pale. "I don't know. That could be dangerous. Americans are out of control. It's too risky."

"Sentio deprivation is no longer just about liberty; it's about life and death," I said, looking into Linda's worried eyes.

She grabbed my hand and led me out of the smelly lab. We walked to an exit door, climbed a flight of stairs, and exited to the outside. Once beyond the campus under the starry sky, walking down Paul Revere Street, Linda let go of my hand and ran ahead.

"What are you doing? Where are you going?" I yelled, and ran after her.

Linda turned and her brown eyes glistened. She ran toward me, her white lab coat lifting in the air like a cape. She jumped into my arms, hugging my neck tightly, sending us into a spin. I went with her force and began to twirl, hugging her tightly, her legs flying in the air. Linda was crying, sobbing as we twirled.

"I don't want anything to happen to you. I'm afraid," she said. "I've seen what the deprived rats do to each other . . . when they're housed together."

I started crying as we continued to twirl round and round. I didn't want to stop. We twirled and twirled. As I slowed, Linda pulled back and smiled through her tears.

"We'll be together for eternity," I said. "We're Sentiomates forever."

I let Linda down, and we wiped our tears.

"Let's talk to Dr. Sol," Linda said.

"Okay," I agreed.

Her brown eyes glistened again, and I embraced her.

"We'll be fine. Everything will work out," I said.

Linda hugged my neck. "You're the love of my life."

I held my tears as Linda released me. She grabbed my hand and led as we walked and then skipped back to the House of Essence.

CHAPTER

56

The next morning I paid a visit to Dr. Sol in his office on the seventh floor. It was the third day of May.

I stood in his office doorway. "Hello," I whispered.

Seated at his desk, Dr. Sol glanced at me, looking up from a book. "Come in, Dasein. Have a seat."

I sat in the armchair. Dr. Sol closed his book and found my eyes. "Dasein, you look upset. What can I do for you?"

I didn't know where to start. I let out a sigh and explained what I'd experienced after arriving in America, including with the interns, residents, medical students, and Anal. I explained my theory about the rats and his sensory deprivation research. I told him that human Sentio deprivation was a form of true sensory deprivation. But he didn't seem to understand.

Then I explained my observations about Anal and the medical students who had darting eyes before being freed from Cogito. "Since their Intentios have been freed to dwell in Sentio, their eyes no longer dart."

"I see," Dr. Sol said, nodding his head. "Great observations. But darting eyes are nonspecific. A hundred-and-one things could explain your observation. It's a clinical observation and nothing more. I wouldn't make too much of it."

I couldn't believe his response. "But what if I'm right?"

"We're studying biomarkers in the deprived rats: their

262

cortisol, growth hormone, glucose, adrenaline, etc. Then we'll correlate their responses looking for causality, which will allow us to understand human responses to sensory deprivation. Humans with slightly elevated cortisol may respond to more sunlight, for example."

"But what about BSP?"

"That's a new and difficult marker to study outside of humans. Since it disappears in most healthy humans, we have a long way to go before we can make correlations with pathologic conditions like depression and low levels of BSP. Don't worry, Dasein. If your observations are true about Sentio deprivation being a form of sensory deprivation, we'll soon have other biomarkers to correlate."

"That could take forever," I said. "So many people might have to suffer needlessly."

"Science demands it; otherwise, we'd have people suffering needlessly from pet theories," he said, paused for a moment, and found my eyes. "What if someone discovered that tiny electrical shocks to the eyelids fixed blepharospasm, blinking eyes, then they decided to eradicate the world of nervous blinkers, applying the shocks prophylactically? We might have a lot more blinkers." Dr. Sol smiled. "We might create more darting-eyed citizens by administering prophylactic strange love."

My chest ached. I looked down at the journals and books on his office floor then found Dr. Sol's eyes. "I guess you're right," I said, realizing my observations were impossible to prove.

"No worries, Dasein. We'll make some sense of all this next year when we look at the deprived rats' biomarker results."

Then a light bulb went off in my head. "I've got an idea," I said, thinking Dr. Sol would like it because my idea would provide new human BSP biomarker data, and it would give us a chance to free the Americans in large numbers. "I propose that we throw a grand strange love party, a rally for freedom, and then study the BSP and Sentio amplitude responses of a small group of students attending the rally who are virgin to strange love."

Dr. Sol grinned. "Now that's an intriguing proposal."

I explained that I wanted to take our discovery to the masses, to the next level for freedom, and—if my observations were true—to save the Americans from the fate of the sensory deprived rats. "We won't have to wait a year for sensory deprived rat data and then several more years for human correlation studies."

Dr. Sol rubbed his chin as if he had a goatee like Uncle Poulou. "Hmm."

I thought he'd understood and liked my idea, but then he narrowed his eyes. "It sounds like you want to have a hippie convention here at Harvard."

I couldn't keep from raising the corners of my mouth. "Linda said my plan reminded her of the hippies."

She'd explained to me the American Sentio movement of the sixties that emerged at the intersection of two streets, Haight and Ashbury, in San Francisco.

Dr. Sol warned me that Americans could react in ways we couldn't possibly predict. Some of the participants might get the wrong idea about an army of lovers.

"I'll print fliers, and we'll get consents," I said. Linda had already mentioned she'd done the same for her French Kiss and Memory Study.

Dr. Sol shook his head from side to side and pursed his lips.

I thought for a moment about Linda and all of my American friends. The potential benefits far outweighed the risks. "Americans are dying every day," I said. "They need hope. And freedom demands taking risks as I took a great risk by following my Compass of Freedom vision, leaving my home in Andorra, and coming to Harvard." I knew in my Sentio from my experiences in America that it was now or perhaps never for many of the citizens.

Dr. Sol stood, looking out his window. A white dove had landed on the tarnished copper cupola of the hospital building. I didn't say anything. After a long moment he furrowed his brow and scratched the back of his head. Finally, he turned into my gaze and agreed with my plan in principle and said he'd approach the administration about my idea. "Two doctors on the human experiments committee trained at UC San Francisco during the sixties. If they respond favorably, I'll seek their approval to have a public gathering for Project Freedom."

He'd named my plan Project Freedom. Smiling internally, I whispered a thank you, shook his hand, and departed.

I met Linda on the eleventh floor. With mixed emotions, I explained. When I told her what Dr. Sol had said about my observations, that darting eyes was a nonspecific finding, she seemed relieved. I admitted I felt relieved too. I told her about my plan to use students who have never been exposed to strange love as a study group. She hugged me and expressed hope that Dr. Sol would gain approval for my plan.

"Our mission," she said.

Her strange love had elevated me. At that moment I wanted nothing more than to make strange love available to everyone. Project Freedom was my—our—mission, my goal since my Compass of Freedom experience at the age of fourteen.

Weeks passed with no word on the project rally. On the last Monday in May, Linda and I got up early, readied for work, and shared a bagel with strawberry cream cheese and a glass of milk.

Chewing on a bite of bagel, I enjoyed the morning view of the harbor from the sofa. Linda sat back in the rocking chair, found my eyes, and said, "Dr. Sol decided our BSP goal should be 50 ug/100ml and our Sentio goal 200 uv because that seems to be the threshold for being able to use one's selective attention agency to deliver the most effective strange love."

I nodded as I swallowed another bite of the bagel. "I agree. We need to get going. I want to stop by Dr. Sol's lab and ask him if he has heard anything from the administration about our rally."

Linda gulped down the last of her milk, then we headed to the sensory deprivation building. After a silent, brisk walk, we arrived and waited for the lift on the ground floor.

I shot Linda a smile. "So, what does Dr. Sol do in his secret, eleventh-floor research lab?"

"He studies professional athletes, and he uses associates to treat the sensory-deprived faculty members at Harvard with his experimental therapy—deep massage with full-spectrum tactile stimulation. Some people jokingly call it S&M."

We hurried into the lift, and Linda pushed #11.

"What do the S and M stand for?" I asked.

Linda pinched my arm as if I were being difficult.

"No, really, I don't know."

"Yes, you do."

I shook my head.

"Really?" Her voice grew serious. "The associates provide the touch that spans from the slightest tickle of a feather to the snap of a leather whip against your back, just beneath the threshold of tissue injury."

Perplexed, I wrinkled my brow. S&M sounded like something my uncle Poulou would enjoy, but I couldn't believe the Harvard faculty members that I knew would enjoy it.

We got off the lift and walked into our lab. Dr. Wolf had Anal hooked up and was preparing to place him inside Zeni, so I walked down the hall and knocked on Dr. Sol's lab door. There was no answer, and the lights were off. I checked his office, two doors down from the lab, and no answer.

I walked back to find Linda and wondered what Dr. Sol thought he'd discovered with his strange tactile therapy, perhaps a biomolecule for pain with a positive side effect.

I asked Linda, and she explained to me that S&M was more like a simulation for pain or surrogate pain, not real pain.

"It's an exhilarating therapy. Dr. Sol requires all his research fellows to participate in therapy, and I used to look forward to my sessions," Linda said.

"What's exhilarating?" asked Dr. Wolf as she stepped around from behind Zeni.

Linda looked at her and whispered, apparently not wanting Anal to hear. "S&M."

Dr. Wolf smiled.

"How about medical students; can we take the therapy?" I asked Linda in a low voice.

"No, not S&M therapy. Sorry."

"Why?"

"Because of an incident between Dr. Sol and a young

female student a few years ago. The S&M research lab has been forbidden to students since then."

I thought about the associates who administer S&M and remembered that I'd probably met three of them in the elevator one day.

"I believe I met some of the associates in the elevator one day. They reminded me of Milly's girls. They were good eye touchers."

"Yes, they're good eye touchers," Linda said, grinning. "Most of the associates are attractive young dancers and performers from New York with a special interest in intimate touch research, and Dr. Sol gives them a nice stipend as compensation for their travel and assistance."

"Do they dance?"

"Well, sometimes. But mostly they deliver and receive tactile stimulation."

"I think it's odd."

"What is?"

"The associates sound like orphans looking for strange love. I see the faces of the orphans that I grew up with everywhere in America. But they will not know what they are searching for unless we help them find it."

"I guess we are all orphans in a way until we find Sentio and strange love." Linda moved her face, almost touching mine, and gave a warm stare with her soft, brown eyes. She knew the secret: living a life for greater freedom for all, by giving love for freedom—

Dr. Sol called my name from just outside the research lab door. He met my eyes as soon as I walked into the hall. "We've been approved for July 4th and have permission to use the main soccer field for our rally. The summer students and faculty are getting notifications about the event today so spread the word."

I whispered as loud as I could, "Hooray!" and embraced Dr. Sol. Our Project Freedom rally was finally approved.

58

Around six in the evening, the last Friday of June, we sat in Milly's new white wicker chairs on the porch at the House of Essence.

Simone smiled. "We're ready for something big!"

Anal leaned over and kissed Simone on the cheek. Milly came onto the porch and got hugs from Lar, Diana, and Barbara. I thought to myself that we'd become gladiator strange lovers. We'd become so efficient in raising BSP, and I loved living around other gladiator lovers. We could make each other's Sentios surge by a simple touch. Diana could boost my Sentio by touching my ear with her lips, and when Linda rubbed my forearm with her soft fingertips, I could feel my sensitivity going through the roof. And our BSP levels had continued to rise, which I believed allowed us to have a greater impact on each other. Strange love had a compounding effect, which was extraordinary to experience.

I got up from my chair, hugged Milly, and joined her on the swing. Diana engaged Simone in conversation and agreed with her that we were ready to do something big. I heard Simone ask Fancy how strange love compared to the love she'd received when she was in Alcoholics Anonymous.

"No comparison," Fancy replied, and shot a smile at me.

Milly's phone rang, and she motioned for me to answer. I picked up the receiver on the table next to the swing. It was Dr. Sol.

"Where is everyone?" he asked.

"We're sitting on the porch at the House of Essence. Simone and I are trying to think of some big things to do." I talked about our group of gladiator strange lovers, and how our capability to deliver strange love had grown.

Dr. Sol chuckled at my suggestions. "I'm finishing up in the lab, and I'll be right over."

Within thirty minutes, Dr. Sol's bald head bobbed as he walked up Double Banger Street's uneven sidewalk wearing a black coat, white shirt, and red tie. By the time he reached the porch, the girls had stood to share hugs with him. Fancy especially loved Dr. Sol; for some reason, she favored him and embraced him first.

After all the embraces, Dr. Sol looked for a seat. I moved to a rocker next to Linda, and he took my seat on the swing next to Milly. He found my eyes. "Is everything ready for the rally for Project Freedom next week?"

I nodded confidently. "Yes, we're ready."

"Simone and the girls will have to dress appropriately, perhaps business attire and white lab coats," he said.

"Yes, of course," Linda replied.

Simone grabbed Dr. Sol's hands, pulled him into an embrace, and gave him a kiss on his lips. When she released him, Dr. Sol struggled to keep from falling into the swing. She'd precessed him.

"We are going to free the slaves of Harvard!" Simone exclaimed.

Dr. Sol dropped back onto the swing, licking his lips. "Yum, peach," he said with a cute little smile. "Yes, Simone will free them or else." He threw up his hands as if he were surrendering to Simone's desire to free him.

I walked over and gave him a high five.

Simone reminded us that although we were far more powerful strange lovers today, the Sentio compatibility issue, the harmony needed to generate an Intentio for strange love, would pose a problem when we began sharing strange love with the public. I winked at Linda because she and I had discussed this concern the previous night.

"Simone, I believe in you. I know you'll figure out a way around this," I said.

The Sentio harmony issue was raised by Sassy because she didn't like kissing guys who smelled bad, had bad teeth, or looked dirty. Linda and I didn't believe this would be a problem with the student rally. But Sassy and Simone were right; Sentio compatibility would be an obstacle when delivering strange love to the masses.

I believed Simone would find a solution, and I could tell she felt the power of our confidence in her. Her face was glowing. She grinned at me.

Linda changed the subject and talked about how much fun we were going to have on the Fourth. She and I had talked and talked about Project Freedom, and I believed she was looking forward to our experiment as a celebration of love and freedom on the day Americans celebrated their freedom from British colonial rule.

Diana smiled at Simone and complimented her for adding the eye touching. Anal beamed at Simone.

"Simone has perfected the fifteen-second French kiss and the thirty-second eye-touching hug," I said, and glanced at Dr. Sol. "And some of the girls are going to deliver thirty-second kisses."

"Marvelous!" he exclaimed.

"After the girls became aware of Sentio through Zeni mapping, their strange love IQ improved dramatically," Simone told him. "I just showed them the kissing technique that Linda taught me." She sounded so modest.

"Yes, the awareness of Sentio, achieved in Zeni, has a much more profound impact than my explanation of the existence of Sentio consciousness with language alone," Dr. Sol said. "I owe that discovery to Dasein. His realization of the benefit of the Zeni experience has had a profound effect on the freshman medical students and my professional athletes too."

Dr. Sol rolled to his feet and gave Milly an embrace, walked over, and kissed Fancy's cheek, then turned toward me with a smile. "I listened to the radio weather channel WBZ earlier. The Fourth of July is supposed to be sunny and clear. We'll have great weather for our Project Freedom rally."

"Awesome. Thanks, Dr. Sol," I said.

Linda got up and excitedly hugged him goodbye.

Later, after everyone had left, Linda and I lay holding each other on the porch swing.

"*Our mission* . . . I liked the sound of that," I said.

Linda repeated in a soft voice, "Yes, our mission. We are going to free the slaves, break through the intimacy barrier in the workplace, and more."

I pulled her into a tight embrace and tickled her. She hiccupped and raised her hand to muffle her laugh. She reminded me not to tickle her, and then she tickled my ribs.

Stretching after Linda's tickles, I leaned back and thought of all the good things we'd achieved. After a few moments I felt a nervous quiver in my chest, and a knot formed in my throat. I swallowed and the knot subsided.

"Why are you so quiet?" Linda asked with concern, and turned touching my eyes with hers.

"Oh, nothing. It felt like something was stuck in my throat."

"What?"

"I guess I'm nervous about freeing the students and faculty. The problem, of course, is that their BSP levels are going to be very low or nonexistent and slow to respond."

"It's just one rally. There will be more," she said with a voice of optimism.

"But will the rally be able to deliver enough strange

love to free their Intentios from Cogito without the laborious freeing experience in Zeni?" I asked. "What if we fail to register any improvement?"

"If we fail, we'll default to Zeni." Linda turned and kissed my lips, caressing my face with her fingertips. "My Sentiomate forever."

I looked into her eyes, and our Intentios merged. We were one.

CHAPTER

59

Our big day arrived. I sat on the window seat wearing my red bandana, lucky white shirt, jeans, and long lab coat, looking out at the harbor, waiting for Linda to change clothes for the rally. Dr. Sol had told the Harvard administrators the purpose of our demonstration was so that we could measure BSP levels of our volunteers' before and after the experience of intimate human touch in the field. In truth, I wanted our rally to ignite a revolution of consciousness, which would spread from city to city, state to state, and all over the world.

I remembered two days ago when Linda, Dr. Wolf, and I had reviewed the Sentio amplitude gains from our recent student trials during which we used thirty-, forty-, and sixty-second French kisses to administer strange love. Oddly, the forty- and sixty-second kisses had proven less potent than the fifteen-second kisses.

The thirty-second French kiss was the most potent form of strange love we'd discovered to date, but because of the time issue, only ten seconds from forty-seconds, it had risks. I preferred the fifteen-second kisses. Simone and her strange lovers wanted to use the thirty-second kisses at the rally, so Dr. Wolf, Linda, Dr. Sol, and I had conferred and gave the okay—with our warning. We suggested to Simone that any of her lovers engaging in the longer kisses needed to carry a thirty-second alarm device. I was nervous about the longer kisses becoming a distraction and a less effective form of strange love.

I wanted our rally to deliver a life-changing aware-ness experience, the Sentio sense of being experience. Linda and I believed the cumulative energy of a mass of people exchanging the most powerful form of love ever discovered would free their Intentios to experience their Sentios. We were also counting on the magic of our sunset experience to assist their Intentios to continue dwelling in Sentio. But would the effect persist? We wouldn't know until our follow-up studies on our thirty-student study group.

Linda descended the bedroom loft steps in her long, white lab coat and with a red bandana around her neck. We embraced then hurried to join the others on the porch. It was late in the afternoon. I led Linda out the front door onto the porch. Our army of lovers stood all around—on the porch, the patio, and the street in front of the House of Essence. Our numbers had grown to more than three hundred. Milly hugged me, and I felt so much love from her. Then Milly hugged Linda. After a few moments Linda and I turned holding hands, facing our group. I lifted our hands above our heads and looked out at our army of lovers, who produced a cheer. They all wore red bandanas; some wore them around their heads, and others around their necks. They cheered for several minutes. I could hear Lar's whis-tled sounds coming from the street.

Simone used a bullhorn from the other side of the porch to congratulate Milly's girls, the students, and Dr. Sol's associates for perfecting intimate touch with strange love intent. Two days earlier, Dr. Sol had allowed Simone to train his S&M associates on how to give strange love for the rally. The associates, about forty in number, stood on the street waving their hands in unison as Simone and the others applauded for them.

I moved next to Simone on the porch while Linda

stepped down to the patio. Linda walked over to the tables on the patio where the students in our study group had queued to have their blood drawn by a team of technicians from the hospital lab. I watched as Linda helped draw blood from a young lady who was in the study group. The group was comprised of thirty students all virgin to strange love. The virgin-students wore white bandanas

Simone finished speaking about Harvard and Dr. Sol, and then she gave words of gratitude and encouragement to the students through the horn. I grabbed the horn and expressed my gratitude and said we needed to get moving. Simone and I joined our group on the street. We marched our army toward the soccer field of Harvard's undergraduate campus where we would soon rally, sharing strange love, and then enjoy a sunset experience. We walked down Double Banger Street, stopping traffic as we cut across Paul Revere Street and continued north. Linda caught up. She'd finished collecting all the blood samples for BSP measures and had left Anal in charge of taking the samples to the hospital lab.

I flashed a big smile of thanks at Linda and held her hand as she walked alongside me. Her lab coat pockets bulged, loaded with extra needles and syringes. I told her how eager I was to measure the Sentio wave amplitudes of the students in Zeni tomorrow and compare the new numbers with the measures we'd obtained last week.

Linda smiled confidently and squeezed my hand. "I know what we'll find."

We walked onto the soccer field and continued up the steps of the large stage while the Harvard faculty and undergraduate students streamed onto the field through the main entrance, joining our troop. Barbara, Izzie, and many others had been handing out fliers and obtaining consents at the stadium entry gates.

Simone signaled for the lovers to spread out. She looked excited and beautiful, her hair fixed atop her head, and she had on her lacy white lab coat with the word Harvard embroidered in crimson, her red bandana around her neck. She smiled nervously as we stood on the platform together facing the sea of people. We played "Imagine" on the sound system while watching more and more people gathering.

Fireworks were planned to begin immediately after our sunset experience, and Tinker informed me everything was set. I looked out at the crowd, and my insides began to shake.

I had an uneasy feeling about strange love and how it would be received. I wondered if my nervousness had something to do with Independence Day and Project Freedom being celebrated together. I realized then the magnitude of the moment. This was my vision coming true. We were starting a revolution of consciousness, the revolution to free Intentio from Cogito, and the world would never be the same again.

As the noise from the crowd grew, I whispered to Linda, "Let's give some strange love in honor of little Jaci." Linda's eyes twinkled as she reached and touched my hand.

A few minutes before sunset, the music stopped just as we'd rehearsed, and I picked up the microphone, preparing to address our army of lovers, the students, and faculty. I saw Dr. Sol climbing the steps in his long, white lab coat. Like clockwork, Dr. Sol was always right on time.

I introduced our team and our purpose for this rally. The crowd cheered. I paused for a long moment and then as the crowd grew silent, said, "Strange love is twice blessed to the giver and the receiver. It's the most authentic and true essence form of love. Unite, my American brothers and sisters! What do we have to lose but our chains to legal Cogito existence and nothingness?"

The crowd erupted in louder cheers. They knew from our brochure on Project Freedom that they would soon be receiving an experimental and powerful form of love.

"Strange love! Strange love!" the crowd chanted.

I could see Barbara, Izzie, Tinker, Diana, Sassy, Fancy, Pretty, Milly, Sophia, and Susan inching closer to the stage, and Anal was approaching, shouldering his way through the crowd. I looked down at Barbara who smiled at me. Behind my friends were several hundred, maybe a thousand, students and faculty. Over on the right side of the field, I waved at the Director, Robin his secretary, and the blue-haired secretary. The bald German fellows and Joe the chef were standing next to them. The chief of security, the man from parking, and Lisa the apartment finder were also among the crowd that was too large to count.

I spotted and waved to Norman Romsky, the professor from MIT I'd met on the plane almost a year ago. I'd called and invited him the week before, hoping he would attend.

"Strange love!" I said in his direction.

The crowd roared again.

Then I repeated, "Strange love is twice blessed. What do we have to lose but our chains to legal Cogito existence and nothingness? I promise to lead you to freedom."

Everyone started chanting, "Freedom! Liberty!"

"What about the IRS, the Department of Defense, and the National Guard?" a man somewhere in the crowd shouted through a bullhorn.

"What?" I asked.

Laughter erupted, and then the crowd grew quiet.

The man repeated, "What about the IRS?"

I located him on the left side of the field. He was a shirtless young man wearing shorts with something sticking out of his waistband.

I tried for a long moment in silence to catch his eyes, but he wouldn't make eye contact with me.

"Our army of strange lovers will rise up and love them back to the Consciousness of Eden," I said.

"The Feds will never let us go," the young man continued. They will pin us against the sea and crucify us."

I responded, "We are gladiator strange lovers. One of us can love ten of them. They do not stand a chance. Our army will grow into millions, and we will free the slaves all over the world."

The cheers were thunderous, and I noticed the sun had dipped toward the horizon. I gave my troops the order for the strange loving to begin. Our lovers began eye touching, then embraced those standing near, sharing hugs and French kisses with the students and faculty. As I looked around at my army of lovers, I was so proud. I wished that my mother, Aunt Helen, and Uncle Poulou could see what we were doing. I was setting the Americans free, like lifting a bird to fly for the first time after mending its injured wing.

I now truly believed we'd found a way to restore Sentio. The Romantics had failed over one hundred years ago. Then the hippies had tried again a few years ago in the sixties, but they'd lost their vision for freedom and love by turning to pleasure and drugs and dropping out. They didn't know about strange love or BSP. I raised my hands above my head giving the peace sign of the hippies, honoring them because their Sentio awareness had changed history, making it easier for us. And now it was our turn.

I turned my eyes into Linda's gaze and smiled—

An explosion rang out. I felt myself falling as the crowd screamed, gravity pulling me to the ground. Then I heard someone shout, "Dasein's been shot!"

Linda lifted my head off the stage, her face twisted with pain, mine and hers. I could feel her panic as she looked down at me.

"You can't die. I won't let you," she said, and cried.

I felt lifeless in her arms and strangely at peace. I didn't sense pandemonium. I could see my followers looking at one another with tears streaming down their cheeks, reaching out and holding hands. I could see everyone. I was floating above my body looking down on them. My Intentio was experiencing my surroundings through the aura of my body.

Linda continued sobbing as she ripped off my lucky white shirt and Dr. Sol began to compress my chest.

"Dasein has made it to the mountaintop." I heard a voice say. I felt joy for a moment, and then I felt the sadness of everyone around me. My lovers—Diana, Barbara, Fancy, Sassy, and the others—had surrounded my body, pulling for me to live, and I wanted to live for them so they could find freedom.

Simone's voice carried through the speakers. "Everyone, please stand still. Please, let's hold hands. We'll find a way to greater freedom for all on this day. Let our Intentios merge for one common cause: to keep Antonio alive.

"When darkness falls, I want all of you to remember that even though Antonio Dasein is no longer visible, his Intentio is still here in every one of us. He emerged in our world through his acts of love for freedom. We will always feel his love when we give and receive strange love for freedom. He is here among us, waving us onward toward the mountaintop of freedom," said Simone through tears, her voice quivering.

"Could someone shut her up?" I heard an unfamiliar voice say. "For God's sake, Dasein's not Jesus Christ."

I heard sirens blaring. The police and ambulance arrived. Lar, Tinker, Anal, Dr. Bock, and the chief of security had pounced on the guy who shot me and had his head pinned on the ground with his arms behind his back.

Linda and Dr. Sol hadn't given up. They were still working to resuscitate me. I heard Dr. Sol yell out that I was breathing then I felt his fingers against my neck. I was back inside my body, and I no longer needed chest compressions.

"I think the bullet pierced his pericardium and missed his heart," said Linda, now composed and speaking like a doctor. She was extracting blood from around my heart with one of the syringes from her lab coat.

"Great work, Linda," Dr. Sol said in jubilation. "The blood extracted relieved his pericardial tamponade. Here's another syringe. We'll leave the needle in till we can get him to the OR and explore the damage in his chest."

I sensed a glow from Linda's face. I imagined her eyes were smiling at me. After a long moment I was able to open my eyes for a second, and she was by my side. Her brow furrowed. The paramedics secured IVs in each arm and then lifted me onto a stretcher, and after carrying me off the stage, they hoisted me into the ambulance. As the vehicle galloped across the soccer field, I opened my eyes again and saw Dr. Sol hugging Linda inside the ambulance, and she was crying.

"He has a good steady pulse one hundred," the paramedic called out to his partner driving the vehicle. "Blood pressure is ninety over sixty."

"Notify Dr. Braunwald's thoracic trauma team," Dr. Sol said to the driver. "We'll need to perform an emergency thoracotomy; I want to take Antonio directly to an OR suite."

The siren blared.

CHAPTER

60

The nurse's station buzzed as the powwow ended.
Cheerful faces gabbed and sauntered in their crimson scrubs
while the medical clerk returned the patients' charts to the
rack. One could set his watch by the evening shift change
routine. At seven o'clock, the day shift vanished, and the
night shift nurses rolled the noisy medicine carts down the
hallway.

Dr. Sol waved at the nurses. The sixth-floor station of
Harvard's finest hospital for the sick and injured had become
his home away from his research laboratory since Antonio's
near-fatal shooting.

"Hello, Dr. Sol," greeted Mrs. Peebles, the medical
clerk, taking a seat at her desk.

"Hello, Peeby. How goes it?"

"Did you get a piece of Georgia's birthday cake?"

He shook his head no. "Tell her happy birthday for me."
He strolled around the counter and pulled Antonio's chart
from the rack.

"Antonio is doing well today," Mrs. Peebles smiled. "He
has company."

"Who?"

"I believe his mother is with him now. Simone, Diana,
Milly, and several of his medical student friends were here
earlier."

"Oh, thanks. I'm on my way to check on him." He shot her a smile, then reviewed Antonio's nurse's notes in the chart for a minute, and returned it to the rack. He shot Peeby another smile, "Later."

Dr. Sol buttoned his lab coat and ambled down the hall. He needed to talk with Antonio's mother about his condition. He stopped in front of the fourth door on the right and peeked inside. He could not believe his eyes. He stepped back and verified the room: 604.

A gorgeous lady with high cheekbones, rosy skin, and long brown hair in a green evening gown sat tall in the chair beside the bed. She looked too young to be the mother. He goggled over his reading glasses as she uncrossed and crossed her long, silky legs.

Surprised and intrigued, he knocked softly with his knuckle then pushed the door open. The lady turned, and her eyes embraced him.

"Antonio sleeps," she whispered with the hint of a foreign accent.

"I need to check; I won't disturb him," Dr. Sol promised.

He closed the door and found it hard to look away from the woman as he moved next to the bed, where his young friend lay motionless under a hospital gown. He picked up the clipboard hanging on the side rail to review the vital signs and most recent lab data.

Four days ago, he and Antonio had stood on the campus stage while students rallied for their groundbreaking medical research. His entire team, a half-dozen of the brightest minds in the world, celebrated. Then a gun went off. One wacko guy, apparently upset because his girlfriend participated in their research, had tried to kill Antonio and Project Freedom with a single bullet.

He replaced the clipboard and was heartened by Antonio's pink complexion, quite a contrast from his pallor in the ambulance. He closed his eyes in gratitude for the deliverance from that horrible moment, and then the memory of seeing Antonio's body in free fall, his lifeless face and blood bubbling from his chest wound, flashed in his mind—

"Is everything okay?" the woman interrupted in a kind and concerned voice.

Dr. Sol opened his eyes. "Yes, everything is fine," he responded, keeping his back toward her. He redirected his attention, gazed toward the monitor screen on the other side of the bed, and then peeked at the chest wound and retention sutures. He lifted the uncoiled chest tube and drained the residual contents. The amount of drainage had improved.

He turned and greeted the lady's eyes.

"I'm Dr. Solomon Sol," he said in a hushed tone. "Antonio is doing well. I think we'll be able to remove his chest tube tomorrow."

"Merci. Thank you," she said.

Dr. Sol thought he heard her stomach growl.

"Are you hungry? I can order you a tray."

She shook her head. "No, thank you."

Looking at her angelic face, Dr. Sol thought perhaps the lady was the mother. He knew Antonio had been adopted and raised under unusual circumstances in Andorra. He hesitated then asked, "Are you Antonio's mother?"

"No, his mother, Marie, went with Dr. Hedrick and his uncle, Poulou, to get dinner. I'm his aunt, Helen."

"Helen Moyen the philosopher?" he asked, surprised. She looked far too young.

She grinned. "I prefer to think of myself as a Sentio being, a being in the world, experiencing subjectivity and objectivity as one and the same."

He smiled and nodded. He still couldn't believe she was the famous philosopher, but who else save Helen Moyen could give a response like that?

"Are you a professor?"

"I hold the William James Chair, and yes, I am a professor of consciousness research." He paused. "I used to do thoracic surgery, but now I research the mind."

"Antonio wrote to me about you."

"Enough about me, I have read your incredible book on freedom. Antonio and I talk about you all the time. I imagined you were much older. You are so young."

He had just finished reading her book *Intentialism*, the philosophy of true freedom, for the third time, the 1976 edition.

She smiled modestly and after an uncomfortable moment of silence said, "Thank you."

He knew from studying her philosophy and her assertions about consciousness that she was a woman of few words.

"Do you mind if we talk?" he asked, hoping she'd agree. "I want your insight on what happened here—"

His pager went off. He reached into his lab coat pocket and recognized the number.

"I'll be right back."

Dr. Sol hurried to the nurse's station and called Milly's number.

"Hello, hello?"

"How is he?" It was Fancy.

"Fancy, sweetheart, Antonio is doing well today," he said. "I'll call you in thirty minutes. Bye, baby."

He hung up the phone, handed his pager to Peeby, and told her to cover for him. He dashed back to 604.

Helen met Dr. Sol's eyes and grinned as he moved quickly and found his chair. She looked at Antonio who remained asleep. "We can talk, and you can call me Helen."

"Wonderful," Dr. Sol responded. He unbuttoned his lab coat and leaned forward, clasping his hands around his raised knee, eager to explore the most brilliant ontological thinker he'd ever read. And he wanted to ask about her philosophy of freedom.

She lifted her large, brown eyes into his gaze as if raising an imaginary curtain and said, "I know you and Antonio found the biomolecule of freedom. Antonio wrote to me about it."

He smiled at her way, a woman of few words and no pretense. "Yes, I—we found BSP. Antonio discovered how the exchange of consensual intimate touch coupled with a unique intention stimulates the body to produce the molecule." Dr. Sol scooted his chair closer and lowered his voice. "Antonio found the only way to increase the levels of the molecule. The peptide precursor is too big for oral administration. We've tried administering the active molecule—injecting, infusing, sublingual—but to little avail. The molecule breaks apart."

"Did you find the molecule's receptor?" Helen asked.

"The molecule acts as a receptor for itself. Antonio

proposed the idea. At threshold concentrations, the molecule induces conformational changes and binds to itself on the cell membrane.

"Antonio named the act of human touch required to produce the molecule, strange love. He told me he had learned a version of strange love growing up at the orphanage in Andorra."

"You do not know what he means to us. Words cannot explain," she said, her voice filled with emotion.

"Antonio has become a great leader at Harvard. I love him," Dr. Sol whispered. "He means the world to me. Our entire team fought to save him. Dr. Hedrick deserves the credit for saving his life."

"Yes, I heard, and I met her. She is a wonderful young lady and reminds me of Antonio's mother, Marie."

"Next to Antonio, Dr. Linda Hedrick is the most brilliant student I've ever taught, and I have been here for twenty years."

"Do you understand what your discovery means?" Helen asked.

Dr. Sol nodded. "I think we found the molecule responsible for the kindness of strangers and altruism."

"But what does your discovery mean in terms of creating greater freedom for all?" Helen pressed.

He stretched out his legs. "From Spartacus to Martin Luther King Jr., men and women have followed the great leaders to new freedoms. Once the biomolecule is restored to its maximum beneficial level, a person will be able to say with conviction: *I have the same vision for freedom as Spartacus and Martin Luther King Jr. had.* And Sentio will become the objective foundation for all knowledge."

She smiled at his conclusion.

"Okay, I can't prove that last statement, but I believe it to be true." When her face grew serious, he expanded on his thoughts. "In the eighteenth century, Rousseau realized that when man left nature, he lost his consciousness of nature and the vision for freedom. Men became jealous of one another and fell under the spell of dictators."

She gave a gentle nod.

His face flushed with crimson pride, and he added, "In the nineteenth century, two of our own from Harvard—Thoreau and Emerson—rediscovered the consciousness of nature and the vision for freedom."

She nodded more affirmatively.

"But then we lost sight of the consciousness of nature, which was written off as a mystical experience. And now our research team has found a way to restore the sensitivity of the consciousness of nature—Sentio, the essence of our being. With our discovery, each man and woman will have the opportunity to pursue truth and true freedom while living among others. They will not need to live alone in nature as Thoreau did. Once we find a way to deliver strange love to the masses, we'll restore Sentio."

Helen sat up tall and gently pushed her hair behind her shoulders. She peered into Dr. Sol's eyes and spoke with authority. "The only infallible knowledge of our empirical world is from sense data passing into immediate perception. Sentio is the consciousness of immediate perception, which projects the sense data, the truth, and the way to freedom. But before you restore their sensitivity, you need to make people aware of Sentio in an experiential way."

Sentio awareness had to come first before attempts to restore sensitivity. He knew that now after what had happened to Antonio.

"Four years ago, my team searched for the Holy Grail of consciousness," Dr. Sol told her. "We went looking for the neuro-electrical wave that represents a single frame of sensory data passing into the consciousness window. To our surprise—though no surprise to you—we found two moments of consciousness for a single stimulus."

"I know you identified Sentio and Cogito: the two consciousnesses," said Helen with a big smile. "I remember feeling so excited the moment I read about your discovery."

Helen Moyen knew more about consciousness than anyone in the world. Her praise and affirming smile meant more to him at that moment than all the awards his discovery had earned him.

"You knew about Sentio long before we discovered it," he said. "I clued in on where to look for the wave after reading your book."

"Thank you. I appreciate your saying that." She lowered her eyes modestly.

"Two years ago, my group discovered the biomolecule of freedom," Dr. Sol continued. "But we didn't understand its complicated mechanism or how it conveyed freedom. When Antonio joined our research team, he had a feeling about the molecule and ran with it. He discovered how to stimulate the molecule's production and how it conveyed freedom. He demonstrated that the molecule improves complex problem solving and raises the voltage of the Sentio wave. Antonio has modified our investigational method to track visual evoked potentials, helping his fellow students connect and attend for Sentio awareness," he said.

"Sentio occurs fast, almost twice as fast as Cogito, but once you tune into Sentio, everything will seem slower—at first," Helen reminded.

Dr. Sol sat up. "Antonio explained the phenomenon to me. I have been working with athletes to improve their reaction times by attending to Sentio, and my two NBA players reported that things slow down when they connect. Even the ball appears to move slower—the players call it the zone."

Helen crossed her legs. "The players are tuned into the faster, more vivid Sentio consciousness and react faster to their environment even though the frames are viewed at their mind's eye speed, set for Cogito consciousness."

Dr. Sol nodded. "Frames acquired from Sentio at forty frames per second are played at the Cogito mind's eye speed at twenty frames per second, and that creates the perception of slow motion. I've discussed this with Antonio."

"Yes, but consciousness in athletic play, all consciousness for that matter, is different than viewing cinema," she cautioned. "Don't forget about the interaction of Intentio in the consciousness experience. Antonio knows as do the great athletes. The experience of life through Sentio translates into excellence in all matters. We can all be geniuses through Sentio. We can experience and react to things before they become apparent to the Cogito mind. A true Sentio being experiences the world twice as fast as a Cogito being. And in high definition with more clarity and without the institutional effect of language."

Listening to Helen, Dr. Sol realized that she was indeed just like Antonio—a Sentio being.

"Does your mind's eye see the world at the faster Sentio frame rate?" he asked.

"I need a moment," she said.

"Of course."

She got up and stepped into the bathroom.

Helen returned to her chair, looked down at the white tile floor for a moment, and then raised her eyes into Dr. Sol's gaze. "I experience the world through Sentio where my Intentio dwells, but I have to use Cogito too. I've seen the gorgeous Eden-like sunsets at the faster frame rate. That is what the biomolecule will do," she noted. "It will raise Sentio sensitivity and adjust the mind's eye speed to the faster frame rate. One day all humans will have the opportunity to enjoy the beautiful garden as intended, where subjectivity and objectivity are one."

Antonio rolled onto his side. Helen walked over to check on him, but he was still asleep. When she sat back down, Dr. Sol whispered. "What you did with Antonio in Andorra—it's amazing." He shook his head in awe. "He is the most brilliant being I have ever studied. His Sentio wave voltage amplitude is off the charts."

She touched the back of Dr. Sol's hand with her fingertips. "I didn't do it alone."

Dr. Sol's entire body tingled and warmed from her soft, lingering touch. She'd given him a dose of strange love. He responded in turn by touching her hand with his fingertips. She produced a warm smile.

"May I ask you something?" he said.

"Of course."

"What can we do to facilitate the process so Americans can find the way to freedom?"

"The difficulty will be in helping people experience and connect to the world through Sentio, as you have figured out. You must free up their attention, Intentio, from language-thinking consciousness, Cogito."

"Do you know of a better way to free Intentio from Cogito?" Dr. Sol asked. Helen's entire philosophy of freedom centered on the attention wave, Intentio, which interacts with Sentio and Cogito.

Helen's eyes were thoughtful. "I compare your dilemma to working with a person who has a passion or an addiction—the freeing of Intentio from Cogito. Antonio's use of your investigational method to connect students to their Sentio sounds promising, as does your work with the athletes. Once people experience their attention within Sentio consciousness, the experience will become a part of their sense of being—the more, the better." Her enthusiasm grew. "Sentio will become a part of them, and they will learn to direct Intentio there and experience freedom from the mundane and language-thinking institutional existence."

"That's what Antonio said, and he believes Americans are addicted to Cogito."

"He's right. Language plays in the mind of a Cogito addict as heroin plays in the mind of an opiate addict, enslaving their Intentio. And you now have a way to free them from their addiction," she said. "Once they're free, you can unleash the power of strange love. Once Americans experience emotional freedom, they will want strange love to restore their Sentio consciousness to the highest sensitivity, the state it was in Eden when Intentio dwelled in Sentio—"

They broke eye contact when Antonio raised his arm and rolled toward the edge of his mattress. He untangled his monitor leads and sat up, his large blue eyes lit with joy.

"Have you been listening?" asked Dr. Sol with a grin.

"Isn't she brilliant?"

Dr. Sol nodded. She was brilliant and beautiful. He had never met anyone like Helen Moyen.

"Her body has followed her mind back to Eden. Aunt Helen, tell him about your discovery," Antonio requested in a soft voice, and motioned for her to come over.

Helen raised up in a ladylike fashion, and Antonio's eyes filled with tears as she approached. She ran her fingers through his curly brown locks, and when she caressed his shoulders, he wrapped his arms around her, and they hugged for several long moments.

Helen looked over at Dr. Sol and then at Antonio. "When you get out of the hospital, your mother, Poulou, and I will tell our story—the journey to freedom at Essence in Andorra."

Epilogue as a Beginning

Around a quarter after midnight, the door of my hospital room creaked open. I could see my mother in a baby-blue and white silk dress; she looked so young with curly, brown hair. Unbelievable. She was talking softly to Georgia, the charge nurse, in the hallway just outside the door. Wide awake, I watched as her silhouette slipped inside the moonlit room. Gently closing the door, she approached with her finger over mouth, tiptoeing past Linda asleep on the sofa.

"Mother," I whispered, "are you okay?"

"Yes," she smiled. "Javier and I are staying in your beautiful apartment, but I couldn't sleep. You were sedated earlier in the evening. Georgia suggested I come back at midnight. I wanted to hold you."

I held out my arms, embraced my mother, and pulled her onto the bed. She snuggled next to me.

"Darling, I love you so much," she said. "I had to be with you tonight."

I found her sparkling brown eyes and whispered, "I love you."

Rubbing my chest softly with her hand, she made a purring sound of love, as she used to do when I was a baby.

"Where are Alex and Polly?" I asked.

"They didn't arrive until late tonight and are staying at Milly's house; she's been so kind to us. Poulou and Helen are staying with her downstairs, and Alex and Polly are staying with Simone and her handsome friend, Andrew. Javier and I are staying with Diana and Lar in your apartment."

I smiled to myself when my mother referred to Anal as Andrew. "Aren't my friends great?"

"They are adorable, and they love you very much."

"And I love them. Did you meet Barbara and Tinker?"

"Yes, and Fancy, Sassy, Pretty, Sophia, Vinay, and the others. They are wonderful people."

"I wish Josephine had come."

"She had to stay at Essence. She was so upset when she heard you'd been shot. All the Sisters and children at Vichy and Essence cried. When Aunt Helen told me, I ran to our room in Villa #4 and cried my heart out—"

My mother's voice cracked, and I pulled her into a tight embrace.

After a moment she continued, "I rocked in your favorite chair. The same chair I rocked you in when you were a baby. After a few minutes I'd calmed and could sense your Intentio in my Sentio. I knew you were alive and okay, and I consoled Helen, Poulou, Josephine, and the others with my revelation that you were okay. Isn't that strange?"

"No, because I wanted you to know I was okay. I willed for you to know."

My mother stared into my eyes for a long moment as if she understood. "Josephine sent you a special get well card from the children, the Sisters, and staff: a group picture signed in love for you. I left it on the window seat at your apartment, which is full of flowers and get-well cards from the people of Pierre. Dr. Frankl called me and said he would share the good news about your recovery with everyone back home."

"I love Dr. Frankl and my family in Essence and Pierre. I have received so much love from so many people."

My mother stroked my forearm with her finger-tips. "Javier sends his love too, and he will see you in the morning."

"How is Javier?"

"He has been so strong for me, but I knew it broke his heart hearing you'd been shot. Earlier this evening, he talked with Dr. Sol and was so relieved; Javier suggested I be with you tonight."

"I have always loved Javier, and I'm so glad he came with you. America is dangerous; you were right about that, and I know why."

She grasped my hand. "Why?"

"Americans are behaving like the sensory deprived rats in Dr. Sol's research lab. Since the citizens' Intentios are unable to experience sensory in Sentio, they are deprived of true sensory." I sighed. "But I can't prove my theory yet."

My mother furrowed her brow at first and then nodded, but she didn't understand the implications of Sentio deprivation as I did. She didn't understand my dilemma, how I'd need objective data to prove my theory. I decided not to talk about it.

"How are you doing, my little Spartacus?" she asked, brushing my hair with her hand.

"I'm doing much better since Dr. Sol said my chest tube could come out tomorrow."

"I mean, how is your Sentio?"

"I have increased my Sentio sensitivity beyond anything I could've imagined." My mother looked surprised, and I pulled her closer. "I'm so thankful. We are so close to freeing humankind."

"Your aunt Helen told me that you and your Harvard team must restore Sentio awareness and the will for freedom prior to deploying strange love to the masses, or the will for pleasure—hedonism—will destroy everything."

I peered into her concerned, brown eyes. "I know, and we will.

"What do you think about our team leaders: Linda, Dr. Sol, Dr. Wolf, Andrew, Simone, and Diana?"

"They are wonderful and brilliant, and I love Linda. When we first met, I felt an immediate connection to her, and she gave me the most wonderful hug."

I grinned. "She is something." I looked over at her sleeping on the sofa.

My mother followed my gaze. "I understand why she is your Sentiomate, and I read your letter about her adoption and her former name."

I met my mother's eyes. "You mean her true essence name, Sophia Lubov—Sophia Love."

"Yes, I knew you would make the connection, just as your name, Dasein, is your true essence name."

"She is the greatest giver of strange love ever! Her love gave me the idea that strange love was connected to Sentio sensitivity through the action of the biomolecule of freedom. And when I needed strange love more than any time in my life, I reflected on her beautiful image in my Sentio, and she saved me."

My mother smiled, laid her head on my shoulder, and drifted off to sleep.

Warmed and filled with my mother's love, I stayed awake, thinking about her concern: hedonism, the belief that pleasure is the purpose of life.

Someday strange love will deliver humankind to a life beyond hedonism.

JC Howell is a new author who writes with a postmodern style and Romantic view exploring the nature of being, love, and freedom. *Sentio* was his debut novel.

Born in America on January 15, 1958, he received his undergraduate education at the University of Tennessee in Chattanooga, completed medical school in Baltimore at the University of Maryland in 1984, and finished his medical residency at the University Hospital in 1987. For most of his life, he has studied, taught, and practiced medicine. Five years ago he began a writing career. *Strange Love in America* brings his story home, where he's at the top of his game.

His thread about love and its connection to greater freedom for all continues in *Beyond Hedonism*.

Strange Love in America

JC Howell

Author website: authorjchowell.com

Publisher: SDP Publishing

Also available in ebook format

Also by JC Howell

Sentio

Available at all major bookstores

SDP Publishing

www.SDPPublishing.com

Contact us at: info@SDPPublishing.com

www.ingramcontent.com/pod-product-compliance
Lightning Source LLC
Chambersburg PA
CBHW030645260626
47157CB00007B/2503